Doug &

Thank-

Support

Hunting Muskie
Rites of Passage

Stories by
Michael Robert Dyet

blue denim press

Hunting Muskie
Copyright © 2017 Michael Robert Dyet
All rights reserved
Published by Blue Denim Press Inc.
First Edition
ISBN 978-1-927882-22-1

This is a work of fiction. Resemblances to persons living or dead are unintended and purely co-incidental.

INCORRIGIBLE: A Short Story - Appeared in *Canadian Voices, Volume 2: An Anthology of Prose and Poetry by Emerging Canadian Writers*. Bookland Press 2010
DANCING WITH GHOSTS: Appeared in *Canadian Imprints: An Anthology of Prose and Poems by Members of Writers and Editors Network (2011)*
RANSOM HEART: Appeared in *Change is in the Wind Anthology*. Second Wind Publishing, April 2012
HUNTING MUSKIE: Appeared in the spring 2012 issue of *Freefall: Canada's Magazine of Exquisite Writing*

Cover Design—Joanne Kasunic/Typeset in Cambria and Garamond

Library and Archives Canada Cataloguing in Publication
Dyet, Michael Robert, 1958-, author
  Hunting Muskie : rites of passage / Michael Robert Dyet. -- First edition.

Short stories.
Issued in print and electronic formats.
ISBN 978-1-927882-22-1 (softcover).--ISBN 978-1-927882-23-8 (Kindle) --ISBN 978-1-927882-24-5 (EPUB)

    I. Title.

PS8607.Y385H86 2017   C813'.6   C2017-905666-2
                                       C2017-905667-0

This book is dedicated to my father who taught me that where there's a will, there's a way.

Other Works by Michael Robert Dyet

Until The Deep Water Stills: An Internet-Enhanced Novel

Table of Contents

Slipstream

Empty Bedrooms

*I*t's our thirtieth anniversary, Mother. Or perhaps anti-anniversary is a better way to put it, since it's about the last time I laid eyes on you. Have you kept track of the years as well? No, that's probably exclusive to the ones left behind. You made a clean break and washed your hands of us.

The practice of speaking to her mother in absentia was a ritual Norah reverted to as each anniversary arrived. It was not, of course, *speaking* in the strictest sense. More in the nature of thought waves launched into the stratosphere in the blind hope that they would find their own way.

So foolish to have promised herself not to fixate on it. She knew, deep down, where uncomfortable truths lived, that she would not be able to keep that vow, since broken promises were what the anniversary was all about.

CoAAH, coo, cooo, co.

The plaintive hooting of the resident pair of mourning doves, regular visitors from Heart Lake Conservation Area which backed onto their yard, reached Norah through the bedroom window. The interrogation embedded in their call—*Who Who Who*—struck her as curiously appropriate for both the reversing tide of time she was caught up in and for the gremlins of blame that refused to be dismissed over a quarter century later.

Reversing tide of time. Not quite on the mark, she decided, but not far off either. It was impossible to frame in words this slipstream she was drawn into in which the past was reanimated so it could co-exist with the present. A kind of temporal echolocation involving tides of fate and momentous events many of which made their mark before she was even born.

If only she could anticipate when it was likely to happen, like a change in barometric pressure when a storm was mounting, she could at least prepare for it. But the slipstream episodes persisted in their randomness. The intervals between them were sometimes years and at other times measured in days. Their point of origin was well defined. It was the first of the three departures, two of which ended in failure, by her runaway mother. That first shock of abandonment had released the power she had inherited to slip free from linear time.

With this blessing, or curse, came precognition. An awareness and a caution, that something momentous was likely to happen.

"Woof! Woof!"

Sawbucks was resting her head on the bed—a wet nose nuzzling Norah's face. Time reassembled itself and reminded her that the here and now had its own particular concerns. *Sawbucks.* Such an irreverent name for a dog. But it was Kevin who gave the Golden Lab her name when she was just a pup. How he happened upon it was a mystery. Nine-year-old boys did not need to be logical.

But seven years had passed since that moment of whimsy. The wilful child had grown into a rebellious sixteen-year-old waging war with life and, in particular, with his father. Father and son were too much alike. Both unwilling to give an inch when challenged. Troy's ultimatum—*clean up your act if you want to live in this house*—had an incendiary effect. Five months had elapsed since Kevin walked out the door without looking back.

"Woof!"

"Alright, Sawbucks. I'm getting up."

The alarm clock registered 5:45 a.m.—a full hour before she needed to get up. The loss of an hour mattered little. Who could sleep when you had no idea where your child was resting his head?

She swung her legs out of bed, rubbed the sleep from her eyes, and shuffled into her slippers. The instinctive glance into Kevin's bedroom on the way past was now hardcoded into her morning routine—a part of her insisting on believing that he would be there. Andie's bedroom had been empty long enough for her to grudgingly make peace with that absence. Thankfully, she was on her own and building a life for herself, although not the kind of life Norah would have chosen for her.

Sawbucks ambled down the stairs beside Norah. She slid open the sliding glass door from the kitchen to the backyard. The chill of a September morning greeted her. Sawbucks trotted past onto the deck, stopped suddenly, sniffed the air and bolted forward. *Skunk! Oh, not again!*

"Sawbucks! Stop! Stop!" She sprinted over the deck and across the lawn as Sawbucks bounded into the gazebo. "Sawbucks! No! No! No!"

The motion-activated light in the gazebo came on. She froze in her tracks at the unexpected sight. Kevin, dishevelled and pencil thin, was hugging Sawbucks as she licked his face.

"Kevin?"

"Hey." Kevin regarded her dispassionately.

"Hey? You've been gone five months and all you can say is *hey*?"

"Just needed a place to sleep. I meant to be gone before anyone woke up."

"Have you done this before?"

"Maybe." He eyed her warily.

The thought of him being there on other occasions, only a few feet away without her knowledge, stirred her anger.

"Our house isn't good enough for you, but the gazebo is?"

"*My house, my rules.* Remember?"

"Your dad's not home. He's in Niagara Falls for a trade show. Be grateful he isn't here to find you sneaking around."

"Like I give a damn what he thinks."

"Look at you. You're skin and bones. You must be starving. Come in the house. I'll fix breakfast for you."

"Don't bother. I can feed myself."

"From what? A dumpster?"

Kevin's eyes dropped to hide his shame.

"Yeah, alright. But just for breakfast. I'm not staying."

"We'll talk about it."

Sawbucks kept Kevin occupied, showering him with affection, as Norah busied herself making bacon and eggs. Kevin wolfed down the breakfast. His eyes periodically stole glances around the kitchen as if storing up images to carry with him.

"Where have you been staying, Kevin?"

"Here and there." He locked eyes with Norah for a moment. "I had a tent in the woodlot in Norton Place Park for a while. But the cops started sniffing around, so I moved. Since then, wherever I can find."

"Do you have any idea how much we've worried about you? Stop this nonsense and come home."

"This isn't my home. Dad made that pretty damn clear."

"You came home drunk again. What did you expect? And he never said this isn't your home. He just said you have to show us some respect. Is that so much to ask?"

His stare hardened now. A part of Norah rebelled as she sensed his resistance mounting. *Who is this person? How did he become someone I don't know?* Living on the streets had changed him. He was constantly on alert as if he might need to cut and run at any moment.

"Yeah, whatever. I can take care of myself. Anyway, what I'd really like is to take a shower. Can I?"

"Of course. God knows, you need it."

"Thanks." He rose from the table, gave Sawbucks a scratch under the chin and went up the stairs.

So how do I convince him to stay, Mother? It's obviously not something I am good at—getting people to stick around. On these slipstream days, she was simultaneously living and reconstructing her own life story. *My Life Thus Far: True Confessions of the One Left Behind.* The connecting thread of the still incomplete narrative was the mystic bond that linked mother and daughter.

But more immediate concerns prevailed. She picked up her iPhone and dialed Troy's mobile number. His voice mail answered.

"Troy, it's me. Call me as soon as you get this message. Kevin's home. Well, not really home. He was sleeping in the gazebo. He says he won't stay. I'll try to keep him here as long as I can. But you're going to have to talk to him and convince him you really want him to be here. It's been five months. Whatever it takes, we have to convince him to stay."

She noticed a missed call from the evening before, and made a mental note to check it later, as she called Andie.

"Hi, Mom. On my way out the door. Can this wait?"

"It's your brother. He's here."

"Kevin? He came home?"

"Yes. Well, not really."

"What? Is he home or not?"

"Yes, he's here. I found him sleeping in the gazebo. But he says he's not staying. I fed him breakfast and now he's taking a shower."

"I doubt he'll listen to me. We don't exactly get along. But I'll be there in twenty minutes. Don't let him leave before I get there."

"I'll try. But you know your brother when he makes up his mind about something."

"Him and Dad both. Too damn stubborn for their own good. Did you call Dad?"

"Yes, but he didn't answer. I left him a message."

"That's strange. He always answers his phone. I'll be there as soon as I can."

Norah had a fleeting sense that something was out of alignment, as if the course of events had shifted sideways from their intended track.

***

Norah called her Remax office as she watched Andie's car pull into the driveway. The office voice mail kicked in.

"Hi, Joanne. It's Norah. Something's come up. I'm not available today. I've got two showings this afternoon for the listing on Morningmist Street. See if Suzanne can cover for me. She owes me a favour. I'm not expecting any offers today. But call me if anything breaks. Thanks."

She met Andie at the door. For a fleeting moment, she could have believed it was Georgia, her sister who had transplanted herself halfway around the world in Australia. All her features were expressive like Georgia's—the eyes that always had a fire in them, a smile that radiated when she was happy and a frown a mile wide when she was upset. The two of them, Andie and her lookalike aunt, were the kind of people that stuck in your memory. She on the other hand was always described as *pretty* which seemed like a polite way of saying unremarkable.

"I really didn't need this today, Mom."

"What kind of greeting is that?"

"Never mind. He's still here, isn't he?"

"Yes. He hasn't come downstairs yet."

Kevin rounded the corner on the staircase as she answered. He had changed into a fresh set of clothes. Andie crossed the room in half a dozen strides.

"You were gone for five months and all we got were two telephone messages. *Don't worry, I'm okay.* As if that was all we needed to know. Do you realize what you've put us through?"

"Nice to see you too, Andie."

"Really? That's how you're playing it? No big deal?" She steered him into the living room and sat him down next to her on the sofa. "Mom says you won't stay. Stop being so damn pig-headed. The world doesn't revolve around you."

"You're starting to sound like Dad. Anyway, it's not your call. I can take care of myself."

"Oh, you can? Look at yourself. You're so thin I can practically see right through you. You look like something Sawbucks dragged in from God knows where."

"Since when did you start giving a damn about me?"

The defiance had not been there five months ago. Norah's iPhone buzzed as she worried over this transformation and what had brought it about. *Troy*, she thought, stepping into the hallway to answer. But it was not his number.

"Can I please speak to Norah Watson."

"This is Norah."

"Norah. I don't think we've met. I work with your husband. My name is Ken Bowen."

"Yes, my husband has mentioned you. Troy isn't here. He's at a trade show in Niagara Falls."

"Yes, I know. I'm here at the show as well. The thing is ... well, Troy seems to have gone missing."

"Missing? What do you mean *missing?*"

"He didn't come down for breakfast this morning. We were worried, so I went to his room to check on him. There was no answer when I knocked. I got hotel security to let me in. Most of Troy's things are there. But the bed doesn't look like it has been slept in."

Norah's early morning precognition took shape and substance. Fault lines grumbled as the earth shifted ever so slightly.

"There must be a reason." She grasped for a rational explanation. "When did you last speak to him?"

"The three of us went for a late dinner last night after setting up for the show. Hollis and I decided to go to the casino for an hour or two. Troy said he was going to drive down to the Falls and take a walk. We didn't see him after that. Did you talk to him last night?"

"No, I didn't." The missed call occurred to her.

"Is that normal?"

"Normal? What are you saying?"

" Sorry. I wasn't implying anything. We just thought we should talk to you before we called the police."

"The police? Do you think that's necessary?"

"Well, it seems like the prudent thing to do."

The synchronicity of events past and present came into focus. The thirtieth anniversary, Kevin's return and now Troy's disappearance. What were the odds it was all just coincidence?

"Norah? Are you still there?"

"Sorry. Yes, I'm here. You're right. You should call the police. Give them my number."

"Yes, I definitely will. Anyway, like you said, there's likely a simple explanation. Troy will probably turn up on his own."

"Let's hope. Thank you for calling, Ken. Please call if you hear anything."

"I definitely will. And let me know if you hear from him. Goodbye, Norah."

The presumptive voice of doubt went to work. *What now, Mother? How am I supposed to find my way through this? You didn't stay around long enough to teach me how to hold things together when the bottom is falling out.*

Andie and Kevin were still sparring when Norah came back into the living room. The look on her face interrupted their debate.

"What is it?" Andie asked. "Who was it that called?"

"It was Ken Bowen. He works with your father. He said your father has gone missing. They haven't seen him since last night."

"How could Dad just suddenly go missing?" Andie was on her feet now.

"I don't know. Apparently, he wasn't in his hotel room last night. That's all they know at this point."

"Did you talk to him yesterday?" Andie asked.

"No."

"No?"

"Don't use that tone with me. And why is that so surprising to everyone?"

"Forget it. So what do we do?"

"Ken's going to phone the police. I guess we just wait for them to call us."

"This is unbelievable." Andie turned to Kevin and pointed her finger at him. "*You* are not going anywhere until Dad turns up. Understand?"

Kevin's expression darkened. "Since when do you give the orders around here?"

"For God's sake, Kevin. Get your head out of your ass. We don't need to be worrying about you right now. You *have* to stay.

"I don't have to do anything. But yeah, I'll stick around."

"Don't just give me a *yeah*. Promise us."

"I said I'll stay, for now. But I'm not taking orders from anyone—especially not you."

***

Secret lives. Her mother had one for thirty years and counting. Kevin had one of his own for the past five months. Even Georgia had one in a manner of speaking—a life on the other side of the world which she knew precious little about. Could it be that Troy had one too? And if he did, what did it say about her, that so many people she loved felt compelled to hide from her?

Self-convicting questions, old and new, continued to circle around Norah as she sought refuge in the gazebo waiting for the police. There was a secret for achieving harmony that everyone knew except her. It was arguably her fault that Kevin had left home. Her failure to prevent the confrontation between Troy and Kevin from boiling over had allowed what followed to happen.

She replayed the scene in her mind. Kevin had missed his curfew again and arrived home, clearly inebriated. Troy met him at the door spoiling for a fight.

"Kevin, do you have any idea what time it is?"

"No, Dad. Keeping me on the clock is your job, isn't it?" His voice was slurred as he leaned against the doorframe.

"Don't be a smartass. It's after midnight. And you're drunk. *Again.* You just don't learn, do you?"

"Can we do this in the morning? I really wanna go to bed."

"You think you can stumble in here at this hour, and there won't be consequences?" Troy jabbed his finger at Kevin. "Let me set you straight. This is my house, and there are rules for everyone in it."

"Wait, let me get a stone tablet and a chisel. Wouldn't want to miss recording the commandments."

"You're pushing your luck, Kevin. One more smartass remark and—"

"And what? What are you going to do?"

Time folded over on itself at that moment transporting Norah to the pivotal night thirty years ago, listening to the angry voices of her parents through the wall on the day everything started to unravel. Driven by that memory, she tried to steer Kevin and Troy away from a full scale blowout.

"Troy, can't this wait until morning? Let's just sleep on it."

"No, it can't. I'm not putting up with this bullshit anymore. You're grounded, Kevin. You come straight home from school and stay put. You don't set a foot outside this house for two weeks. Understood?"

"Oh, grounded. Ouch. I didn't see that coming."

"One more word out of you. I'm warning you, Kevin. One more word."

"Hamburger."

"What?"

"You said one more word: hamburger."

If only she had stepped in at that moment. Troy unleashed a slap to the face that staggered Kevin. It was already too late when she put herself between them.

"Kevin, upstairs. *Now.*"

Kevin stood his ground for a moment with his eyes locked on his father.

"Kevin, please, just go upstairs."

Kevin turned away and started up the stairs. Halfway up, he suddenly pivoted and punched the wall so hard his fist went through the plaster. When she heard the bedroom door slam behind Kevin, Norah confronted Troy.

"What the hell is the matter with you? You hit him. You slapped him in the face."

"What was I supposed to do? You heard him. He mocked me to *my* face. Was I supposed to let him get away with that?"

"But you *hit* him, Troy. How could you?"

"I didn't mean to. But he had it coming. He's out of control, Norah."

***

"The detective is here." Andie called to Norah through the patio doors.

Norah gathered herself as she went into the house. It was critically important, for reasons she could not decipher, that she be in control when the interview began.

"Mrs. Watson, I'm Detective White of Peel Region Police. Niagara Falls P.D. looped us in on your husband's disappearance. I need to ask you a few questions."

"Certainly. But can we not use the word *disappearance*. It's a little early to call it that, isn't it?"

"I understand this is difficult for you. I assume these are your children?"

"Yes, my daughter Andie and my son Kevin."

Detective White paused a moment as he looked at Kevin. "We have a report of Kevin being missing. Did you report his return?"

"He just came back this morning. I haven't had time."

Andie shot a look at Kevin that said *Don't even think about it.* Detective White caught the exchange. "Your son comes back the same day your husband goes missing. That's curious."

"What are you implying, Detective?"

"It's quite a coincidence."

"I didn't really come home," Kevin said. "I was just sleeping in the gazebo."

Andie's look of exasperation did not go unnoticed. Detective White tapped his notepad with his pen.

"I can't help you if you're not honest with me, Mrs. Watson."

"I'm not lying. I found Kevin sleeping in the gazebo this morning. I called my daughter and together we convinced him to stay. It's as simple as that."

Detective White took a moment to weigh Norah's explanation. "Alright, let's move on. When did you last speak to your husband?"

"Yesterday afternoon when he left for a trade show in Niagara Falls."

"He didn't call you last night or this morning? Is that normal?"

"What are trying to say?" Norah felt herself shifting into defence for the third time in only a few hours.

"I'm just trying to gather all the facts. Has he ever gone missing before?"

"No, never."

Detective White paused, flashing a look at all of them, as he dropped the next question.

"Are there any problems in your relationship? Marital issues or financial problems?"

"Excuse me?"

"I apologize if these questions seem insensitive or intrusive. But they have to be asked."

"No. There are no problems. Obviously we've been upset about Kevin. Any parent would be."

"So your husband was upset? Distracted? Maybe even angry about Kevin?"

"This is beginning to feel like an inquisition, Detective. Whose side are you on?"

"We don't take sides. But we have to look at all the possibilities. People go missing for all kinds of reasons. In any event, we'll need a photo of your husband."

"Of course." Norah crossed to the bookshelf, picked up a frame and slid out the photo. "This was taken last year when we were on vacation. Will it do?"

"Yes, it's fine. Thank you. What kind of vehicle does he drive? I'll need the plate number as well."

"He drives a dark green Nissan Pathfinder. But I don't remember the plate number."

"That's okay. I can get it from the system. I think have everything I need for now."

Norah felt a need to re-establish equilibrium. "I'm sorry if I seemed defensive, Detective White. As you can understand, this has been a very emotional morning for me."

"Yes, certainly. I understand. We all want the same thing—your husband back home safe and sound. We'll do everything we can to locate him."

Detective White made his exit. Norah followed him out onto the porch and watched the police cruiser pull away. Something felt wrong about his parting words.

"Well that wasn't what I expected," Andie said. "He could have been more diplomatic."

"Seems to me he was doing his job," Kevin countered.

"Oh, and you really helped. You had to tell him you weren't planning to stay?"

"Keep riding me and I'll walk out the door right now."

"Why am I not surprised? Whenever things get tough, you bail."

"Stop! Both of you." Norah took a breath to gather her wits. "I don't need you two fighting right now. I've got enough to deal with."

"I'm not the one causing problems," Andie replied. "But fine. Kevin, let's stay out of each other's way."

"Yeah, okay. Just don't try to tell me what to do."

It was only later, when Norah had retreated back to the gazebo, that Detective White's choice of words registered with her. *Locate* him, not *find* him. Implying that Troy was not missing, but AWOL. Could it be happening again? Would another letter arrive that she would have to pore over and dissect to find out if she was to blame?

The Keepsake Box

Something was different. A shift in the already tenuous balance of her life. It was the first thought that materialized in Norah's mind the next morning as she surfaced from the few hours of sleep she had managed. The harsh, complaining notes of a crow sounded from the yard, rather

than the accustomed cooing of the doves. But it was something more substantial than that.

Was she still in the slipstream? She cleared her mind to feel for its presence. Yes, she was still in the gravitational pull of it.

The crow squawked again. A bad omen? She entertained the thought but dismissed it. The raucous call seemed fitting for the ironic turn of events—Kevin's return coming on the very day that Troy went missing.

Is one a trade-off for the other, Mother? Oh, don't get me started on all the ways that could be spun. I could get lost in that game of blind alleys and go slowly mad trying to find my way out. But still, why on the same day?

A knock on the bedroom door recalled her to things more immediate. The slipstream went underground.

"Mom? You awake?"

"Yes. Come in."

Andie pushed open the door.

"You are not going to believe this."

"Believe what?"

"Kevin's gone again."

"What! No, he wouldn't. Not now."

"I checked the whole house. He's gone. He must have left during the night. I should have known I couldn't trust his word."

Norah threw back the comforter and slid out of bed.

"Did you check the gazebo?"

"The gazebo? Why would he sleep out there again? What am I saying? Why does he do any of the things he does other than to make our lives difficult?"

"Please, don't start that again. Let's just go check."

Norah threw on her clothes and hurried down the stairs with Andie. Sawbucks came galloping up to them when they stepped out on the patio. She barked frantically, pranced in circles, and raced to the locked gate at the back of the yard.

"He must have let Sawbucks out and gone out the gate. Maybe he hasn't gotten too far. We might be able to catch up with him." Andie opened the gate, and Sawbucks leapt out. "Go, girl! Go find Kevin."

The dog charged down the narrow footpath through the trees with Andie and Norah in pursuit. She burst through to the pathway, cut right, and charged ahead at a full sprint.

"Sawbucks! Wait! Wait for us!"

The Lab came racing back, as if to urge them on, and dashed off again. They followed the path to where it widened into a wheat grass meadow at the back of the conservation area. The dog dodged right and disappeared down a footpath through chest high grass.

"I know that trail, Mom. It's a dead-end side path. Kevin must be at the marsh pond."

At the end of the side path, they found Kevin sitting on the viewing deck, silhouetted by the rising sun, with Sawbucks at his side. Norah held Andie back.

"Let me. Okay? Just wait here."

"Better you than me. I feel like wringing his neck."

Norah approached quietly and sat down beside him.

"You gave us quite a scare. We thought you'd left again."

"I thought about it. But I came here instead. I like it here. It's peaceful and there's nobody trying to tell me what to do."

"I can understand that. Sometimes you just need to be alone." She gave Sawbucks a grateful squeeze. "It's not your fault, Kevin—your Dad going missing—if that's what you're thinking."

"It's not me you need to convince," he answered, glancing at Andie.

"You two need to sit down and talk things out. Neither one of you is seeing the whole picture."

"Yeah, well, there's a lot of that going around, Mom."

"What is that supposed to mean?"

"I'm just saying, maybe you should look in the mirror."

It was Norah's turn to pause. A wave of resentment mounted in her.

"Are you talking about the fight with your father? You're saying it was my fault?"

"He's no saint. That's all I'm saying. You're too busy selling houses to see what was going on."

The wave of resentment crested and tumbled over into anger. How did everything suddenly become her fault?

"What I see is a spoiled teenager blaming everyone else for his mistakes."

That's just perfect, Norah chastised herself. Alienate him even further so he can justify leaving.

Kevin leveled a resentful look at her as if he was going to take the bait. But instead, he shifted his gaze out over the pond as tree swallows skimmed low over the surface, banked at the end, and made pass after pass snagging insects. She studied him while he watched the swallows. In the last year, he had grown into the lanky, athletic build he inherited from his father. The cleft chin and pursed lips were Troy's also. But at moments like this, the thoughtful, faraway expression he came by through her would appear, along with the slight tilt of his head that signaled he was working out a problem.

"Remember a few years ago when we went camping in Algonquin Park?"

"Of course. Lake of Three Rivers campground. We had a beautiful campsite right at the edge of the woods."

"There was one morning in the middle of the week. You and Dad were still asleep in the trailer. Sawbucks wanted out, so I let her out and went with her. The sun had just come up. The birds were starting to sing. For a minute, I felt like I owned the world. And then, all of a sudden, it was there—right at the edge of the woods. Maybe thirty feet away."

"What did you see?"

"A bear. Scared the crap out of me at first."

Norah shuddered at the picture he painted. "But I thought, fuck it. What have I got to lose? So I just ran straight at the bear waving my arms and screaming like a madman. Sawbucks was beside me barking up a storm. The bear turned away and hightailed into the woods."

"What in the world possessed you to do such a thing?"

"It worked, didn't it?" He looked at Norah to gauge her reaction. "It wasn't a conscious decision. It's like there's this other person inside me who is really angry all the time. Except when I'm here. Don't ask me why."

"If you need to come back here again for some quiet time, let me know. I just need to know where you are."

"What is this—the army? I have to sign in and out every day?"

"I didn't mean that. I just mean, no surprises, okay?"

"I guess. But you need to keep Andie out of my face. If she keeps grinding on me, I'm out of here."

***

Something was different. The intuition Norah had awakened to returned but redefined itself later that morning. She was overlooking something important and had been for quite some time. A loose end that had been dangling and was starting to unravel. But what? What could she have failed to notice that was so pivotal to this particular day?

Some parental advice would really help now, Mother. Can you airmail something down the slipstream to help me read the signs and puzzle through what I need to do? But I suppose that is a bit like asking for advice from someone who is morally bankrupt.

The sound of raised voices from the living room recalled Norah from her self-reflection. Kevin and Andie were arguing again.

"You don't know shit about me. So just back off."

Kevin was firing a volley as Norah came into the room.

"I know you're spoiled and full of yourself," Andie fired back. "You need a kick in the ass to wake you up."

"Stop it, you two!" Norah intervened. "Can't you get along for just one day?"

Andie and Kevin exchanged angry glares trying to stare each other down.

"It just irks me that he always needs to be the center of attention."

"Ah, pot calling the kettle black?"

"I said enough! Andie, you should go back to work. I'll call you when we hear something about your dad."

"Just pretend like nothing's wrong? Get serious. I'm not going anywhere until Dad is found. I've already arranged to use some vacation days."

"What about Annaliese? I assume you talked to her. Is she okay with you being here?"

"Considering I haven't seen her in a month, I would say—no, that won't be a problem."

"A month?" Norah looked puzzled.

"We broke up. She moved out. End of story."

"You didn't think that was something I would want to know?"

"Oh, come on, Mom. Don't pretend to be upset. You never liked her anyway."

"That's not true. Where did you get that idea?"

Andie rolled her eyes. "Are we really going to do this *now*, Mom?"

"Do what? What exactly do you mean by *this*?"

Kevin made a dismissive gesture.

Norah swung on him. "You too? Would one of you please tell me what is going on here?"

"I have to call you out on this one, Mom," Kevin answered. "You've always been on the fence about Andie being gay. Dad was okay with it. But you—not so much."

The sudden alliance between Andie and Kevin caught her off guard. How had things shifted so suddenly to make her the odd one out?

"I can't believe this. When did I ever do a single thing to suggest I was anything but supportive?"

"Don't patronize me." Andie was fired up now. "And don't try to play the holier-than-thou card. I accepted long ago that you're secretly ashamed that I'm gay. I wish it wasn't that way. But really, it's your problem—not mine."

"I have never uttered one word to suggest I'm ashamed of you. Not one word."

"I guess you've forgotten the day I confessed it to you. The look on your face said it all. I thought you were going to have a stroke. You probably would if you knew what I know."

The veiled reference fed into the intuition of trouble that had hung over Norah all day.

"What is that supposed to mean?"

"Nothing. Forget it. I'm just venting." Andie was backpedaling now which only raised Norah's suspicions further.

"You can't throw something like that out and just leave it hanging. What did you mean?"

"You're good at that, Andie." Kevin jumped in. "Fire a shot and run for cover."

"Oh, now all of a sudden you're on Mom's side?"

Norah saw the situation spiraling out of control. Accusations and insinuations were flying back and forth like shrapnel.

"We all need to be on the same side. Now is not the time—"

The telephone ringing interrupted her. She crossed the room to answer it. "Hello ... Yes, Detective White. We've been waiting to hear from you ... I see. What does that mean? Alright ... I understand. Thank you. Goodbye."

"That didn't sound good," Andie said. "What did he say?"

"They found some footage, from a security camera down by the Falls, of your father out walking late Sunday evening. That's all. They've put out a media statement declaring him missing and asking if anyone saw him. I guess that's standard procedure."

They were silent for a moment as each of them processed the news.

"Was he alone?" Kevin asked. "On the video footage, was he alone or was he walking with somebody?"

"He was alone," Norah answered. "But why would you ask that?"

"Just curious."

"You're a lousy liar, Kevin," Andie accused him. "Which is odd considering how often you do it."

Kevin stuck up his middle finger to her as a response.

"Enough!! Not another word from either of you!"

Norah turned and stormed out of the room. But Kevin's question lingered in her mind.

***

"Hi, Joanne. It's Norah. I'm just checking in. Anything you need to ask me about? No ... I won't be working today. Maybe not for a couple of days. I have a family matter to deal with. I can't really get into it on the phone ... Oh, you heard the news report. Yes, we are quite concerned ... Thanks, I appreciate the support. Thank everybody for me ... Yes, I'll stay in touch."

It bothered her that Troy's disappearance was now public knowledge. And the reason, she realized, was that Detective White was not entirely off base. It was conceivable that Troy had dropped off the radar intentionally. Gone into hiding to grapple with the consequences of his confrontation with Kevin or to remove himself for a while from their rocky relationship. His late night call to her could fit into that theory. But why not leave a message?

"Alright. Enough navel gazing. You need to get a handle on the situation."

She addressed herself out loud to shake herself into action. *Georgia.* It dawned on her now that this was the call to make. Trust her pragmatic sister to wrestle the situation under control. She went upstairs to make the call.

"Hello?" A sleepy voice came on the line after half a dozen rings.

"Georgia, its Norah."

"Norah! What a surprise. Look at you, calling me out of the blue. And in the middle of the day—your time, of course. It's ... four in the morning here, you know."

"Sorry, I didn't think about the time difference."

"You didn't think? Okay, that's not you. What's wrong? Is it Kevin?"

"Actually, Kevin is home now. Since yesterday."

"Oh, Norah, thank God. You must be so relieved."

"Yes, of course. But ... "

"But what?"

"Now Troy is missing."

"Troy? Okay, define *missing*."

"He's been in Niagara Falls since Sunday for a trade show. But he hasn't been seen or heard from since Sunday evening."

"Have you reported him missing?"

"Yes. The police are looking for him. They've issued a media report about him."

There was a quiver in her voice as she relayed the details.

"Alright, I'm coming. I'll get the first flight I can find. I won't be able to fly direct to Toronto. But I'll move heaven and earth to get there as soon as I can."

"Oh, Georgia. I don't expect you to drop everything and come running. I just wanted you to know."

"Of course I'm coming. There's no *if* about it. You and I, we've had our share of heartache. I won't let you go through this alone."

"Thank you so much. But you really don't have to come."

"Yes, I do. I'm hanging up now, Norah, so I can find a flight and get on my way. Call me if you hear anything else."

"Okay, I will. Thank you, Georgia. Thank you so much."

"Hang tight. I'll be there before you know it."

***

Should she tell her father about Troy or protect him from the distressing news?

Norah wrestled with the question as she pulled into the parking lot of the assisted care home where Joseph now lived. She had flirted with the idea of putting off the visit. But breaking the routine of her Tuesday and Thursday evening visits might tip him off that something was wrong.

How he would react depended on the type of day he was having. He was 83 and slipping more each day into the grip of Parkinson's. Even on his good days the symptoms were increasingly evident.

Should I or should I not, Mother? I really wonder what kind of advice you would give me in this situation? She settled on her decision as she went up the walk to the evening entrance. She had not told Joseph anything about Kevin, during the five months he was away. The same principle applied now. Life was enough of a struggle for him.

"Good evening, Mrs. Watson." The evening receptionist answered the buzzer. "Joseph is waiting for you in the Tranquility Garden."

"Thank you. I'm glad he's feeling up to being out today."

Norah crossed the foyer to the glass door and stepped out into the courtyard. Joseph was seated on a bench peering through the binoculars she had bought for him in the spring when he developed a sudden interest in birds.

She paused a few yards away as it struck her how much he had aged in the last few years. He had always been a rugged looking working man. Chiseled features, squared jaw and one eye permanently half closed—the remnant of an accident early in life he refused to talk about. But age, what it had written into his face, softened the effect. He was fragile now in a way she had not taken note of before.

"Hi, Dad. Sorry I'm late. It's been a hectic day."

She kissed him on the cheek and sat down beside him.

"White-throated finch. Over there, underneath the bush. Did I say finch? That's not right. It's a ... damn, I know it ... a sparrow." He tried to raise his hand to point, but could not. "Over there under the spirea bush.

"Oh yes, I see it. It's quite pretty."

"So how is everybody? Roy, Kevin and ... Sandie."

He was in the habit of saying their names as if to keep himself from forgetting them. But even on his good days he had a tendency to add or drop consonants.

"They're all fine. Business as usual on the home front." She felt guilty for lying to him.

"Good, good. Haven't seen them for a while."

"You'll see everyone at Thanksgiving. The whole clan will be there."

"Thanksgiving? Yes, of course. It's coming up." He paused as he looked through the binoculars again. "Is your sister mad at me?"

"No, Dad. Why would you think that?"

"She never comes to visit. You're here twice a week. But she never comes."

They had been around this subject several times before. Joseph did not comprehend that Georgia had moved away even though she called him from Australia several times a year.

"Georgia lives in Australia now, Dad. Remember?"

"Australia? Why the devil would she go all the way there? What have they got that we don't have, except maybe kangaroos?"

Why indeed had Georgia transplanted herself? There were several possible answers, none of which she cared to entertain.

"You know Georgia. She has always been the adventurous one."

"Damned if know where she gets that from."

Was that a subtle reference to her mother? Subtlety had never been his strong suit. What little inclination he had in that direction had slipped away as he grew older. But she could not rule it out entirely.

"Georgia sends you the flowers every week, Dad. That's her way of showing she cares."

"The calla lilies are from her?" He was genuinely surprised.

"Yes, Dad."

Did he remember why it was always calla lilies? It did not seem as if he did. Memory loss was a blessing when it was the painful memories that drifted away.

"You probably think I've forgotten. But I haven't. My memory is full of holes. But some things you never forget."

"What are you talking about, Dad?"

"It was forty years ago yesterday that your mother walked out on us for good. Forty years. I didn't think I'd live long enough to see that day come."

So he did remember after all, even though he had added a decade to the timeline. It was too much to hope that the vagaries of his memory could be so fortunate.

"I'm sorry, Dad. I thought it was something you'd rather not talk about."

"It is. But we have to, sooner or later, before I forget my own damn name. I suppose you've read the diary by now."

"Diary? What diary?"

"How many diaries do you think I've seen? The one in the keepsake box."

"Keepsake box? Dad, you're not making any sense."

Joseph stared at her for a moment. His expression slowly changed to disappointment. Norah noticed the tremor in his hand that happened when he was agitated. His thumb was rubbing repeatedly against his fingers.

"You're telling me you've never looked in the cedar chest?"

When they had moved Joseph into the home, he had insisted she keep the cedar chest. "*You can give away everything else away if you want. But I won't go anywhere unless you promise to keep the cedar chest.*"

"No, I haven't. Why would I?"

"The keepsake box was your mother's. Her diary was in it. I found it a year before she left."

"Before she left?"

"What?"

"Before she left. That's what you said, Dad."

"No, I didn't. Why would you say that? Are you trying to confuse me? I said *after* she left."

Norah checked herself. Divining the truth in what he was saying was more important than the inconsistencies in it.

"Sorry, I must have misheard you. Go on."

"Where was I? The keepsake box ... the diary ... Right, the diary. Her life story is in it from the time she was thirteen until we met. She didn't tell me much about her life except that she was born an Eskimo. I think they call it something different now. Anyway, she lost her father at a young age. She and her mother had to move to ... damn, Ed-something."

"Edmonton. I know that, Dad. Why wouldn't she have taken it with her when she left?"

"You're asking me? How would I know? I loved her, but I obviously didn't know her as well as I thought I did. All I could think was that she left it for you girls so you would know her story."

"Why didn't you tell Georgia and me about it?"

"Because I read it, and I probably shouldn't have. But how could I not?"

Why did you leave it behind, Mother? Was it for Dad or for Georgia and me? Or were you in too much of a hurry to get away and forgot about it? All this time it's been in that chest gathering dust. Are the answers I've always wanted, about why you left, inside it?

"So tell me, Dad. Why did she leave?"

"I still don't really know. I understand her better. But the pieces don't all fit."

"What pieces? Don't keep me in suspense. Tell me."

"Read it for yourself, Norah. It's not my story to tell."

"Why are you doing this? You know how badly I need to understand. Just tell me."

Joseph took a deep breath and let it out slowly. He appeared to be drifting off. Norah prompted him again.

"Dad ... Dad, tell me."

"Alright, I'll tell you what I know. But don't expect it to tie everything up with a bow because it doesn't."

Joseph paused to summon the courage he needed to tell the story. Norah felt guilty putting him through it. But she simply could not wait.

"Your mother was born in a small village in the North Territories. Or the West Territories. Something like that. Her father was a guide for rich muckety-mucks who went up there to go hunting. There was some kind of accident. Her father was killed." Joseph paused here as if to recharge his memory. "You know how these things work. Enough money can buy just about anything. The man used his money to cover it all up. He agreed to take Alice and her mother back to Edmonton with him.

"Her real name was Alasie, by the way. It got changed to Alice later. Alice's mother was a nanny for the guy's daughters. Wives of rich husbands don't have to take care of their children, it seems. The whole thing was terrible for your mother. She started the diary in the middle of all that stuff."

Some of this part of the story Norah already knew from the letter her mother sent after she left. But she could not confess this to Joseph because he did not know about that letter. It came secretly to Norah and Georgia through a friend of her mother's. But there were some details that were new or better defined in this telling of the story.

"Go on, Dad. I'm still listening."

"What's to say? An Eskimo village –the big city. It's just not the same. She missed her father something awful. And they were second class citizens. Living in a couple of rooms in a huge house. All that money floating around and none of it got to them.

"Alice struggled in school. She didn't fit in. What is they say? Square peg in a round hole. Or is it round peg in a square hole? Same difference. There was something about a rock she used to describe it. About being like a rock picked up from a river and dropped into the city. Sorry, I can't remember exactly how it went."

The slipstream was engaging as Joseph told the story. Her mother's image grew in clarity in Norah's memory.

"After a couple of years, the guy who had taken custody of them lost his wife. I don't remember if she wrote how it happened. Doesn't matter, anyway. These things happen, and what can you do? So they got married."

"Who got married, Dad?"

"Aren't you listening? I just told you. Alice's mother married the guy. It wasn't for love. I suppose it just made sense. He was lonely and Alice's mother was the easy solution. A chance like that for security, she couldn't pass up. But Alice felt betrayed. She never felt like she belonged there. *Invisible*. I think that was how she put it."

Norah was fully wrapped up in the slipstream now. At times Joseph's voice seemed to change its timbre and become Alice's voice.

"Her stepdad ... You know, I never liked that word. You're either a dad or you're not. It's not like you can inherit the role. I mean, really, think about it. It just doesn't make sense ... Anyway, he was a real S.O.B. He made them give up anything to do with their old life. He was the one who changed her name from Alasie to Alice.

"No surprise that all the boys her age were crazy about her. You know how beautiful she was. The first moment I saw her I fell head over heels in love." Joseph paused as he relived the moment. But it faded quickly, so he continued. "It made her stepsisters jealous which didn't help her cause. This part I don't understand. She wrote that she had no interest in those boys. And that she had some kind of secret that made her ashamed. My memory is fuzzy here. Apparently she was born during a ... Damn, what is that thing when it gets dark in the middle of the day?"

"A storm?"

"No! I know what a storm is, for God's sake! I mean when you can't see the sun."

"Oh, a solar eclipse."

"Yeah, that's it. Her mother told her she was cursed or something because of it. Something about an Eskimo folktale that explains an eclipse. The sun goddess—Alina? Mina? Some strange name. She was supposed to be fighting with her brother. He was the moon god. I don't remember his name either. The sun goddess ran away. But her brother found her. Somehow that was supposed to cause the eclipse.

"Anyway, being born during an eclipse was supposed to put some kind of mark on you that you couldn't escape. Superstitious nonsense, it seems to me." Joseph paused here and his expression changed. "She could have had any man she chose. So, why me? Only because I came along at the right time. Because ... "

The slipstream withdrew as Joseph's voice tailed off. Norah tried to hold onto to the image of her mother but it slipped away.

"Dad? Dad? Are you okay?"

"I was never good enough for her. I know that now. I was just a way out of a bad situation. It didn't matter that I worshiped the ground she walked on."

Joseph's voice was edged with bitterness as he emerged from the spell of the story he was telling.

"She loved you, Dad. Don't ever doubt that."

"Did she? Maybe—out of gratitude. But it wasn't enough to make her stay, was it? She was quick to leave when she found someone else. Someone who deserved her more than me."

Norah regretted now making him tell the story that Alice's diary held. It made him relive the worst days of his life and what he viewed as his own great failure.

"There's more in the diary. But you can read it for yourself. I'm tired now. Take me back to my room. I need to be alone."

Inukshuk

Windswept waves of rain clattering against the window in the early morning hours wrenched Norah from a few stolen hours of sleep. She recalled rolling peals of thunder during the night—some nearby, like cannon fire, and others far off, grumbles of discontent. Sila, the god of the weather, was flexing his muscles and making his presence known.

Get out of my head, Mother. I have more important things to concern myself with today.

Remnants of Inuit mythology, passed on from her mother in the years they'd had together, occasionally washed up like driftwood on the shores of her consciousness. Memories dislodged from their place in time as past and present found communal ground in the reverse tide of the slipstream.

Norah had been sorely tempted to retrieve the diary as soon as she arrived home the night before after her visit with Joseph. But what was recorded there she needed to explore in private to discover answers it might offer to the questions she had pondered for so long.

She made her way quietly downstairs while the others were still asleep. The cedar chest was buried beneath an assortment of boxes that had found their way to the basement in the intervening years. She cleared away the clutter and stood a moment staring at the chest. How had she not divined that it contained something important? There was a lock on the lid of the chest but it had been broken. Joseph must have lost the key, she surmised, and resorted to breaking the lock. The contents seemed at first glance to be just old clothes and a couple of quilts. She pushed them aside and uncovered what looked like a miniature sea chest—two feet long by a foot wide and foot deep—decorated with soapstone carvings—the keepsake box. Norah lifted the box clear of the chest and placed it on the floor. She felt a flutter in her heart as she opened the lid and sorted through the contents—jewelry, small soapstone carvings and old photographs. But no diary. Disappointment swept over her. She spread out the clothes and quilts stored in the chest hoping that the diary was wrapped up in them. But it was nowhere to be found. What had Joseph done with it?

Mother, why didn't you find a way to tell us about it? You could have mentioned it in the letter. Why go to the trouble of sending the letter and still not tell us? I don't understand. If you left it for us, why not tell us?

She picked up the photographs and sifted through them until one caught her attention. The resemblance to her mother as she had known her was evident. But this photo was from her teenage years. Alasie was facing away from the camera but with her face turned back toward it. Her expression was resolute and defiant. The physical characteristics of the Inuit were evident in her face—high cheekbones and the eyes obliquely set with heavy eyelids. But there was a perfection of symmetry to her features that held one's gaze. And in the portrait, which extended to the top of her shoulders, Alasie had a blanket wrapped around her which gave simultaneously the impression of vulnerability and seductiveness.

She had an extraordinary beauty. Joseph's words came back to Norah. She had a vision of the look on her father's face when they first met. What was this sudden flare of displeasure she felt? Lingering bitterness over her mother's abandonment of them? No, she realized, it was something more insidious—jealousy. Such beauty was rare and with it came the power to captivate. Alasie had used that power to captivate Joseph and claim him. No matter how much he loved his daughters, that devotion must pale by comparison with the passion he felt for Alasie.

Well, Mother, this is new. I've run the gamut of emotions where you are concerned. But never did I expect to find myself jealous of you. I suppose I can't blame you for that. It's my own baggage. But it complicates matters even more—as if things were not already hopelessly intertwined and entangled.

The wind was driving the rain in slanting sheets against the patio doors when Norah came back upstairs with the photographs in her hand. It was two full days now—forty-eight hours and counting—since anyone had set eyes on Troy. Whether he was absent by choice or by misfortune, on one level it begged the same question. Was it the legacy of loss that haunted their family? Perhaps the careless act, which snuffed out the life of her grandfather, had cast a shadow forward from one generation to the next.

Whether one acknowledged it or not, ancestry was encoded into one's being and not just at the DNA level. The spirits, or however you chose to envision the connecting threads, were passed on through the years. Handed forward or bequeathed or re-conjured, in one manner or another, they lived on.

So, Mother, I am prepared to believe that your spirits can move mountains. What would you have me do? How do I bend fate and bring my husband home?

She leafed through the photographs again and stopped at a photo of a small rock structure beside a river. Memory recoiled and recalled its name. Inukshuk—a symbolic structure her mother had spoken about with reverence.

Really, Mother? Well, why not? I am willing to try anything.

Norah had second thoughts when she came back downstairs after getting dressed. Entirely the wrong conditions for the task, she told herself. She pulled on a rain jacket and stepped out into the yard.

The rock garden, which Troy had spent an entire weekend constructing, provided the necessary materials. She spent the first half hour selecting appropriate rocks and carrying or rolling them to a spot at the back of the yard near the fence. She was drenched within the first few minutes. But the effort of moving the rocks kept her warm. The large rocks that would form the legs were the most difficult to manoeuvre. It took another twenty minutes to tug, push and lever them into position. The remainder of the work—slab rocks forming the body, a longer flat rock for the shoulders and arms, a rounded one for the head—went more quickly.

Norah stood back to appraise her work. The form she had envisioned took shape. It gathered life into itself gradually as if the rocks were shifting and reassembling themselves in response to an ancient imperative.

"Mom! What in God's name are you doing?" Andie crossed the yard and sheltered Norah under an umbrella. "You look like a drenched rat."

"I decided to try and make ... Never mind, you wouldn't understand."

"I know what it is. Or what it's supposed to be. An Inukshuk."

Norah looked at Andie in surprise.

"Don't look so surprised. I know a bit about our heritage—not that you bothered to teach us much. Inukshuk's are an Inuit tradition. If I'm not mistaken, they mean *Someone was here* or *You are on the right path.*"

"You know more than you want to let on. Who taught you that?"

Andie paused, as if she was looking for a way around the real answer to the question.

"Why do you assume someone had to teach me? I'm a reasonably intelligent person. Give me that much credit."

"I'm sorry. Everything I say seems to hit you the wrong way. So you know about Inukshuks. I made one because I'm hoping it will help your father find his way home, although when I say it sounds farfetched."

"Farfetched doesn't begin to cover it, Mom."

"Well, it can't hurt. If nothing else, it keeps me occupied."

"Come inside. The neighbours will think you've lost your mind."

"I don't particularly care what the neighbours think right now. But I'm finished anyway."

***

leaving sydney 2 p.m. your time. arriving dallas 7 a.m. tomorrow. connecting flight @ 9:15 a.m. arriving @ noon. any news?

nothing yet. pick you up at airport?

no. stay put. rental car booked. call you soon.

Norah sat on the bed staring at her iPhone. Such cruel irony, she thought. 9,700 miles between them and they could communicate like they were only minutes away. Troy was probably within an hour or two and yet she could not connect with him. Or could she? What if Detective White was right after all? If Troy was deliberately flying under the radar and not in any danger, she could reach out to him. It was ridiculous that she had not even tried.

troy. are you okay? please answer if you can.

She waited five minutes for a response.

please. just tell me you're okay. we're all so worried.

She waited again to no avail and decided to try calling. His voice mail answered.

"Troy. It's Norah. Please, please, if you're not in any danger, call me. Or call Andie if you don't want to talk to me. Just let us know you're okay."

She disconnected and slid the phone into her pocket. At least she had made the effort, she told herself. No stone left unturned—literally and figuratively.

Andie was waiting for Norah when she came back downstairs.

"I left a message on your father's cell phone," Norah said. "I asked him to call me or you, if he's okay."

"Why? You told the cop there were no problems between the two of you. Were you lying to him?"

"No. Definitely not ... Alright, I'll admit things have been a bit off between us lately. It's not entirely out of the question that he might want some time alone. But I can't believe he would punish us all this way. If nothing else, he would have called you."

"So you're telling me that you did lie to the cop. Dad is missing and you're more concerned about appearances than what might have actually happened to him. Why am I not surprised?"

Norah's store of patience hit its limit.

"I've had about enough of your attitude! Is this still all about Annaliese? If you're upset about her breaking up with you, don't take it out on me."

"What colour are her eyes?"

"What?"

"Annaliese. Do you know what colour her eyes are?"

"What has that go to do with anything?"

"If you cared about her, Mom, if you cared about what she meant to me, you would have noticed. They're hazel, by the way."

"Andie, I'm sorry things didn't work out between the two of you. I'm sorry I didn't notice the colour of her eyes. And I'm sorry if you think I don't approve of who you are. I don't know how you got that idea. I swear on a stack of bibles it isn't true."

"What colour were your mother's eyes?"

Norah was blindsided by the question.

"My mother? What has she got to do with any of this?"

"You built an Inukshuk. Your mother is Inuit. That's no coincidence."

"Did I miss something? You're talking in circles and not making any sense."

"Forget it. It was just a question."

Kevin came into the living room and flopped into a chair beside the fireplace. His presence shifted the focus.

"Heh."

"Heh, yourself." Andie answered. "Nice of you to grace us with your presence."

"What's your problem?"

"You, at the moment."

"Still in a pissy mood? Must be that time of the month."

"How original. Did you learn that from your homeless friends?"

"I really don't give a rat's ass what you think. You wouldn't have survived a day in the places I've been."

Norah felt the edge in his voice and the defiance behind it. He had aged far more than the elapsed time.

"Whose fault is that? Nobody pushed you out the door, Kevin. You decided all on your own to live like a hobo."

"Kiss my ass. I don't have to explain myself to you."

Norah intervened in the exchange.

"What is happening here? This place in turning into World War III." Andie and Kevin locked eyes—each unwilling to give ground.

"Andie, if you can't be civil, go home. I can't take all this fighting. And what was that reference about my mother all about?"

"Nothing. Forget it."

Kevin saw his opening to strike back.

"That's your style, isn't it, Andie? Toss a grenade and run for cover. No wonder your girlfriend walked out on you. You probably turned her back to guys."

"At least I have relationships. That's more than I can say for you."

"Stop it, you two!! For God's sake, your father is missing. We have no idea where he is or what danger he may be in. And all you two can do is fight? You should be ashamed of yourselves. I for damn sure am ashamed of both of you!"

***

Norah closed herself in her bedroom to escape the animosity. The rainstorm continued until noon—a representation of the atmosphere in the house. When the clouds finally left and the sun emerged, she hid herself in the gazebo. Sawbucks settled at her feet.

"Thank God for you, Sawbucks. At least there's one living body that isn't as mad as sin at me."

She pulled out her iPhone and called the police station.

"Detective White, please."

"Please hold. I'll see if he's available."

Norah waited impatiently for several minutes.

"Hello, Mrs. Watson. My apologies for the wait. I was meaning to call you."

"Have you found out anything about my husband?"

"Niagara Falls Police located his vehicle in a parking lot near the Falls."

"What does that tell you?"

"Not much, unfortunately."

"You found his SUV but not him. That can't be good news, can it?"

"I prefer not to speculate on what it might mean."

"That sounds evasive, Detective."

"No, it's not." There was impatience in his voice. "We deal in facts, not speculations. As soon as we have anything substantive, rest assured we will let you know."

"Alright. Oh, there is one thing I neglected to mention. Troy did call me late Sunday evening. He called my cell phone, but didn't leave a message."

"Why didn't you tell me that when I interviewed you?"

"I didn't know the call was from him until I checked later."

"Does he often call you and not leave a message?"

"No, of course not. What are you implying?"

"Any behaviour out of the ordinary we need to know about. It affects the investigation."

"So what does it tell you?"

"Nothing, specifically. But it could be a piece of the puzzle. Is there anything else you left out?"

"No, why would I?"

"I have to ask. It's my job. As I said, I'll be in touch if anything substantive comes up."

"Alright, thank you. Goodbye."

Norah disconnected and put her phone on the seat beside her. She weighed what Detective White had told her. Troy's SUV had been found abandoned. How could that not be bad news? It opened up a series of possibilities all of which could only end badly. As she wrestled with these scenarios, she heard the patio doors slide open. Kevin stepped out on the patio and walked towards the Inukshuk. He examined it closely.

The Inukshuk had turned out to be, without her planning it, an *inunnguaq*—the form of a human being.

"Andie says this thing is called an Inukshuk. What does that mean?" Kevin asked.

"It's an Inuit tradition. They build them as navigational aids. But they also have a kind of inspirational purpose as well."

"So how does it work? Is it supposed to be enchanted or something like that?"

"I don't think *enchanted* is quite the right way to put it. It's more about symbolism. Honestly, I don't really know for sure."

Sawbucks sniffed the base of the Inukshuk, circled around it and sniffed again.

"Aw, Mom. I think she's going to pee on it."

But instead, Sawbucks settled beside the structure and rested her head on the rocks at the base.

"So, about your mother. You never talked much about her except that she left when you were young. I guess you hate her for that."

There was a challenge in his voice. An attempt to draw out emotions she might be hiding.

"Hate? No. But I do have mixed emotions. I don't know as much of her story as I probably should. I know that she was born an Inuit in a village in the Northwest Territories. She lost her father at a very young age which set in motion events that led to her being sent to Ontario and eventually marrying my father. I was six and my sister was thirteen when she left the first time."

"The *first* time?"

"Yes, she came back. She left again a few years later and came back again. But the third time she left, she didn't return. She wrote a letter to Georgia and me to explain why she couldn't come back, although the *why* was never really clear to us."

"Did you keep the letter?" Norah nodded. "So you still hope she'll come back some day?"

How am I supposed to answer that question, Mother? Hope is a dangerous thing. But without it, what do we really have to keep us going?

"The letter is important to me. But her coming back ... I don't think so."

"You say you don't hope for it. But you do. You just won't let yourself admit to it. You do that a lot, Mom—blocking out things you don't want to know."

Norah did not reply. The last thing she needed now was more guilt.

***

The three of them kept their distance from each other for the rest of the day. Norah came to her bedroom in the evening and saw the photos from the keepsake box on top of the dresser. Was that where she had left them? She could not remember for certain, but she suspected otherwise. The implications were unsettling.

The photo on top now was a wedding photo taken on the steps of an old church of indiscriminate denomination. The woman was Inuit but the man was not. It must be the second wedding of Alasie's mother, she deduced. The bride wore a simple beige dress. Nothing in her attire gave any deference to her Inuit heritage. Her expression was contrived—a forced smile of resignation.

The groom wore an expensive, tailored, three-piece black suit, pale blue shirt and a navy blue pinstripe tie. His smile was more suggestive of acquisition and victory than of wedded bliss. His arm was wrapped too possessively around his bride as if signalling ownership. Behind the groom, one step higher, were the children. The two daughters wore elegant, full length gowns that overshadowed the bride's dress.

But the most telling aspect of the photo was not part of the moment at all. Alasie had cut herself out of the portrait—an act of obvious defiance and pain.

Why didn't you tell me about this chapter of your life, Mother? How could you have hidden something so important? Maybe it was an experience you had to suppress. You had to lock the door on that memory forever. Is that it?

The emerging story of her mother's life reopened a troublesome question for Norah: Where should her allegiance lie? Her father's claims on her loyalty were compelling. Languishing in a nursing home slowly but surely slipping into the grip of Parkinson's Disease. In the lifelong equation of sanity, it was hard not to conclude that the emotional turmoil of his relationship with Alice had taken its toll. On the other hand, the tribulations of her mother's life—scarred by death and stripped of her identity—drew the pendulum of sympathy back in her direction. Thirty years had gone by and still that emotional tug of war lived on.

Heart to Heart

Would this unforgiving night never reach its end? A few fitful hours of sleep after midnight were worse than none at all. Wide-eyed awake since 4:00 a.m. willing the minutes to turn into hours. The concussion of a car door slamming punctuated the silence. Muffled voices rising in pitch and another door slam. Who in their right mind would be having an argument at this hour of the morning?

The ping of Norah's cell phone startled her. She opened her eyes and struggled to focus. Had she been half asleep and dreaming? Or half awake and imagining? Or both, courtesy of the slipstream. She felt around for her iPhone on the night table.

arrived dallas. bumped from t.o. flight—overbooked. so pissed! on standby for 10:30 flight. any news?

nothing. found his car. no sign of him.

stay strong. prayers with you.

What day was it? She had to make a conscious effort to remember. Wednesday? No, Thursday. The days all ran together now in one unchanging stream.

CoAAH, coo, cooo, co.

The mourning doves were back. Their soft, plaintive cooing was comforting. But they were farther away this morning—not sitting on the gazebo roof. Norah opened the blinds to scan the yard and was startled to see them perched on the arms of the Inukshuk. The reversing tide engaged and she was back with her mother and Georgia walking along the Humber River near their childhood home. Dragonflies went stitching across the path in front of them. Georgia made wild attempts to capture one—shrieking when it complied and landed on her arm.

What does it mean when this happens, Mother? This sudden remembrance as if the universe has pushed reverse on the time button. Each second bulges like an expanding water droplet. Is there something I am supposed to see that I missed the first time?

Norah was about to turn from the window when she saw Kevin emerge from the house. He crossed the yard to the Inukshuk and sat cross-legged in front of it. The doves remained perched on the arms observing him. He looked up toward her bedroom window as if signaling that he wanted to talk to her. Or was it her discomfort with their last conversation still nagging at her? Either way, she needed to talk to him, she decided.

Ten minutes later, Norah stepped out into the yard. Kevin turned to look at her as she sat down beside him.

"Have you ever made one of these before?" He gestured towards the Inukshuk.

"No," she answered. "I never had a reason to."

"I was gone for five months. You never thought to build one for me?"

Think carefully before you answer, she told herself. It may be the difference between him staying or leaving.

"You weren't really missing. You chose to stay away. But that doesn't mean I wasn't worried about you. Not a day passed that I didn't say a prayer for you."

Kevin turned away from her and occupied himself with scratching Sawbucks under the chin. "What about your mother? Ever make one for her?"

"No. Honestly, it never occurred to me."

"So you never really wanted her to come back. You hate her. Admit it."

"That's not true. I was angry with her. Both Georgia and I were. But we still loved her. You can be angry with someone and still love them."

"Why do you talk about her in the past tense? You hope she's dead?"

"Stop twisting my words."

"Then be honest. I know bullshit when I hear it."

There was intensity in him now that unnerved her.

"We're not going to have this conversation. You're angry. I understand that. But you're throwing out accusations you have no business making."

"Why do people run away from you? Ever wonder about that?"

His question froze Norah. It could not be a coincidence that he had struck at her greatest self-doubt.

"I'll bet your mother's dead. She lay on her deathbed hoping you would come. But you didn't because you've hated her from the day she left."

It happened before she could stop herself. She slapped his face exactly the same way Troy had. But there was no shock on his face this time.

"Wanna hit me again? Go ahead. I can take it."

"Is that what this is about? You think what your father did is my fault? Okay, I'm to blame. I should have protected you."

"I don't need protecting. I've survived a lot worse than that."

"Then what is wrong with you? Why are you doing this to me?"

"Just trying to open your eyes."

"Open my eyes to what?"

"Keep asking that question, Mom. You'll figure it out eventually."

He stood up and walked away from her. The Inukshuk radiated with an electrical current now as if it was joining in the condemnation.

Are you still out there, Mother? And if you are, have you been waiting for me to find you? Enough time may have passed to cancel out the mistakes. But is it enough time for forgiveness?

***

no go on 10:30 flight. crap! confirmed for noon flight. news?

Fate was conspiring against their reunion. Norah pictured Georgia stranded at the Dallas airport walking loops around the hallways with impatience etched in her expression.

nothing new. waiting is so hard. losing my grip on things.

hang in. be there soon.

Three days now since the last sighting of Troy. It was beginning to feel like a countdown clock, this agonizing accounting of time, as things unraveled around her. She heard raised voices in the living room as she came in through the patio doors.

"Drop the act, Kevin. This *nobody understands me* routine isn't fooling anyone. You like playing the outsider. It's all a big grab for sympathy. I'll bet you've slept in the gazebo far more often than you're willing to admit."

"I've slept in places you can't imagine. You'd piss yourself if you knew some of the things I've seen."

"Oh, here we go again. Kevin out in the big, bad world. Lions and tigers and bears, oh my!"

Norah came into the room. Kevin threw at a glance at her, then at his sister and walked out of the room. Norah heard his footsteps thumping up the stairs two steps at a time.

"Why do you keep provoking him, Andie?"

"Why do you keep defending him? He's so damn self-centered."

"He's a teenager. It comes with the territory. Believe it or not, you were the same way when you were his age."

"Ah, now we're getting at the heart of things."

The defiant look in Andie's eyes startled Norah.

"What?"

"I was about his age when I figured out I was gay. You're thinking he might be too. Don't worry, he's not. You only have one defective child."

The accusation stung Norah. She hesitated just long enough for Andie to claim victory.

"You don't have an answer for that, do you?"

***

Get away from it all. The thought crystalized in Norah's mind. Get away from Andie and Kevin who were constantly at odds, away from the house where accusations were flying in every direction, and try to clear her mind. She needed perspective and only getting away for a bit would offer that.

She took Sawbucks and went for a walk in the conservation area. It was quiet during the week once school started up again. Nothing to distract her from puzzling through what was happening. Sawbucks stopped at the trail to the marsh pond and looked up at Norah.

"No, not there, Sawbucks. That's Kevin's hideaway. Let's keep going. There's a better place for us."

She tried to clear her mind as they left the wheat grass field and took the trail that sloped down through the woodlot to the creek and back uphill to the picnic area. Focus, she told herself. On the birds trilling. The wind rustling through the trees. Shadows shifting on the ground. Grasshoppers launching themselves into flight. No troubling thoughts or worries or doubts until she found ground zero of her emotions.

It took fifteen minutes to reach her destination—the Medicine Wheel Garden on the slope that lead to the trail down to Heart Lake. She sat on a bench in the garden and took a long, deep breath. Sawbucks settled her head on Norah's feet.

Alright, Mother. If we are going to have a real heart to heart across the slipstream, this is the place it needs to happen. Yes, I know it technically isn't an Inuit place. It's a place honouring aboriginal beliefs. The Seven Grandfather Teachings— honesty, respect, humility, love, wisdom, truth and courage. All things I think you would value. It's the best I can do right now.

Mother, things are coming unhinged. My husband is missing and I don't know if it is by his own choice or foul play. I'm losing touch with my children. They're convicting me of crimes and deceptions of the heart. It's not fair—any of this. Why I am the enemy now?

Do I hate you? I guess the argument could be made. I am angry with you for good reason. What you did to us, and to our father, was wrong in every way. But I kept your letter. And I've allowed myself to talk to you through the slipstream. You've been AWOL for thirty years. But I've kept your memory alive.

Andie and Kevin keep dragging you into the conversation. Why? They only know you from what I have told them. And I did not have much to tell. So why are they fixated on you? Are you trying to speak to me through them? Is there something you want to say to me? Okay, I'm listening. Speak now, or forever hold your peace.

Norah waited several minutes for any kind of sign that might offer itself. But none came.

"Fine. I didn't really expect it to happen anyway. I really just needed time to myself. Let's go, Sawbucks. There's one more thing I need to do today before Georgia gets here."

She pushed open the gate and entered the yard. The doves were perched on top of the gazebo. One flew down, perched on the arm of the Inukshuk and surveyed her before flying back to the gazebo roof.

"What are they trying to tell me, Sawbucks? Keep the faith? That's easier said than done."

Her iPhone pinged signaling a new text message.

finally here. stuck in godawful customs lineup. may take a while. see you soon as.

***

Norah knocked twice on the door of her father's suite. But Joseph did not answer. She knocked again before letting herself in.

"Hi, Dad," she announced herself. "Decided to drop by earlier today. I have a house showing this evening."

Another white lie. But safe enough, since he was unlikely to see through it.

"Dad. Hello?"

Joseph was seated on the sofa and appeared to be watching television. But the sound was turned down. He swiveled his head at the sound of her voice. The vague expression on his face spoke volumes.

"It's me, Dad. Norah."

"I know who you are. You think I wouldn't recog—recog-*nize* my own daughter?" His difficulty enunciating was painful to witness.

She bent down to kiss him on the cheek, which he grudgingly accepted, and sat down beside him.

"Have you had lunch? Do you want me to fix something for you?"

"I'm not hungry."

"I could make coffee."

Joseph did not respond to her offer. His attention waned for a moment.

Where does he go at moments like this, Mother? Is he thinking of you or just lost in the fog? And while we're on the subject, do you ever think of him? Ever wonder how he is doing?

"I would apologize to her if she just came to see me. I don't know what I did wrong. But I would apologize anyway."

"Apologize to whom, Dad?"

Joseph looked annoyed. He seemed to be picking up on a conversation he thought they had carried on.

"Who else? Your sister."

"Georgia lives in Australia now, Dad."

"Australia? What put it in her mind to go there? We don't have any relatives there ... Do we?"

"No. She just decided to move there all on her own. I guess she needed a change."

"A change from me. Is that what you're saying?"

Was there a subtext to his question? In the disarray of his mind, had he stumbled back to Alice and her comings and goings?

"No, of course not, Dad. Her moving had nothing to do with you. She sends you the flowers every week. That's her way of showing that she hasn't forgotten about you."

Joseph looked over at the table where the flowers were arranged in a glass vase.

"Calla lilies," he said. "They're from Georgia?"

"Yes. She knows how much you love them."

After a pause, she continued, "Dad, can you tell me more about Mother? What she wrote in her diary, I mean."

He looked at her with a mixture of confusion and resentment.

"In her what? ... Oh, the diary. Why would you remind me of that? Can't you see that's the one thing I'd rather not remember? Anyway, you can read it for yourself."

"I wish I could. But a water pipe burst in our basement last winter. It was right over top of the cedar chest. Everything in it got soaked. Mom's diary is illegible now. I'm sorry to ask you. But I so much need to know." She hoped the lie would work.

"I can't. I don't want to remember."

"Please, Dad. Can you try?"

"Why can't you just let it be?"

"Just this one last time. I promise I won't ask again."

"Alright, I'll try. But this is the last time I'm going to talk about her. Where did I leave off?"

"You said she had some kind of shameful secret. And there was the Inuit tale about the Sun God and the Moon God."

"Inuit? What the hell is that?"

"Eskimo. Inuit is what they're called now."

"Right. Let me think."

Joseph did not speak for several minutes. Norah was afraid he was losing the thread of their conversation. But finally he began.

"She was all twisted up about the secret. Don't ask me what it was. I don't remember if she actually said. She felt like she didn't belong in that family. Her mother kept teaching her about their way of life—Eskimo's, I mean. What did you call them? It doesn't matter. Anyway, it just made things worse to keep hearing about the life they used to have."

Joseph stopped as if he had hit a dead end.

"Then what, Dad?"

"Wait, damn it. This is hard for me. She ran away from home. Tried to get back to the village where she was born. She didn't make it. Her stepdad—he had an in with the cops. They caught her and brought her back. After that, he kept her on a tight string. He was a miserable son of a bitch. Should have been thrown in jail for what he did. But if you've got money, you can be any damn way you want. That's the way of the world. If you don't like it, too bad. Not a Christ-damned thing you can do about it."

He was wandering away from the details and indulging his own resentments. Norah gently nudged him back to the story.

"How old was she when this happened?"

"I don't know. What the hell does it matter? Not old enough to make her own decisions."

"Sorry, Dad. Go on."

His sidetracks frustrated Norah. But she realized he had to find his own meandering way through the memories and the emotions they evoked.

"She got into trouble when she was 18. Did something that she shouldn't have."

"What, Dad. What did she do?"

"Stop pestering me, damn it! Or I'll just stop right now. I shouldn't have to anyway."

Norah struggled to reign in her impatience.

"I'm sorry. Just do the best you can to remember."

"She shacked up one night with someone her father didn't approve of. God only knows why. Maybe it was a guy from the other side of the tracks. I don't know. But it pissed him off mightily. He wouldn't have anything to do with her after that. Something about shaming the family name. Like he hadn't already done that himself. Anyway, he sent her away. Got her a job as a nanny in Toronto and washed his hands of her."

Joseph's voice softened now as he came to the part of the narrative that involved him.

"That's when I met her. I was doing some work for the family she was working for. The first time I set eyes on her I couldn't look away. My God, she was so beautiful. I'd never seen anything like her. How could I not fall in love with her? I damn near proposed on the spot ... Anyway, the rest you know. She was too good for me by a country mile and I was a damn fool for believing otherwise."

He had finished telling Alice's story and yet it still felt incomplete to Norah. Was there a decisive circumstance he did not know that would tie up the loose ends? Something he had repressed in his memory? Quite possibly, but it was long lost now.

"Thank you, Dad. I'm sorry for making you relive it all."

Joseph glanced back at the dining room table.

"Calla lilies. They make me feel younger. God only knows why."

***

Norah camped out on the front porch waiting for Georgia. The layers of irony in the circumstances rose in her mind. Georgia was spanning half the globe in a day and a half while Troy could quite possibly be only hours away. Distance could be compressed or expanded the same way time could shapeshift as the reversing tide rose and ebbed.

A blue sedan rounded the corner and slowed down as if the driver was searching for a familiar house. It sped up again and pulled in the driveway. Norah jumped to her feet and ran to greet Georgia as she stepped out of the car.

"It's so good to see you." Norah threw her arms around her sister. "Thank you so, so much for coming. You must be exhausted."

"Let me see your face." Georgia took Norah's face in her hands. "A sight for sore eyes. Little sister, I've missed you so very, very much."

They relaxed into each other's arms for a minute. Living on the other side of the world had not extinguished the perpetual light in her eyes or her flashing smile. But Georgia had grown her hair long. It swept in waves around her face and over her shoulders and made her look younger than when she had left.

Mother, if you are still out there, is your heart swelling at this moment?

"Now, about Troy. Have you heard anything?"

"Bits and pieces. Nothing really. I think it's just another routine case to the police. I'm not sure they really even believe he's missing."

"It's okay, Norah. I don't need the full story right this minute." She turned to Andie and Kevin who had emerged from the house. "Andie, the last time I saw you was your high school graduation."

"Bet you didn't think I'd turn out to be the black sheep of the family."

Georgia flashed a questioning look at Norah who returned it with a *don't ask* expression.

"And you, Kevin. Quite the adventure you've been on. You had us all worried half to death."

"Yeah, the not-so-prodigal son returns."

"I guess you're a bit tired of hearing that, aren't you? You're back now. That's all that matters. Let's go inside. I could use some strong coffee. I've crossed a bunch of time zones in the last day and a half."

***

"So they have video footage of him and they found his SUV. That's the extent of it?" Georgia sipped her coffee as they settled at the kitchen table.

"In a nutshell, yes. I've called the Detective in charge of the case a couple of times. But I've obviously become a nuisance to him."

"Don't let that discourage you. Keep his feet to the fire."

"I thought about hiring a private investigator. Is that crazy?"

"No, I wouldn't call it crazy. But let's put a pin in that idea for now."

Georgia glanced toward the backyard.

"Wait a minute. Is *that* what I think it is?"

"Yes," Norah answered. "An Inukshuk. I know it seems foolish. But I had to do something."

"In the pouring rain, no less," Andie interjected, "if you can picture that."

Georgia gave Norah another questioning look.

"Since you built the Inukshuk, I have to ask. How much have you told them about ... you know who?"

"Really, Georgia? After all these years, that's the best you can manage? She's still our mother. Even if she did—"

"Abandon us. I think that's the word you're looking for. Not exactly mother of the year material. You know she's the reason Dad is the way he is. She broke his heart."

"Do you not love her at all, Georgia?" Norah asked. "Not even when all the doors are closed and no one is paying attention?"

"I moved halfway around the world to try and put distance between myself and her. That should tell you all you need to know."

"And how did that work out for you?" Kevin asked. Norah flashed a warning look at Kevin that he deflected.

Georgia turned to face Kevin. "Excuse me? Do I detect a hint of condescension?"

"Just a question. Don't answer if it you don't want to."

"Ignore him," Andie replied. "He's been on his own soapbox since Mom found him hiding out in the gazebo. Apparently he sees the world more clearly than the rest of us."

"Don't start, you two." Norah reprimanded them. "Your aunt dropped everything to come her and support us. At least let her get her bearings." She turned back to Georgia. "Sorry, they've been going at it pretty much non-stop. I asked them to behave when you got here. But it seems that's too much to ask."

"It's okay," Georgia answered. "You're all worried and on edge. That's understandable. And to answer your question, Kevin. There's a bond between mothers and daughters you can't escape no matter what happens. That much I've figured out. So, Norah, have you filled them in on our family's dirty laundry—that she left Dad, and in the process left us, for another man?"

"Yes, more or less. They know about the letter."

"Mom, you told me about the letter," Kevin said. "But not that there was another man, although it wasn't hard to figure it out."

"Consider yourself fortunate," Andie interjected. "I didn't even get to know about the letter."

Norah instantly regretted her misstep.

"I'm sorry, Andie. I only told Kevin yesterday. I didn't mean to exclude you."

"And yet you did. But don't worry about it. You would be surprised at what I know."

Georgia stepped in to defuse the situation before Norah could puzzle out what that might mean.

"Ah yes, the infamous letter. It's causing as much mayhem now as it did back then. You know, I can't remember what we did with it. How we decided to get rid of it, I mean. Burning it would have been the most appropriate thing. But I don't remember us doing that."

Norah shifted her eyes..

"Norah, don't tell me you kept it? You did, didn't you? You actually kept it."

"I couldn't bring myself to throw it away. It's all we have left of her."

"Isn't that a little like keeping the bullet that killed your best friend? Oh shit, I'm sorry Norah. Blame it on jet lag."

"I know you didn't mean it that way." She turned to Andie and Kevin. "I always planned to share it with you some day. It's all you'll ever have of your grandmother."

Andie's eyes dropped unexpectedly. Norah studied her. What did that gesture signify? It was not like her to hold back anything.

"I guess you kids deserve to hear the whole story," Georgia said. "So you can make your own judgment. Anything you hear from me is biased, to say the least. So where is it, Norah? What's your secret hiding place?"

"A shoebox in our bedroom closet."

"A shoebox? Well, I guess that's a good a place as any. Go and get it. We might as well get it over with right now."

The Riffle of Time

My Precious Daughters,

    I am so very sorry for all the pain I have caused you. Three times now I have left without saying goodbye. Even when I came back, I did not give you any explanation. I expected both of you to simply forgive and forget. That was inexcusable of me. But I could not imagine how to make you understand.

    I am writing to you to beg for your forgiveness. Or at least that you try not to hate me for all the ways I have failed you. I cannot forgive myself for that, so how would it be possible for you not to feel the same toward me? But perhaps you will find it in your hearts, not now but when you yourselves are mothers, to still feel something for me.

    I so wish that I could tell you my life story from start to finish so you could understand why I am the way I am. But there is too much to tell. I can only give you a little bit of my story and hope that it is enough.

    I was born an Inuit in a small village in the Northwest Territories. I expect that you will not have heard that word: Inuit. Many call us Eskimos, but our people do not like that name.

    My father died in a terrible accident when I was just a child. It was a great injustice. But that matters little now. After his death, my mother and I were persuaded, although we had little choice, to move to Edmonton. It was a form of compensation for my father's untimely death. But to us it was as though we were snatched from our world and dropped into a new one with no preparation. Everything was so strange and frightening.

    My mother became a nanny for two children of a wealthy businessman and his wife. She tried her best to shelter me from the shock of so much change. But a few years later, another wave of change crashed over me. The man's wife died and, to drown his loneliness, he married my mother. It was not out of love, but necessity, that my mother agreed to the marriage.

    You must understand that I have always been marked for trouble. When I was only eighteen, after an impetuous and foolish act, I was sent to Toronto be a nanny for a wealthy family—the same path that was imposed on my mother. The flight to

Toronto is forever burned into my memory. Those were the loneliest hours of my life. Every minute put me farther away from my mother and the life I knew.

I had no options now. I had to earn my keep. The family I worked for lived in a big house in Mount Pleasant. I took care of the children as my mother had looked after the children who became my stepsisters. I wrote long, heart-wrenching letters to my mother. I doubt she ever got them. My spiteful stepfather would have kept them from her.

It soon became clear to me that this new life could not last. My heart was not in it. I needed a saviour—someone to rescue me from the wreckage of my life. For once, fate was kind to me. A man, who was a friend of my employer, fell in love with me. He was almost twice my age and had never married. I agreed to marry him. It was the only chance I had for a future. That man, of course, is your father.

I will never speak ill of your father. He treated me well. Better than I had been treated since I was a child. And he gave me the greatest gift of all—the two of you. Did you know it was your father who chose your names? Georgia Norah was your grandmother's name.

But you will remember that I secretly gave you Inuit names.

First you, Georgia. I looked into your eyes as a baby and knew that you would be strong, independent and would travel far. That's why called you Amaqjuac. It means 'the strong one'.

And you, Norah. When I looked into your eyes, I knew you would be fragile and would find life hard but would endure. That's why I called you Tapeesa. It means 'arctic flower'.

I saw the gift in both of you, although you may not see it as a gift. The ability to exist in the riffle of time—that place where past and present, and sometimes even the future, coexist. It connects you more closely to the spirits. I have it because of the chance timing of my birth and I have passed it on to both of you.

Amaqjuac, it lies deep within you. I do not know if it will rise. But it is there whether you sense it or not.

Tapeesa, it is strong in you. You may find it frightening. But do not try to tame it. Make peace with it and it will serve you.

I have spoken little of your father. It is difficult for me to think of him and the pain I caused him. Did I love him? Yes, I grew to love him. But not in the way he loved me. I am marked by fate to be forever different. As hard as I tried to be what he needed, I could not. I ran away looking for my true love. Hating myself for leaving the two of you and always coming back defeated and ashamed. Until this time.

I have finally found where I belong. I will not be coming back this time. I miss you, my precious daughters, so terribly. It tears at my heart to think of you. But I am convinced you are better off without me.

Take care of your father. You are all he has now. You are my gift to him for rescuing me.

Know that I will never, ever stop loving you. Even when I am far away, I will be near.

Georgia took a deep breath and shook her head.

"It's been a long time since I read that letter. Almost like another lifetime. Honestly, I could have gone to my grave without hearing it again."

"Really, Georgia. After all these years, you still can't see her side of the story?"

"That's the problem. We really don't know her side of the story. Just what she said in her letter which isn't much. I'll admit, I don't know if I could have survived all the things that happened to her. But stuff happened to us too, Norah. We grew up in a broken home. And all this marked-by-fate business ... Hell, I don't know what to think. Maybe I should just shut up now."

"You never thought of trying to find her."

Both Norah and Georgia flinched at the tone in Andie's voice. Georgia took up the challenge.

"Clarification, please. Was that a question or a statement?"

"Either or. But for now, let's say it's a question."

"Sure. We thought about it. But it always seemed like she didn't want to be found. And we thought trying would be disloyal to our father."

"I guess that's one way to look at it."

Norah took up the challenge this time.

"That's enough, Andie. You're mad at me. I get that. But you will not speak to your aunt that way. Apologize. *Now.*"

"When and if I have something to apologize for, I will."

Andie paused for effect, turned and left the room.

"Who put a burr under her saddle?" Georgia asked.

"Sorry, Georgia. She broke up with her partner and doesn't want to admit she's having a hard time with it. And apparently, I did something to suggest I have problems with her being gay. She's been raking me over the coals for three days now."

Norah cast a glance at Kevin. He shook his head and left the room as well.

"Wow, if looks could kill," Georgia remarked.

"That's what I've been dealing with. They're both mad as hell at me—when they're not too busy being mad at each other. Thank God you're here. I need someone on my side."

***

Georgia sat in front of the Inukshuk. She placed her hands on the rock forming the head, tracing its shape to feel the edges and the texture of it.

"Georgia? What are you doing?" Norah walked across the yard to her sister.

"Just experimenting. Trying to see if it triggers anything in me. Unfortunately, nada." She turned to face Norah. "The gift, as mother used to refer to it—we haven't talked about it for a while. I have to be honest. It if were anyone else, I'd think they had a screw loose."

"I've wondered about that myself more than once."

They stood, walked to the gazebo and settled inside it. Sawbucks curled up on the floor between them with her head resting on Norah's feet. Georgia reached down to stroke the dog's back as she cast about for a safe subject.

"What does Troy think about it. The *gift*, I mean."

"We don't talk about it much. Never, actually. We've just sort of agreed to stay away from the subject. I'm regretting that now."

"They're going to find him, Norah. It's just a matter of time."

"Yes, but when they do—"

"Don't. Don't even go there. You have to stay positive."

The mourning doves cooed from their perch on the top of the gazebo. They returned more frequently throughout the day now as if they too were waiting for news.

"Okay," Georgia announced. "Time to change the subject. Your choice."

"Anything?"

"Yup. Have at it."

"Okay. What about your love life? Is there anyone special?"

"Off limits. Choose again."

"You said, anything."

"Anything, but that."

"You too? Everybody's cutting me out. Why did you come if you're just going to stonewall me?"

Georgia ran her fingers through her hair as she debated how to answer.

"Alright, if you insist. There is this one guy. Mark. We've been seeing each other on and off for a couple of years."

"What does *on and off* mean?"

"I've broken it off several times. He waits, stays in touch and we start up again."

"So, is it serious?"

"Serious? I hate that word. Why can't it just be whatever it is?"

"Which is what?"

Georgia ran her fingers through her hair again.

"Well, as soon as I got off the phone with you, I called him. He came running. Even offered to drop everything and come with me."

"Sounds like love to me. Is it?"

"He's said it. I haven't."

"Meaning you're not sure? Or you don't."

Georgia stood and walked to the entrance to the gazebo.

"Meaning, I just want it to be uncomplicated."

"And love complicates it?"

Georgia turned back to Norah.

"You of all people should know the answer to that question."

"Don't you see it? You've let what Mother did taint your whole life."

"I'm not like you, Norah. She abandoned us. She walked away like we were nothing to her. You seem to be able to excuse that. I can't."

"I'm not asking you to. I'm just saying that you're letting her live rent-free in your head."

"Oh, and you aren't? Can we get off this subject, Norah? I'm here to support you. I don't want to fight."

Norah felt time uncoupling again. She was simultaneously here with Georgia in the moment and with her that day the letter arrived. The two experiences merged and became one.

Did you really believe we would be better off without you, Mother? Better that it be a clean break so the wounds could heal? Well, that didn't happen. Not for me and especially not for Georgia.

Georgia saw the change in Norah's expression. "It's happening right now, isn't it?"

"Yes. Do you feel it?"

"I *see* it in you. I sort of feel it second hand."

The patio doors slid open. Andie called to them from the door.

"Mom, Detective White is here."

The slipstream withdrew as fear displaced it.

"Norah, don't jump to conclusions." Georgia took Norah's hand. "Let's just go in and see what he has to say."

"He's the officer in charge of Troy's case. He said he'd call if he had any news. But he came in person. That can't be good."

Detective White looked uncomfortable as they entered the living room. He chose to remain standing.

"I don't believe we've met."

"I'm Georgia. Norah's sister. You have news about Norah's husband?"

Detective White turned to Norah.

"I wanted to inform you before the evening newscasts. A man's body was recovered downstream in the Niagara River. The height, weight and general appearance roughly match your husband. But based on a preliminary examination, the Coroner thinks the body may have been in the water too long to fit the timeline of your husband's disappearance."

Norah was too shaken by the pronouncement to respond. Georgia stepped in for her.

"So you need her to come and view the body. Is that it?"

"I'm afraid that won't be possible. The victim was severely assaulted, with some kind of blunt object, before his body was placed in the water. The face, I'm sorry to say, is too disfigured for identification. Does your husband have any distinguishing marks, Mrs. Watson? A tattoo, a scar, or some sort of distinctive birthmark."

"No. Nothing like that."

"What about dental records? They can be helpful in identification."

"No. Troy hated dentists. He thought x-rays were a waste of time. He would go for fillings when had to, but that's all."

"We'll have to rely on DNA matching. Niagara Falls P.D. have your husband's belongings from the hotel. They should be able to get a DNA sample from them. But DNA matching takes time. The system is always backlogged. It could be a few days before we get the results."

"But you don't think it's him, right?"

"As I said, preliminary details from the coroner make it doubtful. But we can't be sure in these situations. The DNA test is the only way to be certain."

"And if it isn't him, what then?"

Detective White looked away as he answered.

"We continue the investigation. And of course, we'll keep you informed if any leads develop."

"So you don't have any leads right now. Is that what you're saying?"

"The best thing you can do right now is let us do our job. Rest assured we'll leave no stone unturned."

Andie turned her eyes to Norah as she replied. "Yes, well, we've been down that road already, haven't we?"

***

The slow exhale of September was in the air. Each day was perceptibly shorter now, or at least it felt that way to Norah. Each minute ticking off the clock counted against Troy's safety. But there was still hope. The body found in the river was not him. The coroner had already weighed in and said the timeline was wrong. That was definitive, wasn't it? The DNA test was just a formality.

Norah resolved to use this period of waiting to break through the barriers that had arisen between herself and her children. She found Kevin sitting cross-legged in front of the Inukshuk yet again.

"You've spent a lot of time studying my Inukshuk, Kevin. I thought you didn't believe in it."

"Maybe I do. Maybe I don't. Haven't made up my mind yet."

"Fair enough. Do you mind if I sit here with you?"

Kevin turned and fixed her with a narrow-eyed stare.

"Why would I mind?"

"Well, it's pretty clear I'm not your favourite person right now."

"You think I'm pissed at you? I'm not, at least no more than at anyone else."

"I'm not sure how to take that. We haven't talked about it—the time you were away. How did you manage? You must have been terribly lonely."

"I found Jesus. Glory, hallelujah! Did you know he was missing?"

"If you don't want to talk about it, just say so. Don't mock me."

She watched for his expression to change but it did not. It was impossible to read his state of mind.

"I wasn't always alone. There are more people than you think living like that. You figure it out pretty quick. Whom you can trust. Whom you can't. Where the shelters are. The Knights Table and Regeneration where you can get a free meal."

Should she take the chance? "I'm glad you're home, Kevin. I want you to stay. But you're different. You keep yourself at a distance. What happened to you?"

"I saw stuff. Stuff you don't want to know about, Mom."

"I do want to know, Kevin. I need to know."

"No, that's not what you need. But if you want to know so badly, okay ... Lots of fights. Guys will jump you for whatever you have in your pockets. You can't let your guard done for a minute especially if you've got a few bucks on you. Some drug addicts, but not as many as you'd think. A lot of people off their meds. You have to be really careful around them."

"I can't imagine how you survived five months out there."

"Depends on what you mean by *survived*. I never got raped, if that's what you're asking. Came close a couple of times. There are some really sick mother-fuckers out there."

Norah tried to hold his gaze but could not. Kevin paused, to let his declaration settle, and continued.

"You can't let it get to you. If you show any fear, you won't last long. You have to put up a kind of wall around yourself. Let all the shit that's going on just bounce off you."

"So how did you spend your time? What did you do?" Norah pushed him for more, sensing there was something he building towards.

"You mean, did I steal? Yeah, when I needed to. Did I do drugs? Sure, once in a while. Don't worry. Not enough to get addicted. I'm smarter than that." His eyes narrowed and looked downwards as if he was visualizing a scene. "One night, about three weeks ago, I saw a guy get killed."

"My God, Kevin. What happened?"

"Two guys got into a fight. That happens all the time. But this time, one guy was getting his ass kicked. So he pulled out a knife and stabbed the other guy six or seven times."

"What did you do?"

"I got the hell out of there like everybody else. You don't try to be a hero when something like that goes down."

"So you don't know for sure that he died."

"Trust me, mom. Nobody reported it. He would have been dead long before anybody found him."

"Kevin, I'm sorry you had to see that. But you're home now. You're safe here."

"Safe? Nobody's ever really safe. Because nobody is every really honest. But I didn't have to be on the streets to learn that."

"What is it you think I've been dishonest about, Kevin? Do you mean Andie—how I feel about the fact that she's gay? Yes, I wish she wasn't. But not because I think it's wrong. It's because I know it makes life hard for her, and that worries me."

Kevin lifted his hand and watched a ladybug crawling across it.

"See this ladybug. I could squash it with one finger. It could fly away and save itself. But it doesn't. Do you know why?" He looked at Norah as he asked the question. "It trusts that I won't hurt it just because I can." He squashed the ladybug between two fingers and flicked it away. "So much for trust."

"Have I done something to make you believe you can't trust me?"

"I'm not your problem, Mom. Well, I guess I am *a* problem. But I'm not *the* problem."

***

Norah stood at her bedroom window looking down on the yard and the Inukshuk. Their latest conversation had done little to bridge the gap between Kevin and herself. She did know what to make of his cool, detached manner when he described his experiences. He had developed the ability to divorce himself from what he had seen and done. But it was a dangerous form of detachment and she feared he would eventually pay a price for it.

She felt restless and unfocused. Partly because of her concern for Kevin and partly because waiting for the DNA results was slow torture. She told herself over and over again that the coroner's opinion settled the matter.

The photos beckoned to her again from their resting place on the top of the chest of drawers. She knew she needed to share them with Georgia or at least offer to do so. It was entirely possible that Georgia would decline the opportunity.

Norah picked up the photo of Alasie as a teenager and studied it again. What was it about her that was so captivating? Was it her exotic features? The perfect symmetry of them? It was not that, she realized, but the impression she exuded of being unattainable. Small wonder her father had been love-struck at the sight of her.

As she lingered over the portrait, Norah discovered something she had previously missed. It appeared at first that Alasie was staring directly at the photographer. But a keener observation revealed that her gaze was focused past and to the left of the photographer. But focused on

65

what? A hoped for or imagined future? An apparition of her father? It was impossible to know and that mystery only amplified the unattainable aura that emanated from her.

Norah's restlessness grew and held her in its grasp. What she needed was answers and certainty. But mysteries, secrets and half-truths were all she was being offered. One thing was clear. Hiding out in her bedroom was not the answer. She put the photos in the dresser drawer and rallied herself to face her family again.

Andie was on her cell phone when Norah came downstairs and into the living room. She quickly disconnected when she saw Norah.

"Sorry," Norah offered. "Did I interrupt something?"

"Nothing important. Just some loose ends I need to get cleared up."

"Loose ends?"

"That's what I said." She held Norah's questioning gaze for a moment before she relented. "With Annaliese. A few things she left at our ... at my place. She's going to pick them up tomorrow. I have to go and let her in."

"That'll be hard for you. Would it help if I went with you?"

"You'd like that, wouldn't you?" There was a challenge in her question. "One more chance to show your disapproval."

"Oh for God's sake. What do I have to do to convince you I have no problem with you being gay?"

Georgia came into the room in the middle of their debate. "Is everything okay?" she asked.

"None of your business!" Andie snapped.

"Whoa, bad timing. Sorry I asked." Georgia turned to leave the room. But Norah stopped her.

"Enough, Andie! This ends now. Whether you believe it or not, I'm sorry you broke up with Annaliese. The only thing I want from you is for you to be happy."

"You're such a hypocrite. How do you live with yourself?"

Norah reached the limit of her patience.

"Fine. Don't believe me. Go. Stay. I don't give a damn anymore! Your father could be dead for all I know. I can't deal with your petty grievances right now!"

"And I can't deal with you, period!"

Georgia tried to defuse the situation.

"Norah. Andie. Let's just take a minute to cool off. Everyone is on edge. Don't say something you won't be able to take back."

Kevin entered the room in the middle of Georgia's attempt to mediate.

"Sounds like a catfight going on in here," he said.

"Oh Christ, just shut up Kevin!" Andie shot back at him. "You're the worst offender of all."

"Andie, the high and mighty. Some things never change. You can kiss my ass."

"And you can go to hell! Or back on the streets. Maybe you'd be happier there."

Georgia put herself in-between Kevin and Andie.

"Hey, come on. This is getting out of hand. Everybody needs to take a breath. We're all family here."

"Really? Family?" Andie turned on Georgia now. "You haven't been around much. What has it been—five years since we've seen you?"

Georgia squared off with her.

"What in the hell is your problem? You're mad at everybody and everything. So you broke up with your partner. It happens. Get over it."

"I should take relationship advice from you? Not in this lifetime."

"What is that supposed to—"

"Georgia, she's right this time." Norah cut her off in mid-sentence. You haven't been around, so it's not you place to pass judgement."

Georgia turned back to Norah.

"I flew 20 hours to be here to support you. And now you're telling me to butt out? Seriously?"

"Why did you really come? Was it for me, or to run from your boyfriend because you can't make a commitment?"

"I came because I thought you needed me," Georgia fired back. "But if I had known it was just to be your punching bag, I wouldn't have bothered!"

"Wow, a left jab from Mom and a right cross from Aunt Georgia. How many rounds is this fight?" Kevin sniped, with a cynical grin on his face.

"Shut up, Kevin! Can't you just, for once, shut up?!" Andie screamed at Kevin.

"Enough!! One more word out of any of you and I'll—"

"You'll what, Mom?" Kevin baited her. "Build another Inukshuk?"

His taunt pushed Norah over the edge. She grabbed the first thing she could put her hands on, a glass figurine off the table, and hurled it across the room. It slammed into the wall and shattered with a resounding crash that silenced everyone.

For What is to Come

The sound of shattering glass echoed in Norah's mind through another tormented night. The confrontation in the living room repeated itself in her dreams. An observer, obscured by shadow, watched the scene unfold. When the last angry words were exchanged and the figurine shattered against the wall, the observer stepped out of the shadow and revealed himself as Troy—looking on and condemning them all, but mostly her, for indulging their grievances when they should have been thinking of him.

Norah awoke with her heart pounding. Did Troy's ethereal presence in the dream mean that he was already dead? The nattering voices of dread argued that it meant precisely that. And if it was in fact his body they recovered from the river, it would mean he had died a violent death.

Norah slipped out of bed and roamed the house. She opened the door to each bedroom to watch Andie, Kevin and Georgia sleeping. The house hummed with their presence—the rise and fall of their breathing intermingling and infusing it with life. What would be become of them, she wondered, if the worst came to pass? The hope they were clinging to was a slender thread holding them together amidst their individual grievances. If that thread was severed, there was nothing to prevent them from drifting apart. Her loss would be multiplied by four.

***

The house was quiet when Norah finally summoned the wherewithal to face the day. The aroma of coffee drew her downstairs into the kitchen. Andie was filling her cup when Norah walked in. Their eyes met for a moment. Andie turned away and went out the front door to the porch. Norah poured herself a cup and went in the opposite direction out the patio doors.

There was a chill in the air that seemed to foretell bad news. Norah shrugged off the sensation and crossed the yard to the gazebo. She did not see Georgia sitting inside it until she stepped in. Her instinct was to turn away, but she fought it off.

"Good morning."

She tried to make the welcome a peace offering.

"If you say so. Apparently, it's not my place to express an opinion."

Norah sat down and wrapped her arms around her coffee cup for warmth.

"I'm sorry, Georgia. About last night. Things got out of hand."

"You think?"

"What do you want me to say?" Georgia stared into her coffee cup. "Fine. Everybody else is mad at me. Why should you be any different?"

An uneasy silence settled between them for several minutes. Georgia finally broke it.

"I envy you, Norah. You're so much better at life than me."

"Better at life? I'm not sure what that means."

"That free-for-all last night. Things like that can't happen unless you love each other. Love is ugly when it gets turned on its head. But it's love all the same. It's not the right time to be telling you. But the life you've built—your marriage, a family, a home—it puts my life to shame. I'm not tied to anything."

"Some people call that freedom."

"Freedom is not all it's cracked up to be."

"What about that guy? Mark. There's obviously something there."

"Yeah, maybe. I'll have to make up my mind about that when I get back home. It's not fair to him to keep stringing him along."

"It's not that complicated. Either you love him or you don't."

"When has love ever been uncomplicated for us?"

The mourning doves flew in from the trees, landed on the gazebo roof and started cooing. Norah felt time come unhinged again and wrench her from the present. But it had no particular destination this time.

Norah reached out and took her sister's hand. Georgia did not resist the gesture. They remained in this pose until the patio doors slid open and Andie called out to them.

"Mom. There's somebody here to see you."

"Detective White?"

"No. Somebody else. Here to see you *and* Aunt Georgia."

Georgia frowned. "Why would somebody be here to see me? Hardly anybody knows I'm here."

"She's waiting on the front porch."

Norah traded a puzzled look with Georgia as they went inside. Kevin came down the stairs as they followed Andie through the house. Andie opened the screen door and stepped back. A pregnant moment passed as they stared at the stranger. Georgia was the first to react.

"Oh my God. I can't believe my eyes."

Norah looked at Georgia and back to their visitor. The veil of the years finally parted.

"Mother?"

"Yes, Norah. I was once. I hope I might become it again."

Norah wrestled with her disbelief. After so many years, without so much as a word, to have her mother standing in front of her did not seem possible. She struggled to reconcile the picture of the Alice she held in her mind with the time altered version standing before her.

"I must seem like a ghost to both of you. I realize I may not be welcome. Would you prefer that I leave?"

Norah and Georgia exchanged astonished glances again. Georgia answered.

"Well, it's not my home. So it's not really for me to say. Norah?"

"What? Oh ... well ... Come in, I guess."

They stood aside to let Alice pass. Andie let them into the living room with Kevin trailing behind. The aura of disbelief went ahead of them and settled over the room.

"Andie. Kevin. This is your grandmother."

"In principle, at least," Alice replied.

The initial shock of the moment subsided and resentment replaced it in Norah.

"We don't see or hear from you in thirty years. And suddenly you show up on my doorstep?"

"I would not have dared to come, unless a door was opened."

"A door?" Georgia asked. "What does that mean?"

"I invited her." Andie's answer caught them all off guard. They turned in unison to look at her.

"You?" Norah stared at Andie. "I don't understand."

"I found Grandma five years ago. It wasn't hard. She's been living in the same place in Scarborough all this time. We've become very close."

"What possessed you to go looking for her?"

"It was when we moved Grandad into the nursing home. You probably don't remember. He insisted you keep the cedar chest. It was obvious there was something important in it. But you couldn't be bothered to look. So I did. I found Grandma's diary."

"Diary?" Georgia turned to Norah with an accusing look.

"I didn't know about it until a couple of days ago. Dad told me about it. I looked for it as soon as I got home. But it wasn't there. Now I know why."

"So when were you going to tell me?" Georgia asked. "Or were you not planning to tell me at all?"

"Of course I was going to tell you. But everything blew up last night. There wasn't a right moment."

"So let me get this straight," Kevin chimed in. "Grandma leaves a diary behind. It sits there undiscovered for 25 years. Andie finds it, and then finds Grandma, but keeps it a secret—until the right time comes for her to spring it on us. For the first time, I'm actually glad I'm home. I wouldn't have missed this for anything."

"Ignore him, Grandma," Andie said. "Stirring up trouble is his thing now. It's the one thing he's actually good at."

"Don't start up again, you two." Norah chastised them and turned her attention back to Alice. "All these years, you've only been hours away. And yet you never bothered to look for us."

"I've always known where you are. Both of you. I made it a point to keep track of you, discreetly of course. Even when you moved all the way to Australia, Georgia—to escape the memory of me, no doubt."

"Oh, well, that makes it all okay," Georgia responded. "You knew where we were. You kept tabs on us. But if Andie hadn't found you, we would have never known you were even alive."

"She had her reasons." Andie came to Alice's defence.

"I'm sorry. I should not have come. Andie, you had the best of intentions. But this reunion was a terrible mistake. "

Georgia bristled at the implication. "We didn't exile you. You made a choice."

"Yes, I did. The most painful one I've ever had to make. I am sorry, Georgia. I left it on you to be the surrogate mother. You should not have had to bear that burden."

Alice stood to leave. But Kevin held her back.

"Before you go, there is something you should see." His tone of voice had changed. The sarcastic edge was gone from it.

Alice turned to Norah. Norah shrugged her shoulders and held out her hands in half-hearted consent. Alice followed Kevin into the kitchen.

"There. By the fence. Mom built it."

Alice gazed at the Inukshuk. She was lost in thought for a moment.

"It's been a very long time since I've seen an Inukshuk. I'm surprised that you believe in what it can do." She caught the reaction Georgia tried to suppress. "I'm sorry, Georgia. I can see you would rather I not talk about it."

Before Georgia could respond, Kevin interrupted again.

"It's your call, Mom. You decide if she should stay or go. But you did build the Inukshuk, so you kind of opened the door. At least that's how I see it."

Norah felt all eyes turn on her. "She can stay," she announced. "For now, at least."

***

Such a strange state of affairs, Norah reflected. Stuck in an agonizing holding pattern waiting for news about Troy. Was he already dead? Still alive but waiting to die? And in the midst of that uncertainty, suddenly reunited with her mother who had known all along where to find her. The house was not large enough to contain all the competing emotions. Thankfully, Alice and Andie had retreated to the gazebo leaving Georgia and herself to puzzle through the turn of events.

"Can you believe it?" Georgia asked. "Radio silence for thirty years and she was only an hour or two away. We could have bumped into her on the street, for God's sake. I can't believe you let her stay."

"What was I supposed to do? Throw her out? Andie would never speak to me again."

"How you could not know about them, Norah?"

"You're going to lecture me about parenting now? You're hardly in a position to criticize."

Georgia scowled and turned away.

"The last person to be giving out relationship advice. Not the first time I've heard that."

"Can we not fight? I'm one phone call away from my life falling apart altogether."

"Sorry. The DNA test. I lost sight of that for a moment."

Norah watched through the kitchen window as Andie crossed the yard and came in through the patio doors.

"The two of you could at least talk to her," she said. "She risked a lot coming here."

"What do you expect us to do?" Georgia answered. "Forgive and forget? Absolve her of everything? That's not going to happen."

"You don't understand her. You're not even trying."

"And you do?" Norah asked.

"Yes, I do. If you care about me half as much as you say you do, Mom, come out and hear her story."

Norah and Georgia exchanged questioning glances.

"Alright," Norah relented. "For your sake, I'll listen."

The three of them crossed the yard to the gazebo. Alice looked to Andie for guidance. Andie nodded and took Alice's hand in hers.

"I suppose there's not much more to say other than that I'm alone now. My partner passed away a year and a half ago."

"Partner?" Norah and Georgia asked the question simultaneously.

"Yes. I'm sorry that you're learning the truth under these circumstances." Alice hesitated, but continued. "It was breast cancer. Such a terrible disease. It should have been me rather than her. But I expect being the one left behind is my penance. I have much to atone for."

Norah felt time halt and split open as so much of the past was replayed in a new light. So this was why her mother had left. She had been living a lie. And also why Andie had bonded with her. It answered many questions both old and new. But it fell short of absolving Alice for abandoning them.

"Well." Georgia breached the silence that had fallen on them. "Now we know. What exactly do you expect of us?"

"Only that you try to understand. Back then it was considered deviant behaviour. But I don't expect forgiveness. I know that's far too much to ask of either of you."

"Is it, Mom?" Andie challenged Norah. But Alice came to Norah's rescue.

"That isn't a fair question to ask. You can't expect your mother to divide her loyalties. I betrayed her father. And I'm sorry to have to say this, what you've accused your mother of in your heart, isn't true. Finding and connecting with me, as much of a blessing as that has been for me, has led you astray. You've gotten caught up in the misfortunes and the terrible mistakes of my life."

"At least tell her about the florist shop." Andie keep her eyes on Norah as she spoke.

"What does a florist shop have to do with any of this?"

"My partner, her name was Catherine, owned a florist shop. We ran it together until she passed away. I've kept it going. It gives me something to do and it keeps her spirit alive."

"That's all very nice," Georgia said. "But I don't see the relevance to us."

"Calla lilies," Andie replied. "The ones Grandad gets every week."

"Yes, I know about them," Norah replied. "They're from Georgia because she can't be here to visit him."

"Wait. What?" Georgia looked puzzled. "I never sent any flowers."

Alice stepped in.

"Calla lilies were in our wedding arrangement. I loved them because they reminded me of my mother. She told me they are meant to teach us to concentrate on the beauty we see around us and remember that it will return even if it disappears for a season. And your father, he loved them for no other reason than because I loved them."

The puzzle disassembled and came together in a new configuration.

"You? The flowers are from you, Mother!" Nora said.

"Every week since you moved him into the nursing home. Yes, I kept track of him too. The flowers are the very least I could do. A small way to honour all he gave to me. I send them anonymously, of course. He would not have kept them if he knew they came from me."

"So Dad thinks the flowers are from me. But they're really from you." Georgia paused to weigh the ramifications. "God, if he ever found out it would kill him."

"There's no reason he should ever find out, Georgia. Let him keep believing they come from you. I'll keep sending them as long as you want."

"I'm not sure I'm comfortable with that."

"What's the problem?" Andie confronted Georgia. "You never see him anyway."

Georgia turned on Andie.

"Watch yourself. If you keep shooting arrows at me, we are going to have a problem."

"I should leave," Alice said. "Nothing has changed. Wherever I go, I bring heartache. Norah has enough weight on her shoulders. I shouldn't be adding to it."

"No, you stay," Andie insisted. "Tell them what you told me about you and Grandad."

"It won't change how they feel, Andie. There are some things that can't be undone."

"Tell them anyway. They need to hear it."

Alice looked to Norah for consent.

"Go ahead," Norah answered. "We've crossed all the lines in the sand already. No sense in stopping now."

"I tried so hard to make myself into what he needed me to be. I did grow to love him. I still do. But I couldn't change who I was. Eventually he realized that I could only give a part of myself. He believed that was his own failure. You can't imagine what it is like to live with that kind of guilt."

Norah and Georgia's eyes met. Neither of them could find the courage or the clarity of heart to respond.

***

Norah sat in front of the Inukshuk trying to stitch together the events of the last few days in some manner that made sense. There had to be a common denominator that tied all the pieces together. But the only constant that carried through it was Troy's absence which had a storyline all on its own.

Was it Troy's body they found in the river? The price already exacted and just waiting to be confirmed. No, she could not let herself even begin to look at that as a cold, hard fact. The DNA test was being done to confirm that it was *not* him.

"You're carrying such a burden, Norah. I am so sorry to have added to it yet again."

Norah felt a hum in the air around her. Was it the Inukshuk? Was it radiating in response to Alice's presence? The mourning doves flew in and landed on the gazebo roof.

"Why did you come, Mother? You hid from us for thirty years. We had written you off. Why show up now?"

"Because your daughter asked me to come. She would not take no for an answer."

Resentment rose in Norah both for days long past and for those only just gone by.

"You turned my daughter against me. You undermined our relationship. It took five years, but you did it."

Alice looked away and let the accusation settle before she responded.

"That was never my intention. Remember, she found me. But it has always been that way for me. I have always been marked for trouble and destined to hurt those I love."

"Oh, yes. Dad told me all about that. Born during an eclipse, wasn't it? The Sun God. The Moon God. The fates conspiring against you. It must be nice to be able to blame all your mistakes on that. You never have to take responsibility for anything."

"I know I can't expect you to understand, Norah. I grew up in a different world that makes no sense to you. Different beliefs. Different values. I have spent the better part of my life caught in-between two worlds."

"That's very dramatic, Mother. But it's really just a roundabout way of saying: None of it is my fault."

"I understand that it must seem that way to you. But what you don't understand, or don't want to accept, is that I do hold myself responsible. Agreeing to marry your father was the most selfish thing I have ever done. It was easier to say yes to him, than to follow the path that was meant for me."

"That's interesting. Marrying him, having his children, was more selfish than eventually abandoning all of us?"

"Yes, because one led to the other. If I had said no, as I should have, your father would have been disappointed and maybe broken-hearted for a while. But he would have found someone else better suited to him."

"And you wouldn't have been burdened with two daughters you didn't want."

Norah regretted the words the moment she spoke them. Alice was silent for several minutes before she summoned the will to respond.

"Tapeesa, if you believe only one thing I say, let it be this. I have never loved anything in this world half so much as I love you and Amaqjuac. That is why I have stayed away. Giving you freedom from me, and the tragedy that follows me, is the one truly selfless thing I have ever done." Alice paused a moment to let her declaration sink in. "I didn't have much, nothing really, to leave for you and Georgia. The keepsake box, the diary, the story of my life—that's all I had to give to the two of you. The keepsake box is one of a kind. My father made it by hand including all the carvings. I trusted that someday it would find its way to the two of you. Such as it is, it belongs to you and your sister now."

***

Norah brought the keepsake box up to her bedroom after the conversation with her mother. She was not ready to accept it as the peace offering, the symbol of selfless love bequeathed, that Alice laid claim to it as being. But it was in some manner the connecting thread, winding itself through the years, which she needed. One thing that survived all the broken promises.

She had paid little attention to the carvings that adorned it, but lingered over them now. They were all animals—a seal, a caribou and a pair of fox—crafted in exquisite detail. How many hours of painstaking labour had gone into them? Hours of love and devotion by a father for his only child.

Kevin was standing at the bedroom door for several minutes before Norah became aware of his presence.

"What is that?" he asked.

"Something your grandfather made a long time ago." She stood, placed the keepsake box in the cabinet beside the bed and closed the cabinet door. "Did you want something?"

"Let's take a walk."

"A walk?" She searched his expression for the sarcasm he had wrapped himself in since he came home. But it was gone. "Where are we going?"

"To the marsh pond."

"For any particular reason?"

"Just because."

"That sounds mysterious. But, okay."

Kevin was silent the whole way to the marsh pond. But it was clear that he had a purpose in mind, as if he had arrived at a decision after no small amount of consideration. He stepped onto the small deck when they arrived and turned to Norah.

"Okay, Kevin. We're here. Do I get to know the *because* now?"

"Look up, Mom."

"At what?"

"Just look up. At the sky."

Norah took a moment to scan the skyline. It was a striking view— full sunlight in a bright, cerulean sky with patches of low hanging cloud, gray underneath and cotton white above, suspended in a manner that made them appear frozen. The cloud edges—in places, wispy tendrils curling and spiraling like smoke, in other places rounded and billowing—stood out in sharp relief against the sky.

"Okay, it's very nice. Is it supposed to mean something to me?"

"It's the clouds. They're perfectly still. And they're not blocking the sun. They're sitting there like someone reached up and stuck each one in place. What do you think it means?"

"I'm sorry. I'm not following you."

"I'm just saying. You don't see a sky like this very often. Seems like it should mean something. Maybe it's shining a special light on something so it doesn't get missed."

Norah recalled the discussions they had over the preceding days and his insistence that she was overlooking something.

"What are you trying to tell me, Kevin?"

He looked away as if he was disappointed in her.

"I've been hoping you'd read between the lines and figure it out for yourself. But I guess I'm going to have to be the one who tells you. Dad's been cheating on you. It's been going on for at least a year that I know of. Probably longer."

The revelation stunned Norah. Her first thought was that Kevin had fabricated the story to strike back at Troy. But his pained expression belied that possibility. Questions piled up in her mind. When and with who? Random encounters or a full blown affair? How could it be that Kevin knew but she did not? The entire landscape of her life once again shifted without warning.

"Who else knows?"

It was a ridiculous question, but the only one she could put words to. Her ignorance of the truth felt as bad, or even worse, than the act of betrayal itself.

"I don't think anybody else knows. But Dad knows that I know. And that should tell you a lot."

"Why are you telling me this now?"

"Because you're worrying about the wrong things. And I don't want you to be blindsided if the truth comes out when you least expect it."

An ominous calm settled over Norah as she reframed the circumstances of Troy's disappearance. Detective White had been right. Troy had never been in danger. He must have left his car in the parking lot by the Falls to cover his tracks while he went into hiding until he was ready to break the news. At this very moment, he might be with *her*—the woman he had been seeing for a year or more—while she waited and worried that he might be dead. He had played her for a fool and she had fallen for it completely.

***

Norah was on autopilot for the walk home. The overwhelming question confronting her now was: *Where do I go from here?* Her mother had reappeared after 30 years. The questions that had haunted her since Alice's departure were answered. Closure of a sort had been gifted to her on that front, even though as many new questions were raised as had been answered. But now a huge fracture had opened in what she had thought was solid ground.

The back yard was empty as they came through the gate. But the patio doors slid open. Andie, Georgia and Alice stepped out along with Detective White. There was a firm expression on the detective's face.

"Let me guess," Norah said. "Troy has turned up but he's not coming home. He has other plans."

Her pre-emptive strike drew a puzzled look from all of them. Detective White composed himself to deliver his news.

"I don't know what you mean. But what I'm here to tell you is, we were able to fast-track the DNA test. I wish I had better news. The body recovered from the river is your husband. I am very, very sorry for your loss."

"What? Troy is ... the body in the river ... what?"

Norah could not process the news. It made no sense with what she had just learned from Kevin. She saw stunned disbelief in Andie and Georgia's eyes. None of it made any sense to her.

"Mrs. Watson, I know this is hard to accept. But there is no mistake. Your husband is dead. It was his body that was recovered from the Niagara River. The DNA test was conclusive."

Norah turned to Kevin searching for reason. But his shell-shocked expression was no help. She turned back to the others. Tears were streaming down Georgia and Andie's faces.

"Norah. Oh God, Norah. I'm so sorry." Georgia saw Norah slump and caught her in her arms to steady her. "You're not alone. We're all here. Oh God, Norah, I'm so sorry."

Alice approached and took Norah's face in her hands. There was an infinite depth of sadness in her eyes.

"Tapeesa. I know too well your sorrow and your pain. My heart is breaking for you."

They became aware of a commotion behind them, and turned at the same time to see Kevin attacking the Inukshuk. Like a man possessed, he wrenched the stones loose and hurled them away one by one. In a minute, the Inukshuk was reduced to a pile of rubble.

Norah willed the slipstream to engage—to halt and freeze-frame everyone and everything. Now of all times she wanted it to happen. But it did not, and she knew it would never do so again.

Dancing with Ghosts

Lightning ricocheted through storm clouds stacked deep in the afternoon sky as the fireflies of memory flickered despite Hunter's attempts to suppress them.

The car skidding sideways off the road, a ferocious flare of lightning, the spine-jarring impact as it slams into a tree, shattering glass as Nate goes through the windshield, that immeasurable interval of waiting, as the storm rages on, before help arrives, strobing red lights bleeding into the darkness, voices that seem otherworldly: can you hear me? Can you hear me?

A discontented rumble of thunder followed as the first droplets of rain splattered on the sidewalk. Such a dismal day for a funeral, Hunter mused, as he steered Nate through the doors of St. James United Church.

He tried to banish the ghosts but the fireflies would not rest. Thirty years on, his memories of that day were increasingly contradictory. There was one moment, before the car left the road, that remained unequivocal. A moment in which it became clear that the underlying assumptions of his life were faulty. Hunter shuffled the memories aside as he and Nate found seats in the back of the church.

"I ... I can't see," Nate protested. "Let's ... move closer up."

"Move to the right a bit. That's better, isn't it?"

"Yes. I can ... see now."

"It'll be a few minutes before the service starts." Hunter's gaze was drawn to the casket at the front of the church. "You remember Charlie Hay, right? He was Niki's father."

"Yeah, sure. Nicki was ... your girl. Everybody knew that."

"That was a long time ago, Nate. I haven't seen her in decades."

"You should have ... married her."

"Marriage wasn't on my radar screen back then. I thought I was on the fast track. Anyway, we were way too young."

The murmur of voices subsided as Niki and her family entered. Silence swept row by row like the shadow of a cloud moving across the sun.

Would she even remember him the way he looked now? *If you have to ask*, a cynical voice in his head muttered. Star high school jock, with his sights set on pro hockey, who had tumbled down the ladder of success to middle-aged bartender. Forty pounds overweight with a scraggly beard he wore to hide the scars both literal and figurative.

Reverend Tull allowed a respectful pause before he took his position at the front of the church. As he started his prologue to the service, Nate's breathing became laboured.

"You okay, buddy?"

Nate shook his head. They stood and slipped out of the pew. Hunter steered Nate into the vestibule by the stairs.

"Here, take one. It'll help."

Nate's breathing gradually slowed as the lorazepam took effect.

"You can ... go back in, Hunter. I'll be okay here."

"No, it's probably for the best anyway. Charlie didn't much care for me. He wouldn't have wanted me at his funeral."

"Niki would."

Was that true? Hunter considered the idea for a moment but quickly dismissed it. Believing in that possibility opened the door to other hopes he could not afford to entertain.

"I doubt it much matters to her one way or the other."

"You have to ... see Nicki. You *have* to."

"Probably better that I don't. I'm just a ghost to her now."

Hunter took a last look up the aisle. Niki turned to look back as if searching for someone. For him? He allowed himself to linger on the idea one more time before turning away.

"Let's go home," he said, not noticing the look of determination in Nate's eyes.

***

Hunter stood at the window of their fifteenth floor apartment watching the storm clouds disintegrate trailing a warm autumn breeze in their wake. A pair of pigeons glided through his field of vision and landed on the balcony railing. He banged on the window to scare them off. But they stared back at him unperturbed, their heads titled slightly giving them a quizzical expression which he found unsettling.

He looked down at the hockey puck in his left hand. The last remnant of glory from his game-winning goal in the Ontario Provincial Junior B championship game. He could still picture the moment if he tried hard enough—a perfect deflection over the goalie's outstretched glove.

It felt like another lifetime now. Humbling to think that his life had peaked that early. In those days, he was certain that there was a future mapped out for him that promised a series of triumphs with Niki by his side. The invitation he and Nate received, to try-out for a hockey scholarship at Ohio State University, had seemed like just one more spin of the wheel of destiny.

It was a Friday morning when they left for the drive to Columbus. Their equipment was stowed in the back of his VW Bug. The VW's brakes were worn down to bare metal. But he had mastered the practice of gearing down in a hurry. Niki had come to see them off. She gave him a goodbye kiss but was reluctant to let him go.

"Good luck. Make me proud," she said. After a moment's hesitation she added, "I wish you weren't taking the VW. Can't you borrow your father's car?"

"Why would I? The Bug will get us there."

"I keep asking you to get the brakes fixed. You never listen to me."

"Don't worry. I got it covered."

In the aftermath of it all, her gentle reproach, and the half-hearted smile that accompanied it, was chock-full of meaning.

A knock on the door drew him out of his reminiscing. He considered ignoring it, but it came again more persistently. Had he paid the rent on time this month? Yes, so there was no harm in answering.

"Hello, Hunter. I wasn't sure I had the right address."

Hunter was speechless for a moment when he saw Niki standing there. "Niki ... Wow, this is a surprise. Come in."

He followed her eyes, painfully aware of how shabby the apartment looked, as she did a quick scan of the room. She took a seat on the sofa and looked away, reaching for something to bridge the years between them.

"I saw you at Dad's funeral. Is Nate okay?"

"Yeah, he's alright now. He gets anxiety attacks. It's part of—well, you know ... I'm really sorry about your father."

"Thanks. It was a shock. He was 78, so I guess it was just his time. Still, we didn't expect it."

Niki cast her eyes down. It struck Hunter that there was a discrepancy between the way he remembered her face and what he saw in it now. He studied her jaw where it rounded into the soft curve of her cheek and the way the curve repeated itself below her eyes. She smiled wistfully and the effect was magnified. She had always been a beautiful woman. Now he noticed an underlying grace he had not recognized before.

"You look good, Niki."

"I wish I could say the same for you. Sorry to be blunt, Hunter, but you look like hell."

"Guess I haven't taken care of myself. Didn't really see the point, you know, after what happened."

"But you've taken care of Nate all these years. I admire you for that."

"Wouldn't have been fair to heap it all on his mother. His father was in the wind before Nate was even born. He does pretty well considering the amount of brain damage. Anyway, my knee was permanently buggered, so they yanked my scholarship. It wasn't like I was giving up a lot."

Niki shifted her gaze out the window. She bit the corner of her lip and twirled her fingers through her hair—gestures Hunter recognized, with a pang of regret, even all these years later.

"You're dying to ask me something, Niki. What is it?"

"I have to know, Hunter, even if it's too late to undo it. Why did you do it?"

He dropped his head and studied the floor.

"Everything was just too messed up. I saw this big future for myself and then it was gone. I didn't have a backup plan. Plus there was the DUI charge. I really didn't have much to offer you."

"I didn't mean breaking up with me. Honestly, I don't think we were meant to be. We were headed in different directions. But that's old baggage." She paused as if marshalling her courage. "I was hoping I wouldn't have to come right out and say it. I ... Do you know what I do for a living?"

"I heard you became a cop. Surprised me a bit at first. But you always did have a lot more going for you than me."

He regretted the last sentence. It sounded like he was angling for sympathy.

"I was a cop for quite a while. But a few years ago I made a change. I'm an Accident Reconstructionist now."

"Sounds impressive. But, honestly, I have no idea what that means."

"I reconstruct traffic accidents to find out what caused them. It's a specialty. I'm good at it."

"That doesn't surprise me. But why are you telling me this?"

She met his eyes as if giving him the opportunity to withdraw the question. Hunter felt the ground shifting beneath him.

"A year ago I pulled some strings. I got the reports and photographs from your accident. It wasn't easy, but I made a few connections when I was a cop."

Hunter crossed the room to the window and turned his back to her.

"That was a bit unethical, wasn't it?"

"Yes. But I couldn't forgive myself for not convincing you to fix the brakes."

"So now you can say definitively that I ruined Nate's life and pissed away my own future. I guess you're glad now that I pushed you away."

Niki came up behind him. He turned to look at her, expecting judgment, but found something else in its place that he could not decipher.

"I discovered something I didn't expect. There's no way you were driving, Hunter."

"That's ridiculous. Why would you even say that?"

"They didn't have the technology at that time. We have computer simulations now that fill in the gaps. It had to be Nate behind the wheel. Why did you take the blame?"

Did she have any right to know the truth he had hidden for thirty years? Maybe, it occurred to him, it was less about rights than about unfinished business.

"You sure you want to know?"

"Would I be here if I didn't?"

"I suppose not. So, the truth ... Nate got offered the scholarship. I didn't. I wasn't anywhere near good enough."

"How is that a reason?"

"You're the reconstructionist. Put the pieces together."

Niki stared at Hunter for a moment before the realization spread across her face.

"You'd rather be blamed for the accident than admit you weren't good enough? Oh Hunter, why?"

"At least this way you remembered me as tragic. Better that than what I really am—just another dumb jock whose ego was bigger than his talent."

"I never saw you that way. But I *was* afraid you were counting too much on that dream."

"I cheated on you. Did you know that?"

"Yes."

It was not the answer he expected.

"So why didn't you kick me to the curb? Not that it matters. I ended up there anyway."

Niki reached for his hand but he forced himself to step away.

"Don't feel sorry for me. I got what I had coming. Nate's the one who lost it all. Me—I'm just collateral damage."

"And if I were to tell what I know?"

"What would it change? I prefer my version of the truth. I've made my peace with it."

"But I'm not at peace with it, Hunter."

"Don't do it for me. Keep the secret for Nate's sake. He's lost too much already."

She hesitated, as if testing the weight of that commitment.

"Alright, if that's what you truly want. But you need to know that I'm here because Nate called me. He said you needed to see me."

"Nate called you?" *You have to see her.* Nate's insistence as they left the church came back to him. "Obviously I underestimated him. Seems like I always have."

"Hunter." Her eyes held a gravity that frightened him. "I don't know if I can live with a secret like that. Where does it leave us?"

Hunter turned from her and looked out the window. In the park below, a rogue gust of wind scattered the leaves. "It's not a good idea to dance with ghosts. Trust me, it never ends well."

Winter Solstice

elusive proof—December 21: 6:15 p.m.

Sketchy eyewitness reports. Hearsay. Circumstantial evidence. Nadine McDavid watched the winter storm rage on from their twentieth floor condo window as she wrestled with the facts. Blinding swirls and backspins of snow whipped around the corner of the building and lashed at the windows. In the parking lot below, the pine trees bordering the grounds were already laden with bear paws of snow. The lamps between them, quivering like winter fireflies in the gusts of wind, cast feeble rings of light. A curving trail of footprints wound through the pines and disappeared where the light faded to ashen gray.

Truthfully, she thought, there was no more proof than these vanishing footprints. Proof could be such an elusive thing. A case like this would fall flat on its face in an evidentiary hearing. And yet, if it was true, if Andrew had been there two days ago and was the one they were looking for, how could she excuse it?

The telephone spared her further debate. She checked the display before answering.

"Hi, it's me. I'm on my way. But the police just closed the highway. Five minutes earlier and I would have been ahead of them. *Five minutes*, damn it."

The howl of the wind in the background muffled his voice.

"I'm not surprised, Andrew. It took me an hour and a half to get home from the office. You should head back to the hotel and stay there tonight."

"Can't. It's booked solid."

"So sleep in your office. You are the manager, after all." She tried to hide the impatience in her voice.

"It's not that bad. I'm doubling back so I can take Tucker Side Road."

"Do you really think you should? Cars can't even get out of the parking lot here."

She realized she had talked herself into the idea of one more day's grace before she had to confront him.

"I can make it. It may take a couple of hours, but I'll get through."

"Alright, if you're absolutely set on it. But be careful."

"Always. See you in a bit. Oh, and—"

"Andrew ... Andrew ... "

The connection dropped leaving her to fill in the blank. Nadine dropped the cordless phone on the table in frustration. Loose ends were her Achilles' heel—an occupational hazard of being a lawyer.

Find a distraction, she counselled herself. She sat down at her laptop and logged onto Explorer. The animated Google doodle caught her attention. A fat lady with a white bag entered from the left and handed a carrot to a pair of blob-shaped figures who in turn planted it on a snowman's nose. She slid the cursor over the doodle.

Winter solstice. The shortest day of the year. She pondered the implications: more lunar hours than any other night of the year. A time when people were more inclined to make bad decisions. *Lunar, luna, lunatic.* Just a myth, of course—the moon and its effect. But a bad time, nonetheless, to be wrestling with doubts and suspicions.

***

snow banks—kilometre 18

"What the hell was I thinking? Can't see past the nose on my face in this godforsaken storm."

The howling wind had finally eased, although the snowfall showed no signs of relenting. Visibility improved enough for Andrew to see a few yards ahead before the headlights' beams diffused in the snow. He had slowed to a crawl for the past twenty minutes. His only points of reference were the snowbanks, now rapidly becoming indistinct, created hours earlier when the plow had made an initial pass down the side road. He kept his Pathfinder centered between them and hoped for the best.

"Full tank of gas. That, at least, was a smart move."

Andrew cautiously accelerated to forty kilometres an hour and tried to calculate how long it would take to cover the distance at that speed. Best guess, he decided, was two hours, assuming the wind did not ramp up again and force him to slow down.

'Really fucked up this time, Andrew. At least a foot of snow already. Gonna need a lot of luck to cheat the devil. Doesn't help that you've already got one strike against you."

What he had done two days earlier, or more to the point failed to do, loomed large now.

"Put that crap aside. Need to have your wits about you. Precious little margin for error now. But you can make it if—"

***

Edana: fathoms deep—December 21, 7:10 p.m.

such a long night this is going to be, richard. i have to bury you tomorrow. commit your body to the earth, your soul to heaven. until then i have to keep myself centered. between life and death.

six feet under. i insisted on that. not necessary, they said. the law only requires two feet. damn the law, i told them. six feet under whatever the cost. they nodded, humouring me, the grieving widow. i tried to explain. he was a ship's captain. it's only right. a fathom down.

they still did not understand. nor can i, for that matter. why you had to die while they live on. a reckless bastard who runs red lights. a gutless man who did not give a damn. he should have stopped. a few minutes more—you might have survived. but he could not be bothered. he lives on while I have to bury you. where is the justice in that?

***

in absentia—December 21: 7:10 p.m.

An SUV crawled up the street, spinning sideways, and turned in the entrance. From twenty stories up, Nadine realized, the profile of most SUVs looked the same. As it passed underneath the light pole, she saw that it was a pastel colour—not the forest green of Andrew's Pathfinder.

Her mind circled back, like a moth to light, to that burning question. Was it Andrew? And if so, was it the incident itself that most distressed her or his act of omission in not confiding in her? But she was guilty herself of convicting him in absentia. She dissected the evidence yet again as she had heard it on the news.

A pickup truck heading west ran a red light at the intersection of Dorchester and Main, clipping the bumper of a dark SUV heading south. The glancing blow appeared to do minimal damage to the SUV. But it spun the pickup out of control and caused it to crash head-on into a Honda Civic waiting on the other side of the intersection.

The driver of the Civic died on the way to the hospital while the driver of the pickup was seriously injured but survived. Witnesses said the southbound vehicle stopped briefly, and sped off leaving the scene of the accident.

Those were the undisputed, courtroom facts. From there conjecture took over. Andrew arrived home that day with a crumpled bumper. *Evidence*. His explanation: someone hit his Pathfinder, while it was parked at the hotel, and left without reporting it. Quite plausible, although conveniently impossible to prove or disprove.

The intersection was on his typical route home and the timing roughly corresponded with his schedule. *Opportunity.* And there was the tangential fact: Andrew arrived home that evening, after the staff Christmas party, with liquor on his breath. Certainly not drunk, but enough that it was questionable whether he would have passed a breathalyser test. *Motive.*

The legal triad was complete.

In 12 years of marriage, there had been nothing to suggest he was capable of such unethical behaviour. If not for the liquor on his breath, there would be no reason to question his honesty. But what were the odds that the facts aligned and yet it was not him?

On the grounds below, the quilt of snow softened the harsh angles and frozen shapes of mid-December. And yet, she sensed, there was something vaguely menacing in its blanketing of the landscape. So much could be obscured or conjured by it—just as hard facts could be whitewashed by what one wanted so desperately to believe.

***

snow drift—kilometre 17.5

The drift across the road was three feet deep. Andrew's Pathfinder had punched halfway into it before coming to a stop.

"Shit, shit, shit! Take Tucker Side Road. Great idea, Andrew."

He shifted into reverse and stepped gingerly on the gas pedal. The tires did not budge. As panic set in, he tromped down hard. The tires let out a high-pitched whine but gained no traction. He shifted from reverse to drive several times as the tires continued to screech.

"Great. Just great. What the hell am I supposed to do now?"

The only answer was the howling wind as it gained velocity again. He pulled his cell phone out of his pocket.

"Dead battery. Unbelievable. Un-bloody-unbelievable ... Alright, think. What are my options? Hunker down here, keep the car running for the night and wait for help to arrive in the morning. That's what you're supposed to do in this situation ... Right, and they find you in the morning cold as a mackerel and dead of carbon monoxide poisoning."

He forced himself to visualize Tucker Side Road in daylight. There were several farms scattered along it.

"Pretty damn sure there's a farmhouse right after the turn from the highway. How far have I come? A couple of kilometres. I can manage that. Follow the tire tracks and the snow banks until I come to a mail box. Sounds like a decent plan. Hat, gloves, boots. An hour to get there. I can manage that."

As he forced open the car door through the drift and stepped out, the driving snow lashed his face. The cold was like a wall of resistance. He questioned his decision a moment, summoned his courage and struck out along the tire tracks into the darkness.

***

Edana: angry wind—December 21: 8:00 p.m.

it has been snowing for hours, richard. the storm of the season, they say. as if that matters one iota. what matters is this—two children to raise on my own. what am i supposed to do now? two children, two lost souls entirely dependent on me. i just want to scream.

but instead, i just sit at the window. watching it snowing hour after hour. trying to lose myself within the angry wind. can wind be angry? you said it can be at sea. i want it to be the wind of my grief and my anger.

i'm transfixed suddenly by a ribbon of smoke. curling and folding from the rooftop smokestacks. it billows and rolls. dissolves into the ash of the night sky. is it you reaching out to me? repeating the dance over and over as i watch? symbolic cremation.

***

forensic evidence—December 21, 8:00 p.m.

"Mr. McDavid. You testified that you discovered on December 19 that your vehicle had been hit in the parking lot of the hotel where you work. Why didn't you report it to the police?"

Nadine paced the length of the living room, trying not to look at the clock, as she imagined herself prosecuting the case. Forensic evidence could make it a slam dunk.

"Well, I was going to. But I thought, what are the odds they'll find the person? I decided it would just be a waste of time."

The long pause here for dramatic effect.

"How do you explain the fact that the paint chips on your bumper match the paint colour on the pickup truck involved in the fatal accident that same day?"

This was her home territory—the courtroom. Lead the accused to the trap you set and wait for them to take the bait. But life was much more of a slippery slope. It had so many twists and turns that were impossible to anticipate.

An irresistible force drew her back to the window. How long since his last call? An hour and a half, so he could still be on his way. But she had called twice and he had not answered. Her heart wrenched when the telephone rang.

"Hello ... Who? No, you have a wrong number ... *I said*, you have a wrong number!"

Naadine returned to her vigil at the window. How well could you really know a person? Time and time again she had seen both men and women passionately convinced of their spouse's innocence even when evidence pointed to the contrary.

And what of her own skeleton in the cupboard? Years ago when she was in law school, long before they met. The baby she decided to abort because it threatened her future. How many times had she tried and failed to summon the courage to tell Andrew? Everyone had secrets that haunted them. Practising law had exposed that reality.

An image of Andrew struggling through knee-deep snow on Tucker Side Road, bent over double and swaying in the wind, lodged itself in her mind. Was it a premonition? Was the script already written? Or was she becoming unhinged with worry?

***

snow blanket—kilometre 18.5

Andrew was covered in snow from head to foot. His feet felt heavy, disconnected from his legs, and his fingers were numb. Clapping his hands together to keep them warm seemed like too much exertion now. He stopped a moment to try and catch his breath.

"I must be close. Must be." In the darkness, he had no sense of how much time had passed. "I can make it ... I can make it ... Look for the mailbox ... Where the hell is that mailbox?"

He willed his legs to move again. Two steps later it felt like the wind picked him up off his feet. But he realized he was sliding rather than flying. When he tumbled over and landed on his back, he realized what had happened. He had strayed off the road and fallen into the ditch.

It was a comfort to be off his feet and not battling the wind. The idea came to him to build a snow fort and curl up inside it. He wondered how long it would take and started to visualize the process. But reason broke through his delusion. He made a bargain with God.

"Get me home, and I'll confess everything. That's it, isn't it? What this is all about? So just get me home and I'll turn myself in."

Andrew struggled to his feet and felt the ground around him until he located the slope. He crawled and clawed his way up to level ground and willed himself to stand. As he did so, he became conscious of a painful headache.

"Alright, on my feet. Still have strength left ... Damn, why can't I catch my breath?"

He looked down to locate the tire tracks and realized he had no sense of direction in the dark and the swirling snow. The awareness that he was utterly lost took hold.. A wave of panic shot through him .

"Oh God. Which way? Which way do I go?" He frantically searched for a point of reference. "Footsteps. I can follow my footsteps back to the car. At least that will be shelter. It's my best chance."

He discerned to his right what appeared to be footsteps and forced his legs to move again. The ball of fear in his stomach receded and grim determination replaced it. He found a slow, laboured rhythm of step after step and focused his energy on it.

***

Edana: storm petrels—December 21, 8:30 p.m.

i know what you meant now, richard. about losing the sense of time while you're at sea. it feels like time has folded in on itself. seems like years since i touched your face. and years to go before this night ends. it's a kind of madness.

i thought death was only absence. but it's presence too. an unrelenting hum. like hydro wires in my brain. it has given me this terrible headache. will it leave when you're buried? i don't want it to. it's all i have of you. can't i hold onto that one connection? like those birds that follow your ship. your sea-friends, you call them. storm petrels. i want a storm petrel to follow me.

where is he? that soulless man who left you to die? is he suffering? i want him to suffer. he doesn't deserve mercy. he'll get none from me.

***

legal cobwebs—December 22, 1:30 a.m.

A thump on the floor above awakened Nadine. It was past 1:00 in the morning, and still Andrew was not home. She went to the window to resume her vigil. The storm had begun to loosen its grip. A ghostly gray-white glow remained in the sky as the last cold embers of the storm released a soft spray of white.

If he made it home, would he confess? And if he did, would she confess as well? It was only right. But all secrets were not equal. Not in the eyes of the law and certainly not in the eyes of the soul. But now was not the time to come unglued grappling with legal cobwebs. It was time to put wheels in motion to find him. She picked up the phone and dialed 911.

"Nine one one. Fire, police or ambulance?"

"Police."

"Hold the line while I transfer you ... "

"This is Sergeant Wilkerson. What is your emergency?"

"My husband didn't make it home tonight. When they closed Highway 5, he took Tucker Side Road—at least that's what he said was going to do." She did not know for certain where he was, she realized.

"When did you last hear from him?"

"Around 6:00."

"Alright. I'll need the make, model, year and colour of his car." Nadine hesitated as the implications of giving that information struck home. "Are you still there?"

"Sorry, yes. He drives a 2012 Nissan Pathfinder. Dark green."

"License plate."

"A K M O 6 4 7."

What if one of the witnesses had reported a partial plate number and they withheld that detail from the news? She may well have just closed the case for them.

"Give me a description of your husband."

"Six foot one. About 190 pounds. Black hair and a mustache."

"Okay, I'll put out a report. But understand, there's not a lot we can do until the snowplows get through. If he stayed in his car, he'll probably be okay. We have your number. We'll call if we find him. If he makes it home or calls, be sure to let us know."

"Thank you. I will."

She disconnected, dropped the phone on the table and went back to her post at the window. Fatigue made her mind wander again despite her attempts to resist it.

What if they had decided to have children? Would he have risked the drive if there were children? Would he have declined the extra drink at the party and headed home earlier?

How long have you been holding that in? The quiet voice of conscience posed the question as if it had been hanging out there for far too long. It had been a mutual decision to focus on their individual careers. Not a hard and fast decision. Not a *never* decision. An issue to be revisited sometime later. But time passed. Life got busy and the years slid by on their own momentum. The question remained tucked away in an emotional closet—until now, when it surfaced with a vengeance, and echoed through the acts of years gone by and the acts of two days ago.

***

snow angel—kilometre 19

Andrew stumbled, regained his balance and stopped as his legs refused to move. He looked around in bewilderment.

"What ... where am I? How did ... how did I get here?"

He raised his arm to wipe the snow from his face. But his hand was lifeless. His legs felt like they did not belong to his body. He dropped to his knees and started to burrow a hole in the snow.

"What the hell am I doing? Get up. *Get up.*"

He struggled to his feet and look around again. His mind rebooted.

"The car. I'm trying to get to the car ... Am I going the right way? Am I ... on the road?" He turned a slow, laboured circle. "No footprints ... They're filled in ... Oh, God, they're filled in."

It occurred to him that the car would be completely covered in snow by now. He could easily have walked past it, within inches of it, and not seen it.

"No ... I would have seen the hump ... Wouldn't I? It must still be ahead of me."

Andrew's legs gave way again and he tumbled to the ground. He flailed with his arms and made it to his knees. Looking back, he saw his imprint in the snow. The contours of it looked familiar, like something long forgotten that reached across time to him.

You can stop. You are safe now. Lie down. Close your eyes and sleep.

"Who said that? Nadine, is that you? ... Are you an angel? My snow angel?"

You are safe. Trust me. Lie down. Close your eyes and sleep.

"It was me, Nadine ... I should have stayed ... and tried to help ... I'm sorry. I'm so, so sorry."

Andrew lay back into the arms of the snow angel. His breathing slowed in its embrace. His eyes closed of their own accord and his fear melted away.

***

Edana: ebb & flow—December 22, 2:10 a.m.

something has changed, richard. i don't know what. i just feel it in my bones. a shiver, as if the universe, or my small part of it, exhaled. like someone suddenly found their way home.

is that the way of it? the ebb and flow of a life? a momentary fracture that heals over just as quickly. is it that instantaneous? surely there must be more. a soul cannot depart that quickly. or can it? is our grip on life that fragile? one turn of fate. one roll of the dice.

i want this night to end. its driving me mad.

***

bad precedent—December 22, 10:30 a.m.

Nadine awoke in mid-morning still curled up in the chair. She remembered awakening late in the night, sometime after two, when a strange, ethereal calm had descended on her. The storm had ended, or moved on, taking her fears with it. It had seemed irrational at first, but gradually and steadily gained credence and was still present now.

It was important to follow their Sunday morning routine. She made coffee, pulled the recliner to the window and settled into it. She watched the continuous plume of snow thrown by the plow as it rumbled down their street. It appeared to her as a wave washing away years of apathy. A chapter had closed in their lives and a new one was opening.

She had set a bad precedent in allowing herself to suspect Andrew of something so immoral. He would never have done such a thing and certainly would not have withheld it from her if he had. Strange, and yet so liberating, that a long night of fear could open one's eyes to reality. Things would be very different now. They would not take so much for granted. And yes, they would have a child. Mid forties's was late, but not too late, for that to happen.

She crossed to the window and settled back into her chair. The sun, hidden for the better part of twenty-four hours, glistened through delicate etchings of frost on the window. Gentle spindrifts tossed fistfuls of snow in the air like a child at play.

Winter Solstice, she thought. *Solstice.* A wonderful name for a girl. Their child would be named *Solstice.*

5 Iron

AJ cocked his head as a thin shadow swept across the practice green. He took one hand off his putter, scanned the sky and caught sight of the hawk gliding in to perch in a large oak. A quick diagnostic—gray back, white rump, russet streaking underneath—sufficed to make the identification: a northern harrier. It stared back at him purposefully and vaguely ominous, as if a portent of what the day would hold.

"I play this course a dozen times every summer. But I've never once seen a harrier here. So, why today?"

Do not read anything into it, he counseled himself. It was just a random occurrence. *Need to talk to you about something, AJ. It's—well, important. Face-to-face kind of thing. So, call me, okay?*

The cryptic telephone message from Davis replayed itself in his mind. It was one of the few times he had ever heard uncertainty in his twin brother's voice. The last time, it dawned on him, was the day Davis called to tell him their father had died.

The harrier launched from the tree and circled the parking lot as the sound of crunching gravel came up the lane. AJ recognized Davis' black Mercedes. He slung his putter over his shoulder, trying to affect nonchalance, as he strolled toward the parking lot.

"Fashionably late as usual," he quipped, as Davis got out of his car.

"Nice to see you too. I guess we're skipping the formalities."

"Sorry, I always feel like I'm starting with a handicap when you roll up in this baby."

"You have to keep up appearances in my line of work. At least, that's what I keep telling myself."

AJ's eyebrows rose. Davis questioning his own assumptions was out of character.

"I'll pay while you get your stuff together," AJ suggested. "My treat today."

"Thanks. I'll meet you at the first tee."

AJ did a reconnaissance of the playing field as he headed into the Pro Shop. They were twins by birth but as different as night and day. Their father had once dubbed them *the go-getter* and *the go-elsewhere* which was apt. Davis was always a step ahead no matter what the field of battle, while AJ sought out the road less travelled.

Shortening his name to AJ from Andrew James had been his way of rejecting their shared middle name and declaring to his father that he would not be judged by the same standards. Davis had countered with the ostentatious Davis J. Halcroft once he had his MBA.

But today the rules of engagement had shifted. Davis did not have his usual swagger. Play along and see what develops, he told himself. It was Davis who had reached out, so the first move was his to make.

"So what's the scoop on this hole?" Davis asked, as AJ arrived at the first tee.

"Long par 4. Pretty straight. Stay clear of the rough. It's a bitch to get out of."

AJ stifled a grimace. They had not yet hit a shot and already he was sounding more like a caddy than a playing partner. "Nice clubs. Are they new?"

"Thanks. Got them a few months ago from one of those custom manufacturers." Davis took a final practice swing.

"That must have set you back a bundle."

Davis aimed a wounded look back at AJ. "They were a birthday gift from Nadine, okay? I wouldn't have bought them for myself." He resumed his stance and executed a textbook swing. The flight of his shot was right to left on a perfect plane.

"Great shot," AJ offered. "And sorry. Didn't mean to imply anything."

"Me either. Let's just play."

AJ teed up and settled himself as he tried to decode what was happening. Davis had the picture perfect marriage including two kids in university. He, on the other hand, had two failed marriages and no children. So why was Davis the one acting defensive?

He caught sight of the harrier passing overhead. It banked left for a moment, as if acknowledging him, before straightening out. Acting on a moment's impulse, he skipped his practice swing.

"That works," Davis said. "You got all of it."

AJ watched the flight of the ball with anticipation. It started on a good line but sliced sharply at the end. Five yards short of Davis' ball, he calculated.

"Can't get rid of that slice." AJ stooped to pick his tee and tossed it away in frustration. "It takes five yards off every shot."

"There are worse things in life than a slice, AJ. It's just a game."

"Easy for you to say, with your custom clubs and your hundred dollar-an-hour swing coach."

"So I've taken a few lessons. Why are you so envious of me?"

AJ was not expecting a direct confrontation. He weighed his options—denial, sidestep or fire back. Long simmering resentment chose for him.

"Your perfect wife, your perfect kids, your hundred and fifty thousand a year job. Seems like reason enough."

Davis gave him a long look. His jaw and his brow tightened. But he made no effort to defend himself. Not a promising start, AJ thought, as they walked the fairway.

Mysteriously, Davis approached AJ's ball.

"What are you doing? That's my ball."

Davis pulled out a 3 Iron, positioned himself and swung away. His shot landed short of the green and rolled up to the fringe.

"You mind telling me what that was all about?"

"I just wanted to not be me for a minute." Davis bent down to replace his divot. "Jarrod got charged with possession of cocaine. He's an addict. I had to put him into rehab."

"Oh man. I'm sorry, Davis. I had no idea."

"Neither did I. What does that say about me as a father?"

So this was the thing Davis needed to talk about. "Don't beat yourself up too much. We did stuff that Dad didn't know anything about."

"You'd be surprised how much he knew, AJ. I damn sure was."

***

They did not speak again until they had teed off on the second hole and crossed the bridge over the creek. AJ was searching for something innocuous to say when he spied the harrier soaring effortlessly overhead. The sight was strangely at odds with the fractious mood that had settled over them.

"Sorry for going off on you back there, Davis. I'll admit it. I've always been jealous of you. I never could keep up with your accomplishments."

"People call me driven. That's supposed to be a good thing."

"You worked hard to get where you are. What happened to Jarrod wasn't your fault. It could have happened in any family."

How strange it felt to be propping up Davis. If their father was looking down on them now, maybe he would see both of them in a different light.

"I'm not sure Nadine would agree with you."

"She blames you? Why?"

"I wasn't paying enough attention to her or the kids. In her words, I was an absentee husband and father." Davis paused. "So, I shouldn't have been surprised that she was cheating on me."

"Really? Damn, you've been through the wringer."

"The thing is, AJ, I didn't have a clue. I was too busy being *successful.*"

"So how did you find out? Or maybe I shouldn't ask."

"We take a vacation to Mexico every year. She blurted it out while we were walking on the beach one evening. I just stood there like an idiot with my mouth hanging open."

AJ pulled a 3 Wood from his bag and lined up his shot. But his mind was not on his swing. So much of what he had thought was clear and defined had shape-shifted in the last half hour. He gave his head a shake to focus and took the shot.

"Nice one. Hole high. You should make a birdie."

The soul-baring moment had passed. Maybe that was all Davis had wanted. The chance to confess his sins and step down off his pedestal.

"Yeah, well, I've been known to three-putt from that distance, so don't hold your breath."

"Why do you do that?" Davis turned toward him.

"Do what?"

"Talk yourself out of succeeding. You've always been that way, AJ. I'm not smarter than you. I just worked hard and believed in myself. But then again, look where that got me."

The old Davis had surfaced for a moment but immediately went underground again.

The harrier passed overhead once more as they reached the green. It went into free fall, as if locked in on prey, but abruptly broke off the dive. The behaviour, which seemed to mirror Davis' self-doubts, puzzled AJ. AJ pondered that question as they finished the hole. He surprised himself by making the birdie and therefore played first on the next tee. He hit a decent drive down the left side. Davis teed up and went through his pre-swing routine. But his gaze was off in the distance.

"I've been thinking lately about the trail I'm leaving behind me, AJ. It's not what I hoped it would be."

Davis looked back at AJ a moment before he coiled and uncoiled through his swing. His ball flirted with the tree line, bounced hard right, and disappeared in the woods.

"Think I'll find that ball?"

AJ shrugged sympathetically.

***

Davis was staring through the trees in the direction of the green. His ball was ten feet deep in the woods.

"Could have been worse," AJ offered. "You can chip out and still make par."

Davis continued to stare. AJ followed his gaze to a narrow opening in the canopy no more than two feet in diameter.

"You're not thinking about trying to shoot it through that hole, are you? That's a suicide shot."

Davis went to his bag, retrieved his 5 Iron and ducked back into the trees. AJ walked out to the fairway. He heard the sound of the swing and watched astounded as the ball threaded the needle through the gap.

Davis scrambled out of the trees to see the result. By the time he located the ball in the air, it was obvious that it did not have the distance to clear the creek. They waited for the inevitable splash. But against all odds, the ball struck a rock in the creek and took a huge bounce toward the green.

"I don't believe it!" AJ exclaimed.

The words were barely out of his mouth when the harrier swooped down. It caught the ball in one claw, at the apex of the bounce, and disappeared over the hill. Stunned silence prevailed a moment before AJ spoke.

"Well, that's one hell of a golf story. You'll be telling it for years."

Davis stood staring at the spot where the spectacle had transpired. What he did next was even more perplexing than attempting the shot. He walked back to AJ's golf cart as if it was his own.

"What? You think my clubs are going to bring you better luck?"

Davis paused, clearly weighing his words.

"Have you ever bargained with fate? I told myself that if I made that shot it would mean I didn't have to tell you."

"Tell me what?"

Davis took a long breath, gathering courage, before he answered.

"A few weeks before Dad died, he called and asked to see me. So, like dutiful number-one son, I went, of course. He took me into his den, pulled an envelope out of his desk drawer and handed it to me. There was a cheque in it for 37,000 dollars addressed to me. It was his life savings. I know I shouldn't have accepted it. But I told myself that if you never knew ... "

Davis looked away, unable to give voice to the half-truth he had tried to live but could not. He nodded toward the clubs. "Take my clubs. Consider them a down payment on what I owe you assuming you ever want to speak to me again."

An incredulous look had spread across AJ's face. Could it be true? Could his father have been so disappointed in him that he had given his life savings to Davis?

"It's not what you think, AJ. I don't know how Dad knew, but he did. I was up to my eyeballs in debt and on the verge of losing my house. Dad knew we'd both lost our way. But he also knew you were the strong one. He knew you could take care of yourself. He did what he had to do, and trusted that I would eventually figure it out and confess to you."

His confession complete, Davis took possession of AJ's clubs and walked on ahead. His stride was less burdened and, somehow, more humble.

AJ struggled to find a foothold in the startling new landscape in which he found himself—no longer the lost son, but the trusted one. He watched the harrier make a final pass overhead with Davis' ball still in its grasp. It circled twice and soared majestically over the treetops gaining altitude until it was out of sight. Understanding came quietly and without fanfare. Why the harrier had shadowed him and what its' odd flight display was meant to teach him.

He picked up the 5 Iron AJ had dropped, lined up his shot and swung. The ball arced right to left and landed on the edge of green. Not a perfect shot, but no hint of a slice.

"That works."

Ransom Heart

William was wide awake at 2:00 a.m., the persistent ache in his chest fending off sleep, when the whistled tremolo of a screech owl rose out of the ravine, beckoning to him. He slipped out of bed and felt his way to the window. All was peaceful in his field of view through the backyard and into the ravine beyond. The half-moon drifted between patches of nighttime cloud. The tranquility that held court over the night mocked him as the owl's call switched to a mournful, descending whinny.

He looked over at DeAnn who reposed in what appeared to be perfect peace. When they had first come here, looking for a fresh start, it was DeAnn who prowled about in the night. Now she had found equilibrium. But the deeper she buried what they had left behind, the more it rose up to haunt him. It did not help matters that DeAnn quickly fell back into her old ways—making monthly treks into the city to Saks Off Fifth Avenue which had become her new favourite place to shop since the chain store moved into Canada.

Extravagant urges tempted him during these sleepless hours. What if he were to slip away, get on a plane and simply disappear for a while? He could cross the Rocky Mountains, find a sleepy coastal town and hide out until the storm had settled.

"Wishful thinking," he muttered, knowing that distance was not an antidote. He retrieved the sleeping pills from the nightstand drawer, swallowed one and slid into bed. DeAnn murmured in her sleep and rolled away from him. The screech owl wailed again, closer this time, from the banks of the ravine.

***

It was only mid-morning but the temperature had already climbed past 80°. The sun slanted through the blinds of Will's office window, at Rambling Creek Golf and Country Club, stenciling a pattern on the wall. Fatigued after another restless night, Will's mind wandered, from the last month's financials he was supposed to be reviewing, to the wavering pattern of light and dark. The phone drew him out of his trance.

"Will, he's here. Can you believe it? He's here." There was an underlying tone of accusation in DeAnn's muffled voice.

"Who? Who is there?"

"Who do you think? Reverend Meagher. Right here in our living room."

A familiar fear materialized and squeezed hard in Will's chest.

"Just Martin? No one else?"

"Martin? You're still on a first name basis with him?"

"DeAnn. Is he by himself?"

"Yes, not that it makes any difference. What am I supposed to say to him? You need to get here. Fast."

"Okay, I'm on my way. I'll handle it."

Will hung up the phone and slumped in his chair. He recalled the tremolo of the screech owl from the early hours of the morning. So this was what it had been warning him about.

He collected himself, pushed aside the image of DeAnn waiting for him with daggers in her eyes, and on his way out, he stopped at the Pro Shop to let Justin know he was leaving.

"I have to go home for a bit. I'll be back in an hour or two."

Justin looked caught off guard. "Dad. You startled me. Is everything okay?"

"Fine. There's just something I have to take care of."

"Ah ... okay."

"What's the matter with you?"

"Nothing. I'm good."

"If anybody asks, I went into town to run some errands. Understand?"

"Got it."

Will ran possible scenarios through his mind on the tense drive home. None of them were good. Thankfully it was only Martin he had to face—not a full delegation from the church board. But that small blessing was not enough to relieve the nagging pain that had migrated into his neck and jaw.

***

As he pulled in the driveway, Will winced at the sight of the ostentatious landscaping makeover of the yard and the custom, designer doors and windows—both things DeAnn had insisted on having done to compensate for the step down from the house they left behind. He imagined what must have passed through Reverend Martin's mind when he saw them.

DeAnn was waiting for him on the front porch. He recognized the wild look in her eyes—a mixture of anger, fear and resentment.

"I can't go through this again, Will. You have to make this go away once and for all."

He shook his head and brushed past her. Martin Meagher was seated on the couch looking distinctly uncomfortable.

"Hello, Will. I imagine I'm low on the list of the people you wanted to see today."

"That's an understatement, Martin." He eased himself into a chair with a grimace. "How did you find us?"

"I didn't. J.T. did. I imagine it wasn't all that difficult. There are only so many Golf and Country Clubs."

"I suppose you've come to tell me that the Board is pressing charges." Will's voice lost all intonation as he voiced his worst fear.

"No, that's not why I came. In fact, the Board doesn't know I'm here."

"Then why are you here?"

"I'm concerned about you, Will. This has to be weighing on your conscience." Martin shifted his gaze to the window, measuring his words. "You promised to pay it all back. If you were having difficulty with the payments, you should have come to me. We could have worked something out."

"It was hard on DeAnn. She couldn't handle being shunned. For a while there, I was afraid she was going to leave me."

"I stood up for you, Will. I took a lot of heat when you left."

"I'm sorry. I really am. I never understood how you kept the Board from filing charges."

Martin's eyes flitted down and back up again. "I told them I'd resign if they did."

"Seriously? Why would you go out on a limb for me?"

"I don't believe you meant to steal from us. You borrowed from the church account and paid it back several times before anyone noticed. I think you just got caught short that last time. But I have to ask. Do you intend to pay back the rest?"

Will hesitated. "It's complicated. DeAnn came from a wealthy family. She expects a certain standard of living. Plus, Justin is going to U of T this fall. Post-secondary education is damn expensive. I know those must sound like empty excuses. And I know that the church is in a bad position ... I'll try to find a way."

Martin stood up to leave. "The church will manage. I'm more concerned about you. You need to make things right or you'll never have peace. Even a hundred dollars a month. Think about it."

Will did not move from his chair for a long time after Martin left. The ransom of conscience felt like a weight bearing down on him. He met DeAnn's eyes, when she came into the room, and attempted a preemptive strike.

"That necklace looks new, and expensive. "

DeAnn ignored the comment.

"Well? Are they pressing charges?"

"No."

"Thank God. I couldn't take that nightmare starting up again. It's bad enough I had to leave the city, where I've lived my entire life, and move to the middle of nowhere."

Should he plead his case? Try to convince her that it could not all be just swept under the carpet. The futility of that effort was too obvious. There were times with her when it was simply better to suffer her incriminating glare in silence.

***

Will tapped a beat on his desk with his pen as he weighed the results of the audit which the Club's accountant had just laid out for him. Howie fidgeted in his chair, distinctly uncomfortable being the bearer of bad news.

"You're sure about this, Howie?"

"The numbers don't add up. Somebody in the Pro Shop is skimming from the till."

"How much?"

"At least two grand over the last few months."

"All right, I'll get to the bottom of it. We only have four guys working the Pro Shop. Justin is one of them, so that only leaves three suspects. FYI, we won't be pressing charges."

"Why not?" Howie asked.

Will spun the pen in his hand as he tried to fend off the sting of divine retribution. "Bad publicity. I don't want the membership getting wind of this. It doesn't go beyond us, understand?"

"It's my experience that these things end up being the worst kept secrets."

"I said *nobody* hears about this."

"I get it, Will." Howie held up his hands in a gesture of submission. "It's your call."

Will turned in his desk chair and looked out at the ninth green. A hundred dollars a month. How long would it take at that rate? Four years—a long time to hide it from DeAnn. He would also have to manufacture a plausible excuse for not putting in the in-ground swimming pool he had reluctantly promised her.

***

Justin was waiting in Will's office for his ride home when Will returned after wrapping up his last meeting of the day.

"Thought you'd be on the practice green– your usual haunt after your shift."

"Too hot today." Justin scooped a golf ball off the desk and spun it in his hand. "I gotta tell you, Dad. I've had enough of the Pro Shop. Another month and I'll be at university, thank God."

"There are worse jobs than a golf club pro shop. Try busting your ass picking tobacco like I did for two summers when I was a grad student. My back didn't stop aching for months."

"Yeah, yeah, I know."

"There's something I need to talk to you about." Will pushed his chair out from behind his desk. "Our accountant says somebody is skimming from the till in the pro shop. Any idea who it might be? Henry? Nino?"

"Why are you asking me? Am I supposed to be your spy?"

"Help me out here. You work with those guys."

"We don't talk much. I mind my business. They mind theirs."

"So you've never seen anything suspicious?" Justin slumped in his chair and fixed an angry look at Will. "What's with the attitude, Justin?"

"You obviously already know. So what's the point of the inquisition?"

"Know what?"

"You don't pay me much more than minimum wage. What do you expect? Don't look at me like that. Like father, like son, right? At least I didn't screw over a church."

Will had no time to respond. Pain erupted in his chest and ricocheted down his left arm. His breath came in gasps as he tried to stand up, staggered toward his desk and collapsed on the floor.

***

"You're fortunate the paramedics got to you quickly, Mr. Stanley." The doctor made notes on Will's chart as he spoke. "You're stable now. But there is evidence of an earlier, silent heart attack. You've been having chest pains for quite some time, haven't you?"

"I thought it was just stress. I've had a lot on my mind."

"You're going to have to make some changes. But we can get into that later when your wife gets here. Your son is waiting outside. I'll let you have some time with him."

Guilt was etched in Justin's expression as he edged into the room.

"Jeez, Dad, I'm sorry. I didn't think you'd take it that hard."

"It's not your fault. This has been creeping up on me for a long time."

"What I said—I didn't mean it. Look, I swear I'll pay it all back. I only spent a bit of it. You're not going to turn me in, are you?"

"No, that would be hypocritical of me. But you have to be the one to tell your mother."

Justin grimaced at the suggestion. "Do we have to tell her? You know she'll go ballistic."

DeAnn entered the room precisely on cue.

"Will, a heart attack? How did this happen? Are you okay? Where's the doctor? I want to talk to him."

"Jeez, Mom. Take a valium."

"Don't you talk to me that way, Justin."

"DeAnn, calm down. I'm going to be fine."

"I'd like to hear that from the doctor. Justin, find him. Tell him I want to talk to him, *now*."

"Wow, slow down." Will sat up and reached for DeAnn's arm. "You can't direct traffic here."

"What is that supposed to mean, Will?"

"Can we just talk for a minute? Sit down, okay?"

DeAnn sat on the edge of the bed and looked from Will to Justin. "What's going on here? What aren't you telling me?"

"Justin. Go ahead."

"Go ahead with what?" She turned her gaze to Justin.

"Don't freak out, okay? I took some money from the pro shop. But I'm going to pay it all back."

DeAnn's face went blank for a moment.

"I don't believe this. It's happening all over again." She turned to Will. "Will, you *have* to fix this."

"I'm not going to report it, so you don't have to worry. But I realized something today. We can't hide from our past. Look where it got us. So I'm going to start paying back the rest of the money that I borrowed . . . what I took from the church. We'll have to cut back for a couple of years. Justin, you're going to have to put off going to university."

DeAnn's eyes narrowed. "Will, we don't live there anymore. I gave up all that for you, in case you've forgotten. We've made a new life here."

"Have we really? It doesn't feel that way to me."

"You're doing this because Reverend Meagher showed up this morning? He won't let them press charges. He said he'll resign if they do. They won't go against him."

"I never told you that, DeAnn. You were eavesdropping on our conversation?"

DeAnn stood and began to pace across the room. "The point is, it's over and done with. You screwed up our lives once, Will. I didn't pull up stakes, give up my dream house and move three hundred miles just to get yanked back into your mess."

"You're never going to forgive me for that, are you?"

"Forgive you? You dragged our good name through the mud. But I stood by you. Now I'm asking—I'm *telling* you—let it go."

"You're not angry because I stole from the church, are you? You're just angry that I got caught."

"Will, don't you dare. Don't you dare make this about me."

"It always was about you, DeAnn. About living up to your expectations."

"I don't have to take this from you. How many second chances do you expect me to give you?"

"Mom, come on." Justin tried to mediate. "Dad just had a heart attack."

"It's okay, Justin. Your mom is right." He turned back to DeAnn. "I'm not looking for forgiveness this time. I'm going to make it easy on you. Just walk away."

DeAnn stopped in her tracks. "What did you say?"

Will swung himself out of bed and stood face to face with her. "You heard me. Get out."

"I rush down here, worried out of my mind, and you tell me to *get out*?"

"I know what you're worried about, and it's not me. I'm only going to say this once more. *Get out.* And let's be clear about this. I don't just mean out of this room."

"Dad, what the hell are you doing?"

"Something I should have done years ago. Taking back my self-respect."

DeAnn hesitated, uncertainty clouding her expression. "Will, you just had a heart attack. You're not thinking straight. I know you don't mean it. We'll find a way out of this. We'll move again if we have to."

"Move wherever you want to, DeAnn. I really don't care, as long as I'm not with you."

DeAnn drew her shoulders back.

"Are you prepared to give up your son?" she said. "If we split up, he comes with me."

Justin's head snapped around to confront his mother. "Hey, when did I become a bargaining chip, Mom? You know what—screw you."

"Justin, step out of the room. This is between your mother and I."

Justin's eyes swiveled between the two of them. A hint of a grin twisted the corner of his mouth as he nodded to Will and left the room. DeAnn leaned toward Will, locking eyes with him.

"You'll regret this, Will. I'll make you pay. So help me God, I'll make you pay."

"Oh, I'm sure you will. You've been holding me for ransom our entire marriage. It took nearly going to jail and a heart attack to wake me up. So, this is your chance."

"Chance for what exactly?" Her jaw was quivering despite her attempt to mock him.

For a fleeting moment, Will felt pity for her. But he brushed the feeling aside. This day had been a long time coming. He was not about to deny himself the moment of victory.

"The bidding is open. Name your price."

The Thing with Feathers

The rhythmic patter of rain on the window, quickening with the restless gusts of December wind, became a timpani roll for the gathering storm of Hannah's thoughts. She had a perfect right to be angry and indignant. So why was she unable to summon the feelings? Standing back and withholding her emotions was not the proper response.

Reality reasserted itself, in the form of her BlackBerry buzzing, and reminded her that she was in the teacher's lounge where gazing distractedly off into space was bound to draw strange looks. She rummaged around in her purse, pulled it out and answered.

"Hi, Hannah. It's Julie Riley. I'm not interrupting a class, am I? I think you have a free period right now."

Evan's guidance counsellor. Hannah drew a quick breath to clear her head, instinctively bracing herself.

"No, it's fine. What has my prodigal son done this time? Not another fight, I hope."

"No, nothing like that. But I do need to speak to you and Scott. Today if possible."

Evan, her only child, was square in the middle of the turbulent teen years. It was too much to ask, it seemed, to have a well-adjusted child. Or perhaps, too much to expect for someone not so very well adjusted herself.

"I don't know if today will be possible. Scott may not be able to get time off. But I'll call him and find out. Can you give me some idea what this is about?"

"Well, it's difficult." Julie paused. "No, I think it's best to wait until you're both here."

Hannah took a moment to compose herself after disconnecting with Julie. She so much did not want to hear Scott's voice after what last night had revealed about him. But parenthood once again took precedence. The looming decision would have to wait.

Her BlackBerry shimmied on the table. She picked it up. "Hi, it's me." Scott, unexpectedly, with an edge to his voice.

"Scott. I was just about to call you."

"So you've heard already. I guess it's true—bad news travels fast."

"What? Heard what? What are you talking about, Scott?"

"Well, basically, as of today, I'm unemployed. Me and about 100 other people."

"No! Really? What on earth happened?" A less than sympathetic response, she realized.

"The radio station has gone tits up. At least, that's the bullshit they're shoveling to us. All kinds of rumours are flying around."

Why did this have to happen now? It earned Scott a measure of sympathy. "I'm sorry. That's awful. But you've been there a long time. At least you'll get a decent severance package."

"Didn't you hear me, Hannah? They're claiming the station's bankrupt. Nobody's getting squat."

"Can they do that? Just slam the door in your face?"

"The union will fight it. But I'm not holding my breath. Anyway, I just got home. You said you were about to call me. About what?"

Last night's revelation flared in her mind. The implications of Scott coming to the school struck her. What better way to confirm what she had discovered?

"Evan's guidance counsellor wants to see us."

"Oh, great. Sometimes I think he gets into trouble deliberately just to get me riled up. What the hell did he do this time?"

"She couldn't say on the phone. But she said it's important."

"Honestly, I don't know if I'm up to it today, Hannah. Can you handle it this time?"

"Do you have a problem with coming to the school, Scott?"

"It's not that. It's just ... um ... Okay, I'm on my way."

"I'll meet you at the front entrance in half an hour. Bye."

Hannah disconnected and slid her BlackBerry back into her purse. The trap was set. But now that it was, she wished it were otherwise. What she really wanted was more time to turn over the options in her mind.

Hope is the thing with feathers—
That perches in the soul—
And sings the tune without the words—
And never stops—at all—

Emily Dickinson's anthem on the fugitive nature of hope rose in her mind without beckoning, although not altogether unwelcome given the direction in which it turned her thoughts. Dickinson was her enigmatic soul mate over the reaches of time—always at the ready with just the right verse to interpret her state of mind.

How long since she had last given in to the temptation? It must be close to a year. Going there was both rationally and emotionally reckless. She had lived in these parallel existences—the inner world where she could fashion and reorder events to suit her rebellious desires, and the outer world of reality where control always eluded her—most of her life. The two existences had become interdependent.

She picked up her BlackBerry, opened Google and typed in the name: *Joshua Redding*. The usual social media site hits, Facebook and LinkedIn with their fast forward snippets of life, showed up first. Her eyes scanned down to the next listing and hung on the word: *Obituary*.

Joshua Norman Redding Obituary

Drifted away peacefully on September 28, 2015 at Grand River Hospital with his wife and children by his side. Joshua was born on June 5, 1968 to

> Howard and Joanne Redding in Toronto. He
> married Cynthia Elizabeth Anderson in 1990.
> Joshua and Cynthia were blessed with a son,
> Norman James Redding and a daughter, Anna
> Elizabeth Redding.

An oppressive weight of sadness descended upon Hannah that made it difficult to breathe. She felt cold, foreign fingers of fear closing around her heart and a rising wave of sorrow that threatened to shipwreck her. She drew a deep, laboured breath, checked the rogue emotions as she had learned by necessity to do, and willed herself to continue reading.

> Joshua is survived by his wife and children and
> brothers Jonathan and Jordan. The family will
> receive friends at the Henry Walser Funeral Home
> on October 3 from 1:00 to 3:00 p.m. and 7:00 to
> 9:00 p.m. Funeral service will take place on October
> 4 at 1:00 p.m. at Emmanuel United Church with
> interment following at Woodland Cemetery.
> Donations to the Canadian Cancer Society will be
> greatly appreciated.

The voice of reason rallied to rescue her. This knowledge, however unwelcome and vaguely sinister, had no effect on her tangible life. It was nothing more than the closing of a portal in that parallel existence that was sustained by will alone. Any emotions that washed over her were fabricated and as insubstantial as wind.

Because I could not stop for death—
He kindly stopped for me—
The carriage held but just ourselves,
And Immortality.

Drifted away peacefully. Despite the reality check, the latching of locks and the soul-quieting words of Dickinson, those three words burned to the touch. Why should they, a mere statement of fact dressed in the language of loss, have such power to pierce her heart?

"Are you okay, Hannah?"

Reality closed in again. Hannah looked up and saw Ellie Lewis standing over her.

"Oh, yes. I'm fine. Just lost in thought for moment."

"You're sure? You looked ... stricken, I guess, is the word."

"I'm fine, really. But thank you."

Ellie studied her expression for a moment longer. "Alright, if you say so." She moved on to the door and left the lounge.

It was a perilously close call. The clashing of worlds had lifted the veil of her emotions and left them exposed. But it was not the time to sort through the rubble of this quake. Here and now, the foremost concern was Scott and the secret he was keeping. For some time she had had her suspicions and, despite her efforts to push them away, they would not be denied. Yesterday evening she had resolved to uncover the truth for better or for worse.

While Scott was in the shower, she took his BlackBerry off the night table and accessed his recently called numbers. There were months' worth of calls. He had not thought to cover his tracks. And there it was—one unfamiliar number that appeared regularly on Thursdays.

There was no turning back once the discovery was made. She placed his BlackBerry carefully back in its place on the night table and used her own. Punched in *67 to activate call block, tapped in the number and waited breathlessly for an answer.

"Hello ... Hello? ... *Hello.*"

The possibility that she would recognize the voice had occurred to her. But she was not prepared for the voice she heard. She quickly disconnected.

Now here she was, the next morning, possessed with this new knowledge that she did not know what to do with. Strangely conflicted about the way separate spheres of her life suddenly overlapped. Was the voice really who she thought it was? Doubt crept in. But the means to resolve it were at hand. Scott was on his way here. It was not, strictly speaking, the scene of the crime. But it was an opportunity to bring both suspects face to face and watch for the signs that might betray them.

***

Hannah met Scott at the front entrance as planned. She kissed him on the cheek, to maintain the semblance of routine, while surreptitiously studying his expression.

"Thanks for coming. I know you didn't need this after what you've already had thrown at you today."

"One shit storm after another," he replied. "Just that kind of day, I guess."

"I've got someone covering my Grade 12 English class. We can go straight to Julie's office."

"Any idea what this is all about?" Scott asked, as they walked down the hall.

"Sorry, no. But we'll find out soon enough."

In more ways than one, Hannah told herself. She was more than a little concerned about this latest crisis with Evan. "Did you hear anything more about the station?"

"Rumours up the ying yang," he answered. "Got a text from our union rep. Apparently they hired back a bunch of people under another company name. God only knows what game they're playing."

Hannah noticed that his eyes were fixed on the hallway ahead of them. Was there a mounting wariness about him or was it just the cumulative effect of the day's events? She kept up her part of the conversation as they walked.

"Sounds like it's going to be messy. I guess all we can do is wait and see how it all falls out."

As they approached the school office, the door opened and Janine Bradley, the vice principal, stepped out as if on cue. The momentary halt in her usually confident stride, simultaneous with the sudden stiffening of Scott's posture, spoke volumes. Their eyes locked ever so briefly before falling away.

"Hello, Hannah. Scott." Janine's guard was back up. "Evan again?"

They had had several meetings with Janine about Evan, over the past couple of months, in the hope of staving off another suspension. How exactly those encounters fired up an attraction, and how she had managed not to notice it, was a complete mystery to Hannah.

"Yes," Hannah replied. "We're on our way to see Julie."

"Let me know if there is anything I can do to help."

Stop sleeping with my husband. That would be a good start. The temptation to blast it all open rose up for a moment. But she was nowhere near ready for that confrontation.

***

"Thanks for coming in on such short notice."

Hannah read concern in Julie's expression which underscored the seriousness of the meeting. Evan, seated across from Julie and slumped in his chair, threw a quick sideways glance at them.

"What did you do this time, Evan?" Scott fixed his glare on his son.

"Scott, don't make this an inquisition." Hannah turned to Julie. "What is this about?"

"Evan, tell your parents what you told me this morning about your girlfriend."

"Girlfriend?" Scott asked. "You have a girlfriend and you didn't tell us?"

"What? I have to tell you everything I fucking do now?"

"Hey, watch your language." Scott leaned toward Evan. "You're already on thin ice here."

Thin ice. Hannah let the irony slip by unacknowledged for the moment. "It's okay, Evan. Just tell us the problem."

"She's not my girlfriend anymore. Her family moved away. But ... we had sex a few times."

"You used a condom, right?" Scott jumped back in. "Tell me you were at least responsible enough to use protection."

And did you, Scott? Hannah swallowed hard to keep the words from spilling out.

"Yeah ... except for the first time. I wasn't really expecting it to happen."

"Oh, Evan. Please tell me you did *not* get this girl pregnant." Hannah winced as she heard the unintended condemnation in her voice.

"No, but ... There are rumours going around that ... " He looked imploringly at Julie for help.

"That she was, or is, HIV positive," Julie replied. "We've been aware of the rumours for some time, although of course we could not officially confirm them. It's a sensitive matter."

Silence fell on all of them for a moment while the reality sunk in. Scott was the first to break it.

"Jesus! Who is this girl?"

"Evan does not wish to reveal the girl's identity. And I have to respect his decision. I know who she is. But there are legal liability issues involved, so I can't tell you. In any event, since she isn't a student here anymore, my hands are tied."

"Evan, you have to give us her name. And then let's goddamned well find out where they moved to." Scott was on his feet and pacing now. "We need to know if this is true and we need to know *now*."

Hannah was lost for a moment absorbing what she had just heard and deciphering the intersection of it with the silent revelation of a few minutes ago in the hallway.

"Jesus, Hannah. I could use some support here."

"Sorry, Scott. Yes, I agree. Can we find out where they moved to?"

"My advice to you is that you focus on getting Evan tested as soon as possible," Julie answered. "Even if we could locate the family, they would probably not be particularly receptive to your questions."

"Yes, of course, you're right." Hannah struggled to get the words out through the jumble of her emotions. "Scott?"

"Yeah, okay, that makes sense. Come on, Evan. We're going straight to the doctor."

Evan stood up slowly with shame in his eyes. "Sorry, Dad. Mom. Guess I kinda fucked up."

"That's the understatement of the year," Scott fired back.

Anger flashed in Hannah's eyes. She levelled a withering look on Scott.

"What?" he asked.

Julie pulled them aside. "A word of advice, as a friend. Whatever is or is not going on between the two of you, put it away for now. Evan should be the only thing on your mind."

If only it were that simple, Hannah thought.

***

Evan was secluded in his room watching a movie on Netflix—something violent judging by the sounds escaping under his door. Scott had retreated to his man cave in the basement. On the surface, an evening like any other, it occurred to Hannah, except for the frantic few hours that had preceded it.

It began with an urgent call to their family doctor. He directed them to a special clinic where they sweated out two hours waiting for a *point of care* test. She wondered, as the nurse explained the test to them—a simple needle prick with immediate results—why no one else saw the irony in that phrase. Evan's result was "reactive" which translated to "inconclusive." The more detailed blood test that necessitated had a two-week wait for the results.

Alone now in the living room, with only a glass of wine for comfort, Hannah wondered how the order of her life had so completely unravelled in the last 48 hours. Scott's indiscretions were the most perplexing. Round and round the idea she went, as if there was a precise angle at which, if she could happen upon it, the light would be just right to solve the puzzle. *Drifted away peacefully.* Her rebellious heart made one of its quantum leaps and landed her back in that other existence. Why were those words so laden with sorrow? *Passed away peacefully*—she could have wrestled that into submission. But "drifted away" painted a picture. The life slipping out of him. The final, agonizing *I love you* from his wife before he breathed his last.

Why cling to this unrequited love for someone she hardly knew? A relationship that ran aground before it ever began years and years ago. She should have let go of it, at the very least, when she joined her life to Scott's. Why was her feet-on-the-ground life never enough for her?

Footsteps sounded on the stairs. Scott was coming up from his man cave. Reality asserted itself. Here was the man she loved, had a child with and had built a life around. Did it matter so very much if she was not irrationally, beyond all reason, hopelessly *in love* with him? Scott found Hannah in the living room and sat down next to her.

"What are we going to do, Hannah? What are we going to do if the test comes back positive?"

"I don't know," she answered. "I guess we cross that bridge when—if—we come to it."

"Hell of a time to be out of a job. Feels like I'm not holding up my end of the bargain."

"We'll manage. One way or another."

Vague reassurance was all she could summon for the moment. In her mind, she knew already what she had to do tomorrow.

***

Hannah was up early on Saturday morning. Her cover story—that she needed to catch up on work at school after missing most of Friday— slid by without question. How ridiculously easy it was for them to deceive one another.

She struggled to numb her mind on the drive to Kitchener. Listen to the radio. Read every sign on the 401. Watch turkey vultures gliding on wind currents overhead scanning for roadkill. Anything to distract herself from the risky act she had committed herself to carrying out. The most obvious problem in her hastily conceived plan occurred to her only as she was turning into Woodland Cemetery. How was she going to find his gravesite? Wander around all morning hoping to stumble on it? Hannah was on the verge of abandoning the whole idea when she saw a city worker emptying garbage cans. She pulled up next to his truck and rolled down her window.

"Excuse me. If someone was buried here, say two or three months ago, where would the grave likely be?"

The man stared at her as if she was quite mad. "You're coming to visit a grave, and you don't even know where it is?"

"Sorry, it's ... complicated."

"Yeah, I imagine it is. Well, the newest area of the cemetery is over that way. But if it's a family plot, it's anybody's guess."

"Thanks."

She turned in the direction he indicated, drove until she came to new graves and parked. Her courage faltered as she stepped out of the car. What was she doing here? Following her rebellious heart one final time.

She started at the newest graves and criss-crossed from row to row reading headstones. Fifteen minutes passed before she found his grave. An elegant headstone of speckled gray was already in place.

Joshua Norman Redding

1968—2015

Cynthia Elizabeth Redding

1970 –

Sorrow rose like mist from the sacred ground on which she stood as the years fell away. She was once again the shy, self-conscious and yet emotionally reckless young woman who wanted nothing more than to be rescued by love. But also unable to relinquish at any price the core of who she was beginning to know herself to be. And he, Joshua, was as much imagined as real. She saw what she wanted to see in him. There was unquestionably an aura of gentleness and vulnerability about him. He too was still discovering who he wanted to be.

"Excuse me ... *Excuse me?*"

A voice broke the trance that held Hannah in its grasp. She turned and saw a woman staring at her.

"Do I know you?" she asked.

"No," Hannah answered, hesitantly.

"Why are you standing over my husband's grave?"

She was caught in the act with no reasonable excuse to offer for her presence. Intruding on this woman's grief and raising suspicion without cause. What could she possibly say to justify herself?

"I'm his sister."

The words slipped out before she could catch them. She had forgotten that moment until now. The conversation, over glasses of wine, during which Joshua had shared that he and his sister were given up for adoption at the ages of two and four. Adopted by different couples and separated ever since. He spoke passionately of how he intended one day to find his sister.

"You're Clara?" The woman's expression softened.

"Yes." Hannah was committed to the deception now.

"Oh, my God. I'm Cynthia—Joshua's wife. He tried so hard to find you. He searched for years and years. You must have been searching too. Clara, you missed each other by only a few months."

Coming here was a terrible misjudgment, Hannah realized.

"I'm sorry for your loss." She was casting about desperately for a way to disengage herself from the situation.

"Thank you so much," Cynthia answered through tears. "But you, you lost him twice. I am so, so sorry. It's cruel that you didn't get to meet him."

Drifted away peacefully. It struck Hannah that this was the woman who had crafted those words. The one who had the right to the emotion they invoked. Never imagining how they might land on the heart of someone she had never met.

"I ... I'm sorry ... I have to go."

"Oh no," Cynthia implored. "Please wait. Can't we talk?"

"I'm sorry ... I just ... I can't ... I'm sorry, I have to go."

Hannah turned and began to walk away, resisting the urge to run.

"Clara, please ... Please?"

Hannah turned and saw the tears streaming down Cynthia's face. She could not continue to play out the immoral deception. But the lie was planted and she had to own the consequences. She went back, folded Cynthia in her arms and held her for a few seconds while past and present, real and imagined, desired and forsaken become one. And when she could contain herself no longer, she turned and fled.

***

The house was mercifully quiet when Hannah arrived home in the early afternoon. She was emotionally wrung out and wracked with guilt. Her BlackBerry had been off, a conscious choice, the whole time she was away. She turned it back on now and picked up Scott's message.

"Hey, it's me. Ah ... Evan wanted to play in his hockey game today. I told him that was out of the question because—well, obviously. He asked if he could at least go and watch. I couldn't see any harm in that. So, we'll be back around three-thirty ... Love you. Bye."

Not "I love you"—just "Love you". A shorthand version of those words that meant so much, and yet could be tacked onto the end of something by habit alone.

Drifted away peacefully. One last foray down that road, she promised herself. Already there were reasons enough, painfully puzzled out, to explain why those words carried such a heavy weight. Was there anything more?

For each ecstatic instant
We must an anguish pay,
In keen and quivering ratio
To the ecstasy.

Leave it to her muse to boil it all down to its essence. It was not fair or just. But it was truth—unrepentant truth. The time had arrived to stop trying to fathom why for so long she had had feet in two different worlds or what it was about her, what flaw or susceptibility, made it so. Close the door finally and be done with it. Marshall all her emotions, rebellious or otherwise, to fight for the life she was left with however scarred that life might have become.

Hannah heard the sound of Scott's car pulling in the driveway, bringing Evan and himself back to her. She walked across the room to the door and opened it wide.

Scars of Humanity

Hello from above our magnificent planet earth. The perspective is truly awe-inspiring ... I have seen some incredible sights: lightning spreading over the Pacific, the Aurora Australis lighting up the entire visible horizon with the city glow of Australia below, the moon setting over the limb of the Earth, the vast plains of Africa and the dunes on Cape Horn, rivers breaking through tall mountain passes, the scars of humanity, the continuous line of life extending from North America, through Central America and into South America, another crescent moon setting over the limb of our blue planet. Mount Fuji looks like a small bump from up here, but it does stand out as a very distinct landmark.

Was it an unconscious intuition, that these words might be her epitaph, which caused mission specialist Laurel Blair Salton Clark to mine her poet's heart for this eloquent soliloquy?

It was by no means a new question. But Laurel Hyatt Thorne found herself circling back to it yet again as she studied her reflection in the bathroom mirror. It had to be more than mere coincidence, logic argued, that she shared both a name and a birth date with astronaut Clark. But that alone was not what forged the cosmic connection she felt to her. *The scars of humanity.* Laurel stepped into the shower, tilted her head back and let the jets of hot water stream over her face. There was a vague comfort in losing herself in the billowing clouds of steam. An errant screech like a cry of pain interrupted the moan of water rushing through aging pipes. Laurel's thoughts detoured momentarily conjuring the image of Kate the day they first met. Three days earlier, the Columbia space shuttle had broken up and disintegrated, in welcoming skies over Texas, spiriting away the lives of its seven crew members.

One day earlier, astronaut Clark, stealing a few minutes away from her duties, had sent an e-mail message to her family with what would become, in effect, her dying words.

She was still under the spell of that momentous day when she met Kate. In one of those rare moments of other worldly perception, she knew instinctively that Kate had her own carefully guarded scars of humanity. And now, six months later, Laurel was still keeping their weekly assignation despite all her better instincts.

Another screech emanated from the pipes. This time it seemed like a voice of condemnation calling her to account for living a dual life.

Kate was lying on the bed pecking out a message on her BlackBerry when Laurel emerged from the bathroom. Laurel's eyes lingered on the watercolour portrait of an eagle, perched on a branch with its wings spread wide in a protective posture, that hung on the wall above the bed. It had always felt portentious to her.

"Just got a text message from my sister. She works for First Energy down in Ohio. Something funky is happening to their distribution lines. Three of them have disconnected in the last half hour."

"Disconnected from what?"

"From each other. All on their own apparently. They can't figure out why."

"And that affects us how?" Laurel asked. "This is Mississauga, after all."

"The border is just an imaginary line where the power grids are concerned. My sister says there are a whole series of interdependencies. One grid connects to another. And that one connects to a couple more. It's like a spider web spreading out for thousands of miles."

"Whatever. I have to get going. I'm running late."

Kate pointed her BlackBerry at Laurel, snapped a photo and held it out for her to see.

"So what?" Laurel asked, with an undertone of irritation. It made her uneasy to have a physical record of their time together.

"It's your *I can't wait to get out of here* expression. I thought by now you would have started to figure things out."

"What is there to figure out?"

Laurel regretted taking the bait. Giving voice to her annoyance only corroborated that there were undercurrents at work which she did not want to confront.

"Do you realize you hardly ever say my name? Why is that? So you can keep on pretending I'm not actually a woman?"

"Kate, Kate, Kate. Is that better?"

"Are you this bitchy with your husband after sex?"

"I'm *not* going to have this argument with you. I have to go."

She dropped the towel on the bed and reached for her clothes. Kate slid across the bed and took Laurel's face in her hands.

"Laurel, I hate this part. I play the bitch because that's what you want. I make you resent me so you can flip the switch and go back to your regular life. I know that's what you need, so I do it."

Laurel pulled away. "You're the one who seduced me, remember? I was perfectly happy being heterosexual."

Kate rolled out of the bed and threw open the drapes. "How long are you going to keep up this 'I'm bisexual' charade?"

"Excuse me?"

"Have you ever had an orgasm with your husband—or with any man for that matter?"

Laurel felt a momentary surge of resentment towards James at the mention of him. It felt like, against all reason, he was complicit in her affair.

"I've been married for eight years. Do you really think I could have got away with faking it that long?"

Laurel finished dressing while she fended off Kate's accusations.

"Hell, yes. Men are totally clueless."

"How would you know? Have you ever been with a man?"

The taunt slipped out before Laurel could catch it. Kate paused, turning to look out the window, before responding.

"Be careful what you ask, Laurel."

"Can I take that as a *no*?"

"Depends. Does my father count?"

"Is that supposed to be a joke? It's sick."

Kate did not respond at first. Laurel felt a sudden shift in the tide of their argument, as if the energy had suddenly drained from the room.

"Yes, I suppose it is." Kate's voice was subdued and devoid of emotion.

"My God, you're serious ... Kate, I'm so sorry."

"For what? For what my father did to me? Or for ever getting involved with me in the first place?" Kate turned back and tilted her head to study Laurel. "Wow, it just hit me. I just gave you the out you've been looking for, didn't I?"

"No, I wasn't ... I could stay awhile. If you –"

"I'm still a total stranger to you, aren't I? You don't know me at all even after six months. I don't want your pity. If you can't see that, well, I guess this thing between us has run its course."

Laurel was caught off guard. Could this really be the end? Could it happen so abruptly—all the intertwined emotions disengaging at the same time?

Kate turned back to Laurel with a sad smile. "Have you figured it out yet?"

"Figured what out?"

"Why you had a lesbian affair."

Laurel had replayed the images of that first day a dozen times in her memory.

"Honestly, no. I'm not sure I even want to understand."

"A piece of foam the size of a briefcase."

"What? You've lost me."

"Yes, I have. But that's not the point I'm making. The Columbia space shuttle explosion. It happened three days before we met. A little piece of foam was all it took to destroy a billion dollar piece of technology and erase seven lives. I remember thinking: Damn, if life is that arbitrary, I'd better grab whatever I can get right here and now. I think you felt the same way."

Kate took Laurel's face in her hands and kissed her. "I'll miss you, Laurel, more than you can possibly imagine. I'm going to turn away now because I don't want to watch you go."

Her hands lingered a moment before she turned and walked to the window.

The lights flickered, as if affected by the emotional charge in the room, as Laurel struggled to accept what was happening. So this was the end? No goodbyes. Just the dimming of the lights as the final act faded to black.

***

Laurel drummed her fingers impatiently against the wall in front of the elevator. The relief she felt was rapidly being undermined by a spiraling sense of loss. *Does my father count?* A shocking confession, if it was true. Ironically, it had vaulted them into a new level of intimacy. How could the relationship end on a note like that?

The ring tone of her iPhone yanked her back to the present. She fumbled in her purse, found the phone and answered it.

"Hi, honey."

Guilt lodged in her chest her at the sound of James' voice.

"Hi. Wasn't expecting you to call." Laurel glanced at her watch. Still enough time to make it home before him. "What's up?"

The elevator door opened. She stepped in as she spoke, nodding to a Fedex courier preoccupied with something streaming to his Bluetooth.

"I'm on my way home. Should be there in about twenty minutes."

Laurel's heart skipped a beat.

"On your way home? It's only four o'clock."

"I had an off-site meeting today, remember? Told you I'd be home early."

Laurel realized that there was no chance she was going to get home before him.

"Laurel ... Laurel?"

"Yes."

"Thought I lost you there for a minute. Where the heck are you?"

"In the elevator. I'm going down to the lobby to meet a courier." She glanced at the Fedex courier who raised an eyebrow inquisitively.

"They don't come up anymore?"

"Apparently not."

The elevator stopped at the sixteenth floor, but no one got on. Laurel jabbed the close button with her thumb.

"Hold the door!" A young man in a torn denim jacket jammed his leg in the door and forced his way in. "You deaf? I said, hold the door."

Laurel shrugged and stepped back to make room. She noticed fresh scratches on the man's hands before he jammed them into his pockets. The elevator stopped again at the fourteenth floor where the Fedex courier got off.

"Anyway, I called to find out if you want me to pick something up for dinner."

"Yeah, sure ... Um, I might have to step out for a few minutes to run an errand."

"For what? Maybe I can do it on my way."

Think, Laurel, think. She watched the elevator floors passing by, like seconds on a count-down clock, as she wracked her brain. The elevator ground to a halt at the eighth floor. At the same moment, the lights went out and the emergency light flickered on.

"Oh, shit."

"What's the matter, Laurel?"

"The elevator just broke down. I think we're halfway between floors."

"That sucks ... What the hell?"

"James?"

"That's weird. The stoplight I'm at just went dead. And I think all the store lights ... Looks like ... Something must have ... "

"James? You're breaking up."

"Damn, my cell battery ... "

The connection dropped leaving Laurel with dead air. She frowned at her phone, sneaking a glance at the young man.

"What the hell are you looking at?" His expression darkened and suspicion rose in his eyes.

"I think there's been a blackout," she said. "We may be stuck in here for a while."

"Son of a bitch." He slammed his fist against the wall and looked up to the ceiling. "There has to be an emergency door up there."

He crouched, jumped straight up and knocked the plastic ceiling panel away. His jacket flapped open as he did so, giving Laurel a glimpse of a handgun jammed in his waistband. Her heart sped up at the sight.

"What kind of elevator doesn't have an emergency door?"

"Not much we can do but wait," she offered. He stabbed at the open button several times. "That's not going to help. Even if it does, we're between floors."

"Shut up, bitch. If I want your advice, I'll ask for it."

Laurel dropped her eyes to the floor, silently protesting the random alignment of events that had landed her in this predicament. Trapped in an elevator with a stranger who, by all appearances, was fleeing the scene of a crime. Her last words to James a lie. Her last words to Kate so inadequate.

Her iPhone rang. She glanced sideways at the young man as she answered.

"Laurel, its Kate. The power went out. Did you get out of the building?"

"No. I'm stuck in the elevator between floors."

"That just figures. I'm a curse to you, aren't I? ... Laurel, I'm sorry. I didn't mean what I said. Or, at least, I didn't mean it the way it sounded. I don't want things between us to end that way."

"Ah ... this really isn't a good time to talk about it."

The young man locked eyes with her. Choose your words carefully, a voice in head whispered.

"Are you okay? Are you alone in the elevator?"

"No."

"Are you in trouble?"

"You ... could say that."

"Should I call 911?"

"Yes, that would be a good thing to do."

The man pulled out his gun and pointed it at Laurel.

"Hang up. *Now.*"

Laurel hesitated. He snatched the phone from her hands, dropped it on the floor and stomped on it.

"What would be a good thing, huh?"

"Just ... something we've been planning."

"Something what?"

"Um, just a trip we've been planning. A vacation."

"You're lying." He lashed out and struck her on the forehead with the heel of the gun. Laurel slumped to the floor and lost consciousness.

***

As she slowly regained consciousness, Laurel became aware of a throbbing pain in her head. It took her a few moments to recall how she had come to be in a heap on the floor.

"Get up." She looked up into the face of her assailant. "I said *get up*."

He grabbed Laurel by the arm and yanked her to her feet. The pain in her head flared and made her unsteady. A grinding sound reached her ears along with muffled voices.

"They're prying open the elevator doors. I'm betting there are cops out there because of your phone call. This is how it's going to go down. You're my ticket out of here. Do what you're told and you may just live. Screw me over, and you're dead. You wouldn't be the first person I've killed today. Do you understand? *Do* you understand?"

He jammed his gun against her head to make his point.

"Yes. Okay, I understand. Whatever you say."

"Fucking right. Whatever I say goes."

Laurel struggled to settle her nerves. She pictured herself high above planet earth, peering out the capsule window, following the continuous line of life across the continents. The blue planet, illuminated and protected by the crescent moon and dotted with lights that flickered like candles, was a portrait of serenity.

The elevator doors parted a few inches. Her captor wrapped his arm around Laurel's neck and held the gun to her head. Her breath came in short gasps.

"Hello? Anybody in there?"

"Yeah, we're here."

Laurel heard grunts as their rescuers forced the doors fully open. The elevator had stopped three feet above the floor level. A hand holding a large flashlight appeared followed by a head peering up at them. She saw enough of his police uniform.

"Back off. Everybody out there *back off*."

The man quickly withdrew his head. Laurel heard hushed voices.

"Two people: a man and a woman. He's holding a gun to her head."

"Is she okay?"

"Couldn't tell. I didn't get a good enough look."

Laurel's captor bent down while keeping her in front of him. Together they stooped low enough to clear the door frame and climb out into the hallway.

"Back up! All of you, back away! Get that goddamn light out of my eyes."

Laurel could make out two figures in the hall which was illuminated only by flashlights.

"Please, do what he says. He said he'll kill me."

"Fucking right, I will. You, throw me that flashlight ... Alright, all of you, down on your knees. I'm taking the stairs and she's coming with me. Anybody tries to follow us—I shoot her and you."

A piece of foam the size of a briefcase. Kate's words echoed in her head. How strange that the repercussions of that moment were even now still rippling through her life.

"Come on, you're smarter than that. You know we've got all the exits covered. Give me the gun and we can work this out."

"This is not a goddamn negotiation. I have the hostage. I call the shots. On your knees or I start shooting."

"We can work this out. Nobody has to get hurt. What's your name?"

"Like I'm going to fucking tell you that. Get it straight. I'm the guy calling the shots. Anybody comes at me, you'll be scraping her brains off the wall. If you think I won't do it, go check out apartment 1610."

"You've got to work with us. We need a show of good faith. Let her go and we can talk."

He raised his gun and fired into the ceiling.

"On your knees. *Now!* Or the next bullet is in her head."

The shadowed figures dropped to their knees. Laurel's captor began to edge backward down the hall pulling Laurel with him.

One of the police officers unexpectedly called out. "Hey, is somebody there? This a police situation. Go back to your apartment."

"Yeah, like I'm going to fall for that crap," Laurel's captor growled. But he swung the flashlight behind him anyway. "Get back! Get back or I'll shoot!"

Laurel twisted her head around in time to see a figure, clutching a kitchen knife, lunge toward them. Two shots rang out. She heard a gasp, a moan and the sound of a body dropping to the floor. Her captor fired twice in the other direction toward the police, shoved Laurel away and bolted down the dark hallway. Laurel covered her head as she tumbled to the floor. A beam of light blinded her momentarily. The police officer behind the flashlight knelt beside her while his partner pursued the gunman.

"Are you okay? Were you hit?"

"No. I think I'm okay."

The officer pointed his flashlight at the prone figure on the floor a few feet away.

"Damn. He shot her twice in the head." He helped Laurel to her feet. "Don't look. She was dead before she hit the floor. She probably saved your life. It's rare, you know, for a total stranger to do that."

In the few seconds of silence that prevailed, Laurel saw with clarity the sequence of cause and effect that led irrevocably to this moment. History denied and reimagined, promises carelessly made and recklessly broken, all aligned like telltale constellations in the night sky and all leaving behind their own telltale scars of light.

She knew, as she forced herself to turn toward the body, that the chance was now lost for final words from the heart. Kate's fearless hand, still clutching the knife, convicted her.

God's Honest Truth

The last embers of November daylight were expiring over the treetops as David Hamm rounded a bend on Point Pelee's DeLaurier Trail. Overhead the rolling bugle call of a late-season sandhill crane resonated over the marsh. David raised his eyes and followed the crane's sleek profile—elongated neck slicing across the sky like a spear and three foot, slate gray wings carving the air with graceful power.

"Reluctant to leave, are you?" David said to the crane as it abruptly banked to the east. "There's a lot of that going around."

He continued on the winding trail, passing swamp ponds with blankets of algae and cloaked in shadows, until he came to the viewing platform. He rested his arms on the railing and leaned out to watch a snapping turtle haul its cumbersome body out of the canal. The snapper, raising itself on its stubby legs, swiveled its prehistoric head slowly toward him. Its inscrutable gaze posed the question: *Are you sure?*

"A bit late for second thoughts," David answered. "I've accepted the job and handed in my resignation here. It's a done deal."

The snapper regarded him for a full minute, as if waiting for him to finish.

"So why haven't I told Lyndsay? I will. Just have to find the right time and the right words. She'll be upset at first, but she'll come around."

The snapper turned away and levered itself further up the bank. David leaned back and scanned the length of the canal. It still amazed him to think that the DeLaurier men, squatters on this land 170 years ago, had dug the canals by hand to drain the land for farming. The act of leaving Point Pelee seemed, at this moment, like turning his back on those indomitable men who had claimed the land by taming it.

He turned his attention back to the turtle. It occurred to him that snappers could live for thirty years. It was quite plausible that this grizzled old-timer was the same one he had seen here when his father brought him to the park when he was only five. It had been a mesmerizing experience for a child with an innate passion for the natural world.

Pelee became his obsession. He was a familiar figure as a teenager riding his bicycle down Mersea Road, past the Sturgeonwoods Campground and Marina and past the cottages perched on the breakwater overlooking the lake, heading for the park.

Point Pelee was the only place to which he had applied after earning his Master's degree in biology. And yet now, less than two years after he had realized his dream, he was leaving for reasons that he still could not clearly articulate. He knew only that a momentous shift had occurred in him like tectonic plates colliding in the subterranean depths of the earth. He was restless, discontented and anxious for change.

The buzzing of his cell phone stirred David from his thoughts. He pulled it out of his pocket to check the number—Lyndsay calling from the Leamington Days Inn where she worked. She was probably just bored or needing to vent her frustration because the new registration system had gone fubar again. He slipped his phone back into his pocket.

There was no denying that the two of them had been out of sync. It seemed at times as if Lyndsay had something she needed to tell him as well. Or had she sensed that he was harbouring a secret and was waiting for him to come clean?

A ping from his phone signaled that a message was waiting. He pulled out the phone again and logged into his voice mail.

"David, it's me. Have you heard? You must have. Can you believe it? Call me as soon as you can."

The alarming tone in her message grated on David. What could be so urgent that she needed to talk to him right now. This was Leamington after all, he reasoned. A sleepy town on the shores of Lake Erie where nothing of consequence ever happened. Whatever the issue was, it could wait, he decided and slid the phone back into his pocket.

A cool breeze came gliding in over the marsh. David raised the collar of his jacket as he listened to the wind muttering through the trees, tugging at the last few clusters of leaves. He sensed in that rustling the first real intonation of the change of the seasons. Winter came late here in the southern-most region of the province. He heard himself reciting the geographic details.

Point Pelee Provincial Park has the second warmest climate in Canada after the lower mainland of British Columbia. You may find it hard to believe, but right now you are standing at the same latitude as Rome and the northern border of California. In some areas of the park, you'll find Prickly Pear Cactus growing.

The reality that his days were winding down, in this place that was home in every nuance of the word, came into sharp focus. How was it possible that all the pieces of his life for twenty four years had fallen perfectly into place, and yet now he was preparing to leave it all behind? The answer, in principle, was that the job that awaited him at the Ecosystems Branch of the BC Ministry of the Environment, was too good to pass up. In career terms, it made all the sense in the world. But in emotional terms, it felt like a wild leap in the dark.

How to break the news to Lyndsay, and convince her to pull up stakes and come with him, was the most worrisome obstacle. David twisted the engagement ring on his finger as he pondered the problem. He knew exactly how she would react. She would tilt her head to the left, squint her eyes and start probing him for some underlying reason.

On his way back up the trail, David stopped at the old DeLaurier house—a two storey, gable-roofed structure with board and batten siding. He felt at peace each time he stood in this spot as if there was a mystical connection across the years to the people who once called it home.

David's cell phone vibrated in his pocket again. He chafed against its insistence on disturbing his effort to make peace with leaving Point Pelee as he pulled it out and checked the number. It was his parent's phone number. Odd that they would be calling him at work, he thought. A chill ran up his spine but he dismissed it and slid the phone back into his pocket.

He had not yet broken the news to his parents. In truth, he was more worried about their reaction than Lyndsay's—his father, in particular, who had his own secret burning a hole in his conscience. Their conversation two months ago reverberated in David's mind.

They had been in his father's workshop tying flies. Albert held the early black stonefly nymph he had just finished up to the light and admired his handiwork.

"Not my best effort, but not half bad," he announced.

"Looks good to me, Dad. I can picture a hungry rainbow jumping all over it."

A look of consternation leaked across Albert's face. David paused in the fly he was working on.

"You okay, Dad?"

"Think I could make a living doing this? I've made some pocket money from it for years. Could be there's a business in it. You think?"

"Maybe. You'd have to make a lot of them and round up some regular customers."

"I wouldn't mind spending eight or ten hours a day down here. Beats the hell out of punching the clock at the Heinz plant. I've had my fill of that."

The plant was a century old and woven into the fabric of the town. Say *Leamington* to anyone in the province and chances are they would reply with one of three things: Tomato Capital of Canada, Heinz Plant or Point Pelee Provincial Park.

"You've only got a few more years to go there, Dad. It's probably best to stick it out and get your pension. Then you can do whatever you want. No pressure—you can putter around down here at your own pace."

Albert dropped the stonefly nymph on the workshop table. A look of defeat washed over his face. Then his father told him his dark secret.

David continued on to the parking lot and climbed into the park pickup truck. The image returned of the snapper twisting its neck to look at him and question his motives. Was he making the right decision? There was still time to reconsider. But something he could not put his finger on declared that the door was already closed on that possibility.

***

The aging headstones of the DeLaurier cemetery floated to the surface of David's thoughts as he drove through Leamington. They were hidden down the Anders Footpath which few people bothered to explore. A few simple stones, surrounded by a white picket fence, in a peaceful, out-of-the-way spot.

A car horn startled David out of his reverie. He realized he had missed Erie Street and gone clear to the edge of town. As he turned around, he glanced at his watch and saw how late he was. Lyndsay would already be home by now.

His cell phone buzzed again as he was stopped at a traffic light on Erie. He slipped it from his pocket. Lyndsay again. Something was definitely up. But he could not very well answer now after ignoring her other calls. He tossed the phone on the passenger seat as he passed the Heinz plant. There were crowds of people milling around the doors and spilling out onto the grounds.

"What the hell? Is there a wildcat strike? Maybe that's what Lyndsay and Dad were calling about. I'm already late. Guess I should swing by Mom and Dad's place and find out what's going on."

Ten minutes later he pulled up to his parent's house and was surprised to see Lyndsay's car in the driveway. Lydia met him at the door.

"David. Thank God, you're here. Your father is so upset."

"What's going on, Mom? Is there a strike or something?"

"You haven't heard? It's all over town. The plant is closing next June. Can you believe it? Warren Buffet spends 28 billion to buy the company and turns around and closes our plant. Just like that—700 people out of work."

"Closing? It can't be."

The idea seemed absurd. But as he followed his mother into the house, the people milling around outside the plant started to make sense.

"David, why haven't you answered your phone?" Lyndsay crossed the room to him.

"Sorry, the battery is dead. I forgot to charge it last night."

"So you didn't know until now?"

"No, I had no idea." David approached his father. "Dad, I'm sorry. I was by myself most of the day. I would have come home right away if I had known."

"Nothing you can do about it, David. Nothing anyone can do."

"The union will fight it, won't they?"

"Sure, but precious good it will do. It's a done deal."

David flushed at his father's choice of words. Lyndsay caught his reaction and shot him a questioning look.

"I've been trying to tell him it'll be alright." Lydia appealed to David. "Tell him he'll find another job. He won't listen to me."

"I'm 56, Lydia. Who the hell is going to hire me? Thirty-five years' experience at the plant isn't worth a plugged nickel now. Seven hundred other people in the same sinking boat and most of them are younger than me."

"You're a shift supervisor. That says something. You're a respected man in this town."

Respected man. David saw how those words stung Albert.

"Respect doesn't go very far when all you have is a Grade 10 education, Lydia."

Lyndsay gave David a *do something* look.

"I understand how you feel, Dad. It's a shock. Give yourself time to come to terms with it."

"And we'll be here for you," Lyndsay offered. "Whatever you need. Right, David?"

"Well ... yeah, of course. Of course we will."

"David? What's the matter with you?" Lyndsay's eyes narrowed and her head tilted.

"Nothing." He turned back to his father. "They'll have to give you severance pay. You'll get a big settlement. You'll have a lot of time to figure things out."

"David's right," Lydia joined in. "The mortgage is paid off. We have some rainy day money—with that and your severance pay we'll have some time to figure out what to do."

Albert pressed the heel of his hand into his forehead. David saw that he was summoning all the courage he could muster as he lifted his eyes to face them.

"Albert. What is it?"

"There's no good way to say this, so I'm just going to put it out there. Remember a few years back—that summer I went on fishing trips pretty much every weekend?"

Lydia's expression changed. She looked past him as if at some unseen threat.

"I wasn't fishing. I was going to the casino in Windsor. I got caught up in it and couldn't stop myself. Got us in debt up to our eyeballs. I had to remortgage the house to get out from under it ... I'm sorry, Lydia. You can't imagine how sorry I am."

The burden of his secret lifted from Albert's shoulders. But David could see that it was anything but a relief. Albert was bracing himself for the worst when her eyes met his again.

"I knew you weren't fishing all those weekends. I thought ... I thought there was another woman ... I'm ashamed that I thought you were capable of that. Can you forgive me, Albert?"

"You're asking me for forgiveness? I should be the one doing the asking. I stole our future."

Lydia did not answer. She simply took Albert's hands, drew him to his feet and began to slow dance with him as if it was a perfectly natural thing to do.

"Lydia? What the blazes are you doing?"

"Dancing with the love of my life. I don't need money, Albert. I just need you."

Lyndsay took David's arm and whispered in his ear. "We should leave them alone. Let's go upstairs."

Lyndsay's demeanour changed when they were out of earshot of Albert and Lydia.

"David, what's going on with you? You've been distant and distracted for weeks."

Not the ideal circumstances under which to break the news, David realized. But he could not put it off any longer.

"Nothing bad. I've been offered a new job."

"They promoted you at the park?"

"Not at the park. I mean a *new* job."

"Wait, you mean out of the blue somebody offered you a job?"

"Not out of the blue, exactly."

Lyndsay's eyes narrowed. "That's what I'm talking about. You're being evasive. What the hell is going on?"

"I heard of a job in BC with the Ministry of the Environment. It was a really good opportunity, so I applied."

"British Columbia? Did it not occur to you that you should discuss it with your fiancé before you went after a job that would turn our lives upside down?"

"I didn't know if I would even have a chance at it. I didn't want to say anything until it was actually on the table."

"So when do you have to give them an answer? How long do we have to talk about it?" David hesitated just long enough to tip his hand. "You've already accepted it, haven't you? Without even talking to me about it. You just assumed I would drop everything and come with you?"

"No, it's not like that."

"Then what is it like, David? Explain it to me, because I don't get it."

Gears engaged in David's mind for the first time. All his ambivalence came into focus. In that same moment, Lyndsay stumbled upon the truth.

"Oh my God. You don't *want* me to come with you, do you? Answer me, David!"

"No, I guess I don't. I'm sorry. I'm really, really sorry, Lyndsay."

"No. You don't get to play that card now. Out of the blue you tell me it's over. No discussion. Just *boom*, we're done? And you expect me to believe you feel guilty?"

"I know it sounds crazy. But I really didn't know until right now."

"Do you expect me to believe that, David? Do you really think I'm that naïve?"

"It's the truth. God's honest truth."

As David said it, it sounded ridiculously hollow. He realized that on some level he had to have known for months but had not found the courage to face up to it.

"Is there someone else? Is that it?"

"What? No. I wouldn't do that to you."

Lyndsay was struggling to keep from breaking down."

"Then why? There has to be a reason. Did I do something wrong?"

Why? The question thundered in David's mind.

"I guess I just always went along with it, with us being together, because it seemed right. I never stopped myself to ask if I really loved you. And when I did, well ... I'm sorry. I can't tell you how sorry I am."

"BC—as far away from me as you can get without actually leaving the country. That about says it all."

"I'm sorry. I ... I don't know what else to say."

Lyndsay turned her back on him and started down the stairs. But halfway down she stopped, as if transfixed by something she saw. David went down to the landing beside her. From their vantage point, he saw Lydia and Albert still slow dancing in the living room. The full awareness of what he was giving up came crashing down on him.

Lyndsay turned back to him with a look in her eyes he could not decipher.

"One last dance, David, for old time's sake?"

Her sudden calm unnerved David. He made no attempt to resist as she took his hands in hers. For several minutes they mimicked the scene unfolding downstairs. Lyndsay stopped, drew close to him and whispered in his ear.

"A little God's honest truth for you, David. You're going to be a father."

David's entire world shifted on its axis. The image of the crane banking to the east came back to him with new meaning. But there was no time to process it. Lyndsay's eyes went wide with surprise as she stepped back and realized there was nothing solid beneath her foot. Her arms reached out instinctively.

"David!"

It was already too late when he realized what was happening and made a desperate lunge for her. Their eyes locked as a choked scream escaped from her throat and her backward free-fall began.

Saint Jude

Jude Neale's life intersected with mine for what amounts to a heartbeat in the grand scheme of things. Truthfully, *crashed* into my life would be a more accurate description. A flock of geese, on the way to their nighttime roost at Heart Lake, were passing overhead like the drawing of the shades on the waning day. But the chattering blackbirds on the hydro wires scattered like buckshot when Jude thundered by me in his rusted Ford F-150 pickup truck.

I was on the way home from seeing *Les Misérables*—an ironic choice given what it had to say about the bridges we burn before we know the consequences. It had started me tallying up the failings that had led to me being divorced and alone with two daughters who would rather be at the mall than with me every second weekend. My mind was not entirely on driving when Jude's truck nearly sideswiped me.

Jude blew through the red light at Dixie Street as a Honda came through going north. He probably could have rammed it and kept right on going. Swerving to miss it was his undoing. His pickup hit the center median, ricocheted back to the curb lane and fishtailed wildly before rolling twice and wrapping itself around a pole.

My first instinct was to make the obligatory 911 call and stay out of harm's way. I am not by nature the get-involved type. What made me change my mind? Best guess, it had to do with intersecting fates and the forces they exert on us. Both Jude and I had been trying to keep our heads low and steer clear of trouble when our lives collided.

I did not know that the police were only a few minutes behind him, although it was obvious he was on the run. I stopped my car in the curb lane, flipped on my four way flashers, called 911, and ran to the pickup. The airbag must have been faulty because it had not deployed. Jude was pinned behind the steering wheel. Pebbles of broken glass were embedded in his blood-splattered face and blood was tricking from his mouth and nose. My stomach heaved at the sight, but I could not turn away.

There was no chance that the ambulance was going to make it in time. I felt a bit like the angel of death, although I could find no words to play the part. I did the only thing I could conceive of in that dire situation. I reached out and took hold of Jude's hand. His eyes rolled sideways and met mine with that conflicted resignation I later heard about from the people I interviewed. His face relaxed when he saw me, as if it was an unexpected blessing not to die alone.

The sun slid below the horizon as the lights went out on Jude's life. Something broke loose inside me as the police came screaming onto the scene. I saw, in Jude's all-or-nothing run from his pursuers, my own attempt to escape from the increasingly obvious ruin of my life.

I did not realize until much later, when the police had finished taking my statement, that Jude had pressed something into my hand before he died. It was that final act that led me to Jessie Neale.

***

It was two weeks after the accident when I finally located Jude's mother in the small Northern Ontario town where she had spent her entire life. The news of Jude's death had already reached her. She was more than willing to talk with me.

"I was drinking when I carried Jude. This was thirty years ago, so you understand, I knew I shouldn't. But put yourself in my shoes. Three kids under six and a fourth on the way. Shane was a drinker and a nasty drunk. He smacked me around just for the fun of it. We were scraping by on his welfare cheques. Months behind on the rent. But the owner was too scared of Shane to do anything about it. I didn't know liquor could hurt Jude that much. They have a name for it now, I think."

"Fetal alcohol syndrome," I offered.

"If you say so. I'm not educated, so I wouldn't know."

Jessie stared out into the yard from her lawn chair on the sagging wooden porch. I followed her stare, wondering if it reached all the way to Jude's mangled body in his truck back in Brampton.

"So you were the one who found him, Mr. Sullivan?"

I was expecting a tragic sadness. But there was only her studied resignation, as if she had made peace with it already.

"Edward. Call me Ed. No, as I told you, I'm a newspaper reporter. I was assigned to cover the story."

It was a plausible enough deception. More believable at any rate than the real reason—that I was searching for some meaning for my own tattered life in that chance encounter. I had not yet decided if I should give her what Jude had entrusted to me.

"No, you were there. Your eyes say it."

I began at that moment to suspect that the chain of events, which brought me to this northern Ontario town, started long before the last two weeks during which I had been trying to piece together Jude's final days.

In the back of my mind, my conviction that putting the pieces of the puzzle together would somehow open a new door for me was losing momentum. Truthfully, that conviction began to erode when I spoke to Fossey, the bartender at Hannigans, where Jude was drowning his sorrows on the last night of his life.

Fossey was reluctant to talk to me. He was naturally suspicious of someone interested in a dead man. But I loosened him up enough to find out that, somewhere between Jude's fifth and sixth beer, he stared too long at a woman. Long enough for her boyfriend to take offence.

The bouncer made them take it outside. He said Jude, although he was nowhere near the size of the other guy, messed him up pretty bad.

He paused, scratched his chin and spoke about the look in Jude's eyes. *Like this was the last straw.* I sensed empathy which was odd for someone in his profession.

"Jude was scrawny from the get-go," Jessie continued, "Barely three pounds when he was born. I knew from the start he wasn't right. But what could I do? We were just poor white trash. I sorely loved him, even more than the others. I knew in my heart he was marked for trouble."

Jessie must have been waiting an agonizingly long time to unburden herself. She opened up to me, a complete stranger, so unguardedly.

"School was no place for Jude. He couldn't pay attention long enough to learn anything. The teachers were scared to death of him. He was a holy terror when he got mad. They pushed him along to the next grade just to be rid of him.

"By Grade 5, I gave up and stopped making him go. He went when he wanted to, which was hardly ever. He just went out the door every morning to fend for himself. I prayed he wouldn't get beat up by the bigger kids. But that was the least of his troubles. He was small but he'd fight like a badger. I was proud of that. I know it was wrong. But somebody had to be on his side. If not his mother, who then?"

Jessie's eyes squinted as she reached back and grieved those lost days. Honestly, I really did not know how to respond. Just listening was the kindest thing I could do.

"He was eleven the first time the cops picked him up. He was throwing stones at the Community Centre windows because they wouldn't let him into the Penny Sale. Everybody treated him like an outcast. After that, they'd bring him home about twice a month and dump him at the door like a leper.

"He took off when he was 15. Went God only knows where. I called the cops but they didn't do a thing. Good riddance as far as they were concerned. Shane hardly noticed. But I worried myself sick. I prayed and prayed for him. Precious good it did. God never gave a damn about us."

The bitterness in her voice made me shudder. It frightened me to know that there was a farther latitude of heartache than I had yet reached.

"Jude came home three months later. Still with the devil in him, but there was something different." Jessie's voice became quieter now. "He lost something while he was gone. I tried to talk to him about it. But he just looked at me with that down-deep-inside hurt that there's no talking about.

"That was when the fighting started between them. Jude got it out of Mary that Shane was messing around with her and made up his mind to protect her. I think it gave him a reason to stay. Jude would get between them every time Shane went near her. They'd end up in the backyard beating the pure living hell out of one another."

I sensed a tide of emotion rising in Jessie now that was hauntingly familiar. My conversation with Constables Reynolds and Colt echoed in my mind. They got the call around 9:00 p.m. Jude was gone by the time they rolled up. But they knew where to find him. It was not the first bar fight he had been in. They kicked in his apartment door, but Jude jumped out the second story window.

They spotted him again at a donut shop around 2:00 a.m. Jude made a break for it before they could corner him. Colt's eyes drifted upward, as if he was reliving the scene, as he described it. He said Jude slowed down like he was going to give himself up. But something made him keep going. They lost him when he jumped a fence into a construction site.

"Are you still listening?" Jessie's voice recalled me to where I was. I flushed at the realization that I had stopped paying attention.

"I'm sorry. Yes, I'm listening."

"It was a Saturday night fifteen years ago. I knew this was going to be the last fight. Neither of them was gonna stop until one of them couldn't get up. I prayed that Jude would win. You think that's sinful—hoping someone will die? Well, maybe, but I've lived long enough to know that there are times when you just have to choose sides.

"Shane was losing, and it pissed him off. He called Jude a worthless son-of-a-bitch and a poor excuse for a son. That didn't bother Jude. He'd been called far worse. But then Shane said something that set the fire burning in Jude. 'You're no better than your drunken whore mother.' Jude hit him awful hard and Shane went down like a shot buck. Jude kicked him in the head twice ... and that was it."

I tried to imagine what Jessie must have felt at that life altering moment. But it was too far outside my reality. Her gaze was glassy now. She was lost in the memory of that day when Jude set her free and condemned himself.

"'You gotta go, Jude,' I said to him. 'Before the cops get here. This will always be your home. But don't you ever come back this time. Promise me, Jude.'"

I wondered if I should tell her about Jude's last hours. I imagined trying to tell her that Jasperitis and Hallcroft picked up Jude's trail around eight, and the 45 minute high speed chase began. Hallcroft said Jude ran a couple of stoplights on Mississauga Road and could have shaken them. But every few minutes he slowed down as if he was daring them to catch him.

The chase continued on Highway 401. Jude swung onto Highway 410 and headed in my direction. Hallcroft said Jude gave them the slip temporarily when he veered right at the last possible moment and took the Bovaird exit. *We damn near bought it trying to follow him. How the hell he got that rust bucket pickup to make that turn, I'll never know.*

I could not find the courage to describe it to her. Instead, I opted for a hollow reassurance.

"I can imagine how difficult that must have been for you."

"I really don't think you can. But that doesn't matter. I went into our bedroom and got the Saint Jude charm my mother gave me when I married Shane against her will. You know Saint Jude? He's the patron saint of lost causes. I put the charm in Jude's hand and told him not to ever go anywhere without it. My last words to him were: 'Jude, I love you with all my foolish heart. I'm god-awful sorry I let this happen. But you gotta go now. If you love me, don't you ever come back.'"

Jessie lapsed into silence now. Jude could have just looked the other way. He could have let his sister fend for herself. But he chose to answer the call of love, and willingly paid the price. The story Jessie had lived with for so many years, waiting for someone to tell it to, was finished.

I reached over, opened Jessie's hand and put the charm in her palm. Jessie did not look up. But I felt her spirit rise and close itself around that priceless icon. As I stepped off her porch, I realized I was going to have to rethink the conclusions I had arrived at about why people become who they are, the uncompromising nature of love, and what it takes to own the life you are given.

"Jude was a love child."

I turned back to her, puzzled by this parting comment.

"Jude didn't kill his father. Shane was his daddy in name only. I never got the chance to tell Jude that ... Maybe when I'm gone, if I'm forgiven my sins, I'll get the chance. Do you think?"

The Blank Deed

Three cormorants, wings folded downward like flags at half mast, cut recklessly across the path of the *Sam McBride* as it churned across the harbour toward Toronto Island. Lauren watched Jonathan's grandfather, his eyes narrowing with concern as he followed their flight. Were the cormorants a harbinger of things to come or a reflection of the past she was compelled to confront?

Lauren studied the old man's noble, weathered face. It was expressive, and yet, inscrutable. The experiences etched there were beyond her understanding. She searched for traces of Jonathan. There was a slight resemblance

"Are you okay, Grandfather? This must be terribly hard for you."

"And for you."

"Am I crazy to be doing this? Everyone seems to think so."

"Our people, the Anishinabe, believe we can't be separated from the cycle of living things—life, growth, death and rebirth. So no, you're not crazy."

"Anishinabe? Jonathan told me he was half Ojibway."

"Ojibway, Mississauga, Chippewa. We've been called by many names."

Lauren turned her eyes to the island. A rising dread gripped her as the ferry neared the Ward's Island dock. It felt disrespectful to be chasing after Jonathan's ghost. But the journal hidden in her handbag urged her on.

There were a handful of passengers on this Thursday morning in late September. They filed towards the bow as the ferry manoeuvred into the dock. Lauren held back, waiting until they had all disembarked, before she guided Jonathan's grandfather over the gangplank onto the dock.

"Thank you for coming with me, Grandfather. Do you mind me calling you that? I know we're only related by marriage."

"It's fine. You're Jonathan's wife and the mother of his child."

"*Was* his wife."

He cocked his head slightly.

"Sorry. I don't quite know how to refer to myself yet."

He nodded and crooked his arm in hers as they started down the path toward the Ward Island Clubhouse. Gulls skittered off the path ahead of them, protesting the disruption. Their plaintive shrieks sounded like cries of distress.

Lauren: You know that I keep this journal. So you'll know, I hope, to look here when they come to you with the news of what I have done.

I know you will be angry and wounded. Please, keep reading, if you can. This is my last will and testament—literally all that I have to leave you. A paltry inheritance. And yet, in some ways, more than I ever had to offer before.

I will not say that I am sorry. People spit out those words so often as if they erase all the harm. But they never do. Apologies will not change what I feel. I have descended, slowly at first and then in terrible leaps, into a dark and unspeakably lonely place.

"This was not originally an island." Grandfather made a sweeping gesture which encompassed all they could see. "It was a long sand spit running from the mainland. A great storm in the 1850's flooded the end of the spit and created the eastern channel. The western channel was deliberately opened to let boats come into the harbour."

He paused a moment, his expression quizzical, as if straining to collect and assemble his memories.

"In times long past, this place was always changing. The sands would come on the current, settle for a while and wash away again. Life ebbs and flows, and so does the land. But your people built hard shorelines, and filled in marsh land, calling it *land reclamation*. We don't believe in such things. We believe that harmony with all created things has been achieved and should not be disturbed."

"So you think Jonathan chose this place because it represented harmony to him?"

"I can't be certain. What did Jonathan tell you about his childhood?"

"Just that his mother was from the reserve, but left to marry a Hagersville man. He told me he has a younger sister who married when she was 18 and went back to the reserve. He thought she was foolish for going back."

Talking about him in this way, in the past tense, felt dismissive and disrespectful. Yes, he was gone. But she was not yet ready to close that door.

"Did you know that his father died tragically?" Grandfather asked.

"Yes. His car went off the road as he was driving home from work in the winter. Jonathan had just finished university and started his first job when it happened."

"He told you that? It's not true. Jonathan was only nine when his father died."

How many lies had he told her?

"Tell me more. Jonathan didn't like to talk about his past."

"Childhood was difficult for Jonathan. He was caught between two very different cultures. He felt he had to choose one or the other. I wanted them to come back to the reserve with us. But his mother felt she couldn't turn back. The only job she could get was waiting tables at the bar in the town hotel. It didn't pay much. The bank took back their house.

"Even then she wouldn't give in. She rented a two room apartment above a store. The three of them lived there from that point on. Jonathan was ashamed of their situation. He made up his mind to get an education, get out of that place and never look back."

One piece of the puzzle fell into place. Jonathan's obsession with money and with maintaining appearances, she realized, had grown out of that experience.

What is it I want to say to you? Is it to thank you for being the only pure thing in my life? Or a last, desperate cry for pardon? No, I said I would not ask for forgiveness.

I want you to understand, if you can, how I came to be in this dark place. So, where did it begin? Or, should I say, what was the beginning of the end? It was two years ago when those young rebels from the reserve took a stand and occupied that subdivision in Caledonia. I paid little attention to native land claims until then.

I scoffed at them at first. Remember? Such fools—dredging up old grievances. But something in me, lying dormant, flickered. The heritage I ran away from because I was caught in between. Because they took everything away from us—my mother, my sister and me.

"I only saw him once after that, until the occupation at Caledonia," Grandfather continued. "He came home for his mother's funeral. She died suddenly of a heart attack. Life just wore her out."

Lauren realized it was her turn to fill in the missing history, or at least, the part of it in which she had shared.

"Jonathan already owned the Harbourfront condo when we married. I didn't realize how much he had tied up in investments until the financial crash came earlier this year. We lost a small fortune in a matter of weeks. On top of it all, the company he worked for went bankrupt."

Grandfather nodded and drifted off in thought. Should she continue? Perhaps he knew the details already. "A law clerk's salary doesn't go very far in Toronto, especially when you have a lot of debts. We moved to a bachelor apartment on Jamieson Avenue. Jonathan hated that place. I kept saying it was only temporary—and it didn't matter where we lived as long as we were together. But it must have felt like his childhood all over again."

Lauren paused to watch barn swallows darting under the Algonquin Island Bridge where it arched over the channel. Emerging on the other side, they wheeled and twisted in an intricate choreography. Had Jonathan stopped to admire them?

You sensed the darkness growing in me. Talk to your family, you said. I did not want to go back there. But I had to. Grandfather opened my eyes to what we had lost. Not just the land—the Plank Road, Block 5, the Burch Tract—but our identity that was tied to it.

I could see, as we talked, that he was ashamed of me even though he denied it. For trying to bleach the Ojibway out of myself. For trying to win on their terms. Trying to build a fortress of money.

But I kept going back to him. Obsessed with learning all I could, even though it felt like self-abuse. Like crashing up against my betrayal over and over again. Finally, he came to the Toronto Purchase. What we gave up, without knowing what we were agreeing to, because we lived by a different creed. And there I was, living on that very land playing by their rules. Betraying my heritage day after day.

I know you tried to help. But I could not let you in because I was trapped in between my love for you and what I owe my people.

"Algonquin Island is entirely man-made." Grandfather gestured toward the island. "They dredged the harbour for boat traffic and used the sand to make the island. But I know that's not what you want to hear from me."

"Jonathan spent a lot of time with you. What did you talk about?"

Grandfather was slow to respond. It was important to him, she realized, to filter his memories and sound the depths of them before he spoke.

"About history. How our two races were thrown together and misunderstood each other—especially about the land. Jonathan found all of this very troubling. But it was when I started telling him about the *Toronto Purchase* that something seemed to break loose in him."

"What was the *Toronto Purchase?*"

"I'll have to give you a bit of a history lesson. The American Revolution pushed United Empire Loyalists across the border into Canada. The British needed land for them. Our people did not have any concept of land ownership. To us, all land belongs to the Creator. Our ancestors thought the White Men were asking permission to live with us. They didn't realize that they were giving up all of their rights to hunt, fish and carry on their lifestyle. They would never have signed the treaty if they had fully understood.

"That first treaty was never actually signed. It came to be known as *The Blank Deed*. Early in the 1800's, the British restarted negotiations and made sure they got signatures this time. A parcel of land 14 miles wide and 26 miles deep was ceded in that treaty."

Grandfather paused now as he watched a couple in a canoe glide by them in the channel. He was searching for self-assurance.

"Jonathan stopped coming to see me after that. It was like he had crossed an invisible line and couldn't turn back. Maybe I told him too much. But we had come so far together ... I believed I was helping him."

"He had convicted himself, hadn't he? That's the invisible line you referred to."

"Yes, I think you're right, although I did not see it at the time."

Does the way I reacted seem out of proportion? It must. Because the walls I was crashing through were buried deep where you could not see them. Walls I built all those years ago living in shame. The three of us in two rooms. Not White, not Indian—we did not belong anywhere.

I fought my way out of it. Wrestled an education out of their system. Learned economics and the world of investments. Built my equity and leveraged it again and again. I came to love the risk. Every time I dodged a bullet, I was beating them at their own game.

Until the bloody U.S. banks brought it all crashing down with their greed and mismanagement. They sent us all into a tailspin. I should have just pulled out the money that was left and got out of the way. But I waited too long. All this year, from February on, I have not been able to sleep. Up all night trying to find a way out of it.

Finally, it was all gone. All our savings, the condo, everything. The banks took it all. All those years back, I resented my mother for letting herself be a victim. And there I was, with all my education, every bit as helpless as she was.

They had reached the Snake Island Bridge. Lauren imagined Jonathan standing on this very spot—thinking that, if he crossed over, he was committed to the act. If she crossed it now, would she be gifted with the ability to forgive him?

"I'm not sure I can do this," she whispered.

"If you don't do it now, you will find you have to come back. I'm sorry, Lauren, but I would not be able to come with you. I can only make this journey once."

Then it must be now, Lauren decided, for she could never face it alone. She took his arm in hers again and together they crossed the bridge. A path through the middle of the wooded thicket brought them to a clearing on the south side of the island. The Toronto cityscape appeared across the harbour.

Grandfather stopped and closed his eyes. A shudder passed through him. He sat on the ground drawing Lauren down with him.

"Here. This is where his soul departed."

What had she expected to feel? Something untamed and extravagant—anger, grief, despair or some unwilling mixture of all of them. But instead, she felt a pool of sorrow, its depth unknown, spreading out around her in widening circles. She became acutely aware that she was on hallowed ground.

Reaching into her handbag, she withdrew Jonathan's journal. Turning to the last entry—his final words for her eyes only—she began to read. As his passionate plea for understanding washed over her, she realized that forgiveness was not hers to offer or withhold. The legacy he bequeathed her, as painfully bittersweet as it was, made him more fully her beloved than ever before.

And now, out of all the madness, calm.

I am not caught in the middle anymore. In a way, I am free. Nothing more to lose. All of my inheritance, the only kind that really matters, squandered. All of my bridges burned.

Lauren, my life is a blank deed. I do not belong anywhere anymore. I am a man without a homeland. All that remains is to go to the island, which was once sacred to our people, and pay my debts at the barrel of a gun.

Someday, when our daughter is old enough to understand, tell her that her father, with his last breath, prayed for her and her mother. That they might live, not as he did, but as he ought to have. You are my legacy. To you I pass the deed. In the oneness of all things, that none can undo, I will love you forever, Lauren.—Jonathan.

The Reckoning

I *can hear the sirens now. They're coming for me. They've been coming for thirty* *years. Their wailing sounds like the personification of grief. Strange how your* *senses expand when you know the end is near.*

So quiet in here now—just faint crying and soft moans—after all the chaos I *brought. It's surreal—serenity turned inside out. This sense of floating above it all* *after the horror of the moment. I wish he could be here to marvel at it. It's time to* *write the ending. I should feel dread. But staring down the barrel is so much easier* *than I expected. No need for prayers to summon the will. Just one last act of courage.* *One—two ... three—*

Six Hours Later

"Son of a bitch."

Quentin grimaced as he levered himself up in bed. His head was throbbing and his left eye was swollen half shut. Pain ricocheted across his chest when he took a full breath. He did a quick inventory: a cracked rib or two, definitely a black eye and a couple of loose teeth.

"How bad do I look, Chelsea?" He turned, expecting Chelsea to be watching him. But she was not in the bedroom. His glance landed on the alarm clock on the bedside table: 3:30 p.m.

"Damn, I've slept half the day away."

"Chelsea? You out there?" He eased himself onto his feet, crossed to the door and scanned the small apartment. "Chelsea? Serves me right, I guess. She's had her fill of patching me up."

He shuffled to the bathroom, swallowed a couple of Tylenol and took a quick look in the mirror.

"How many punches did I take? You'd never guess looking at me that I won the fight."

As he made his way back into the bedroom, the closet door ajar caught Quentin's eye. He reached over and opened it wide. Half of Chelsea's clothes and two suitcases were gone.

"Shit. Not again."

He grabbed his iPhone and punched in her number. It rang four times before she answered.

"What?!"

"I know, I know. I should have listened to you."

"I told you last time, Quentin. No more chances."

"Is this about yesterday afternoon?"

"It's about everything. The fights. The drinking. Throwing your life away. You're a lost cause, Quentin. I'm done with you, and all your baggage."

She disconnected before he could respond. Quentin slumped back in bed, pain rattling through his rib cage again, as those two words echoed in his head: *Lost cause.* "You'll have to come back for the rest of your stuff. I can wait you out, Chelsea. God knows I've had lots of practice."

Quentin leveraged himself out of bed again, kicked the closet door shut and made his way into the kitchen. The empty coffee tin was placed conspicuously on the table. He stepped on the foot pedal to open the garbage can and saw Chelsea's handiwork—the last half of the tin's contents dumped into it.

"Nice touch. So, no coffee ... Might as well check the World Cup scores. Big game today—England and Italy."

He settled himself at the computer desk in the living room and logged on to the Toronto Star website. The front page headline jumped out at him. *Four Dead in Mississauga Murder-Suicide.*

"Great. This day is just full of good news."

He scanned the story, only half interested, until his eyes fixed on one paragraph.

The gunman, now identified as Casey Kent of Mississauga, shot himself before police arrived at the scene of the incident on the twelfth floor of a City Centre Drive office building. He had been dismissed two days earlier. Company officials declined to comment on the reason for his dismissal.

"Holy shit. Casey Kent. There's a name I hoped I would never hear again."

A memory flooded back from too many years ago, breaching the walls he had erected to keep it buried. A foolish dare, and an even more foolish response to it that nearly went terribly wrong. The night in the holding cell at the police station. His father cuffing him around, after finally coming to get him out, and the confrontation that followed.

His eyes flicked to the date at the top of the page. June 14, 2014. Gears engaged in his memory. Last night at the bar—that face in the crowd. The mask of the years fell away.

How many did I kill? I think it's three. Three lives, innocent of any wrongdoing, banished from the world. They just got caught, literally and figuratively, in the crossfire of bullets and of retribution. Maybe it was their destiny to die that way.

But did I have the right? Did what I suffered, and carried with me, bestow that right on me? That hardly matters now. It was all for him. So he can never forget and never sleep peacefully again. The same day all these years later. He can't possibly miss the connection.

They'll say it was about revenge for being fired. Which it was and wasn't. Cause and effect, who is to blame, as if it is ever that simple. There are always stories within stories and everybody's misinterpretations.

They'll learn, finally, that not all questions have easy answers. Too much time has passed to follow the trail of overdue redemption. But there isn't much time left to deconstruct what I have done. I can hear the sirens now ...

Twelve Hours Earlier

Quentin threaded his way through the bar to the table he had his eye on.

"We don't have a problem here, Al, do we?"

Al was a regular, a heavy drinker who took offense easily after a few beers. Tossing him out, if it came to that, would not be a problem. The guy he was exchanging insults with might not be so easy.

"Not with me. Dickhead here, that's another matter. He threw a chicken wing at me."

"Really? Come on, Al, grow up." He turned his attention to the table. "Hey bud, I'm Quentin. What's your name?"

"I'm Nick. Your friend here's had a few too many."

"Yeah, maybe. But it's my job to make sure everybody gets along. Do me a favour and leave him alone."

"You're a bit old for a bouncer, aren't you?"

The other men at the table laughed and exchanged glances. Quentin took a step forward and leaned over Nick.

"I was kicking asses when you were still in diapers. You just think about that."

"Wiping asses?" Nick turned to his friends with a grin. "Did he just say he was wiping asses?"

Another ripple of laughter went around the table. Quentin leaned in closer.

"Funny guy. Just leave Al alone, and finish your beers. This is your last round, understand?"

"I don't think so." Nick pushed his chair back and stood up.

He was bigger than he looked sitting down—about six foot two and a muscular 190, Quentin judged. But nothing he could not handle.

"You wanna take this outside?"

"Alright, old man. Let's go."

Quentin was halfway to the door, with Nick and his entourage behind him, when Chelsea intercepted him.

"What the hell, Quentin? That guy's half your age."

"Seen his type a hundred times before. Trust me, this won't take long."

"Why do you have to fight him? Just throw him out. Simon will back you up."

"I fight my own battles, Chelsea. You know that."

"You need to ask yourself what battle it is you're really fighting." Her expression softened for a moment as she waited for his reaction.

"I don't know what that means, and I don't really have time to talk about right now."

Chelsea shook her head and turned away from him.

Quinten took a quick scan of the bar. It was an old habit from his hockey days in the American League—take the pulse of the crowd and feed on it before you start swinging. One face caught his attention. A disconcerting sense flickered that he should recognize the man. But he shrugged off the sensation and went through the door.

Half the occupants of the bar emptied onto the sidewalk and formed a circle around the two of them. Quentin sized up his opponent.

"I'll give you the first shot, old man. Give me—"

Quentin landed a right to the jaw that sent Nick sprawling to the sidewalk. He rubbed his jaw as he stood up.

"Not bad for an old man. But we're just getting started."

Quentin swung again. But his adversary dodged the punch and came back with a left that staggered him. A collective murmur went through the onlookers.

Old instincts kicked in as Quentin realized this was going to be a last-man-standing affair. He lunged forward with a shoulder block, knocking his opponent off his feet and stepped forward to press his advantage.

Nick rolled sideways and kicked out his right leg. He caught Quentin flush on the ribs with the heel of his cowboy boot. Quentin backed away gasping for breath. Pain shot through his chest with each gasp. Nick was up fast and landed two lefts.

"Had enough, old man?"

Quentin went low with two shots to the stomach that left Nick doubled over, giving him the opening he needed. He grabbed Nick's head in his hands and drove a knee into his face. Nick went down groaning, and stayed down this time. Quentin straightened up slowly and collected himself.

"You guys, scrape your friend off the sidewalk and get him out of here. I don't want to see any of you here again." He turned to the spectators. "Show's over. Go back inside."

Chelsea approached him with judgment in her eyes.

"Told you I could handle it."

"You don't get it, do you, Quentin? No matter how many times I say it or how many ways I say it, you just don't get it."

"It's my job. What was I supposed to do?"

"That's the problem. It's *not* just a job with you. Are you ever going to stop trying to prove yourself?" She spun around and stomped back inside the bar before he could answer.

Don't think or feel. It's not the least bit personal. It's just the accumulation of past sins and the balancing of the scales after such a long legacy of injustice. And, yes, striking out at him when he is most vulnerable.

It was so clear in his eyes last night. The self-doubt he tried so hard to hide. He looked straight at me and still did not recognize me. How is that even possible? But he will remember after this day of reckoning.

Breathe. In and out, slow and easy. Step outside yourself and be the agent of retribution. Best not to aim. Random is better. Now. Do it now! Again! Again! While the moment thunders and you live within the heart of it. Again! Again! ...

... nough. Drop the gun. Let it be.

My God, the screaming and the sobbing and the chaos. Did I really do this? Tear the fabric of the everyday and unleash such terror? Am I really the author of this nightmare? And my God, so much blood. How many did I kill?

Nineteen Hours Earlier

"Why not, Quentin? You always say no, but you never tell me why."

Quentin's face strained as he curled the weights—left arm, right arm, left arm, right arm.

"What difference would it make? We've been together six years. Doesn't that say enough?"

"If it doesn't make a difference, why not do it? Nothing fancy, just you and me at City Hall."

Chelsea sat on the couch, cradling a beer and watching him go through his routine. It occurred to him that maybe he should give in. She was a good looking woman, more or less tolerant of his lifestyle, and only 38—ten years younger than him. He was not likely to do better. There really was no good reason to keep saying no. And yet, there it was still—the instinct to keep his options open.

"I just don't see the point, Chelsea. What is it going to change?"

"God, you make me so crazy! You hate anything new. Like those dumbbells. They're ancient. I bet you had them when you were in the American League. Tell me you didn't."

"And that's a problem, how?" He glanced sideways, in time to see her roll her eyes.

Left arm curl, right arm curl, left arm, right arm. How many reps was it? The argument had made him lose count.

She smacked her beer down on the coffee table.

"You can't see past the tip of your nose, can you?"

"What the hell is that supposed to mean?"

"Forget it. I'm tired of arguing with you. Besides, I have to go to work. Jack wants me in early tonight." She unfolded herself from the couch and headed for the bedroom.

"Nice ass."

"You're not the only one who thinks so, you know." She threw it out like a joke, but with just enough of an edge to leave him wondering. "Don't be late. You know that pisses off Jack."

"Yeah, yeah."

Chelsea stopped and turned back to him. "Keep it up, Quentin. Keep it up and see what happens."

Quentin continued with his arm curls—left arm, right arm, left arm, right arm.

A minute later she stuck her head out of the bedroom door. "I know more about you than you think I do, Quentin. A lot more."

Quentin stopped in mid curl. What the hell did she mean by that?

Eighteen Years Earlier

"Come on in, Quentin. How's the shoulder?"

Coach Wallace gestured to a worn chair in front of his desk. Quentin was still in his equipment except for his skates.

"No problem, coach." He dropped into the chair. "Thought we had that game in the bag. Our penalty kill sucks—that's the problem."

Coach Wallace tapped the edge of his desk. He stood, turned away and adjusted a plaque on the wall.

"How long have you been in the American League? Seven ... eight years?"

"Ten." Quentin knew the routine. Traded again. The only question was where.

"We brought you in because we needed to get tougher to protect Kubina. But he's with the Lightening now, and he's not coming back. So—"

"I don't need the song and dance, coach. Just tell me where I'm going this time."

Coach Wallace turned back to Quentin and leaned forward on his desk.

"Home, Quentin. You're going home."

"Home?" The words did not register at first. "You mean, I'm done for the season? My shoulder's not that bad, coach."

"That's not what I mean. We tried to arrange a trade. But no one wants you. You've had a good run, Quentin. Ten years in this league is a lot. But it's over. It's time to move on."

How many times had he been in the dressing room when a guy walked in with that look on his face? Too many to count.

"You know I can still kick the ass of anyone in the league. There's always a place for a good enforcer. Always some hotshot kid that needs to be protected."

"I'm sorry, Quentin. All the teams want younger guys. Same thing happened to me. Guys like you and me, we're just hired guns ... You could maybe go to Europe. Might catch on with a team over there and buy yourself a few more years, if that's what you want. I know a couple guys other there. I could make a few calls, see if anyone's looking."

"Europe? You gotta be kidding me."

Reality sunk in. He was thirty years old and washed up. Just another thug on skates no one would remember by the end of the year.

He flashed back thirteen years. Acting on a dare from his buddies after football practice. Hanging Casey Kent by his ankles out a second floor window of the high school. Casey screaming in fear and pissing himself. The instant time froze as he lost his grip on Casey's right ankle. An agonizing few seconds before his buddies reacted and helped him pull the kid back in. His father's words the next morning at the police station still etched in his brain.

"What the hell is it with you and this kid? Every time I turn around, I'm getting a call from his parents or the school about something you did to him. And now this stunt. You could have broken his goddamn neck."

"I wouldn't have dropped him. I—"

A backhand slap to the face silenced him.

"Did I say you could speak? Keep your mouth shut. You're goddamned lucky I didn't leave you here. It's what you deserve." He paused, his liquor-fuelled stare fixed on Quentin. "I'm through wasting my time with you. You'll never amount to anything. A lost cause, if I ever saw one. And a goddamn poor excuse for a son."

He had made a solemn promise to himself that day to prove his father wrong and not let that encounter be the defining moment of his life. But his father's prophecy had come true. He was a failure, a lost cause, a nobody.

Here I am at the precipice. I thought I might feel doubt. Might not be able to go through with it. But what I feel is the privilege of truth and what it empowers me to do. It is not something I chose. It is what I am called to do.

Coming almost face to face with him was the moment when it all came into perfect alignment. Seeing what he had become and that time was running out for him. That was the instant when everything coalesced.

A divine moment of clarity. Why I've never been able to hold onto a job. Why I've been engaged twice, but never made it to the church. How I let myself get so deep in debt I can't answer the phone or a knock on the door. All the ways and means I've found to sabotage my life. That one day, that one moment—when he made feel worthless, born to be a victim—that was the nexus from which I've never been able to escape.

But now I've been given a vision. A new and final purpose for my life. You can't fight this kind of thing. It's already written. The gods, or fate, choose your poison, have decreed it. I am the tool of unconscionable fate. The loop has to be closed. So, don't think or feel ...

Three Days Later

Sparrows foraged on the ground around the open grave oblivious to its significance.

A gust of wind blew one of the roses off the casket startling the sparrows which took flight. Quentin bent down, picked the rose up and put it carefully back in place.

"Jesus, Casey, it was thirty years ago. If it was eating away at you all this time, why didn't you come looking for me? I'm not that damn hard to find ... I suppose that's not really true. Five teams over ten years— Portland, Chicago, down to San Antonio, over to Oklahoma City and back north to Syracuse. Toughest son of a bitch in the league and proud of it.

"A dozen years working the steel mills in The Hammer until that work dried up. Finally found my way back here to Mississauga three blocks from where I grew up. Working as a bouncer, the only thing I'm qualified to do, at the same bar where my father spent most of his spare time, until he dropped dead of a heart attack."

Chelsea wandered into his thoughts. He wondered again why he had resisted the idea of getting married. Maybe it was too much like a contract. Being a free agent was the only control he had over life now.

"Probably should be me in there instead of you. Anyone who knew us both would have put good money on me being the one to check out that way."

He needed to think of some parting words. Something to pay his respects in some manner, or at least grasp at an explanation for why things had come to where they had for both of them.

"I guess everybody lives by some kind of code. Mine? The only thing my father ever taught me—always be the last man standing. That's it. That's really all I've got ... At least you got a good turnout. Me— probably not. Chances are there won't be many roses on my casket."

Another gust of wind blew a rose off the casket. He bent down to pick it up and realized it was the same rose.

"So, what? Is this supposed to be some kind of cosmic sign?"

"You tell me."

The voice startled Quentin. He spun around and was speechless to see Chelsea standing there.

"How did I know you'd be here? I know a lot more about you than you think I do, Quentin Aaron Morrissey. You're not the closed book you think you are."

Incorrigible

Huck Fryman stopped to rest, halfway on his trek back from the barn, to let the pain in his leg subside. The pain came in waves of late, each one cresting higher than the one before. He squinted to look up at the sun. Coming on to two o'clock, he judged.

He had forgotten something. There was a buzz in his memory that would not let up. He could not remember why he had gone to the barn in the first place.

"What the hell?"

There was something inside the hollow fence post he was leaning on. He reached inside and pulled it out.

"My fence pliers? Right, that's where I kept them, back when I was still working the farm. The boys thought it was flat out stupid. But I always knew where to find them."

He resumed the journey back to the house, oblivious to the mourning doves that scurried out of his way as they fed on thistle seeds in the overgrown pathway. The door to the shed was open. How many times had he told Vera to keep it shut to keep the coons out? Or was it Vera who kept telling him?

Huck lit a cigar as he settled behind the wooden desk that balanced precariously on three legs. The pain flared again as he sank into his chair. Out of the corner of his eye he saw the mouse peer tentatively around a box. It surveyed the scene and took the measure of him. Satisfied that all was well, it skittered across the floor to the crackers in their usual spot.

"Huckleberry, I've told you a thousand times. You shouldn't feed the mice."

Vera's voice startled him, but resonated in his ears like a finely tuned bow string.

"I swear you make less noise than a feather in a wind storm. After 60 years you'd think I'd hear you coming."

"Don't go changing the subject on me. I'm wise to your wily ways."

"Ever seen one in the house? No, because they know this is where the food is. There's a method in my madness. And for the love of Lucifer, for 60 years you've called me Huck. Now out of the blessed blue I'm Huckleberry?"

"Time was you'd be tickled pink if I called you that."

"Well, no more. I'm Huck and leave it at that."

"You'll always be Huckleberry to me."

"Have it your way. I'm not of a mind to argue," he relented, resisting the fond smile that tugged at the corners of his mouth.

"Are you of a mind to clean up this shed? Every newspaper that came into this place in the last ten years is still here. What will people think?"

Huck scanned the confines of the shed. Small motors of every size, shape and make rested on stacks of yellowing newspapers. A path barely wide enough to navigate wound from the shed door to a desk littered with spare parts.

"You think I don't know what people say? Crazy, old motor man. Couple bricks short of a load. I don't give a good goddamn. Nobody but you ever understood me, Vera. I expect that's not likely to change."

"Huckleberry, what am I going to do with you? I won't be around forever, you know."

Huck's brow furrowed. His bad left eye, on the side where the cow kicked him many years back, drooped half shut.

"You're always talking that way. But you're too stubborn by half to go before me."

The sound of a pickup truck, navigating the potholes that punctuated the long, gravel lane in from the road, blew in through the hole in the window.

"There's a customer for you. Let them haggle for once. They won't buy unless you do."

"My price is my price. They buy or they don't. It's all the same to me."

"Incorrigible. You're perfectly incorrigible."

The shed door opened with a screech like a startled cat.

"Good afternoon. Mr. Fryman?"

A barely perceptible nod was the only reply.

"Mr. Fryman, I'm Jack Willis—the new Chief of the Volunteer Fire Department. Can I call you Huck?"

"No."

Unprepared for such a dubious welcome, the fire chief paused to reconsider his tack.

"Mr. Fryman, I think you know why I'm here. You've had warnings before and a citation, if I'm not mistaken. You've got to clean up this shed. All these old motors lying around ... I could smell the gas before I opened the door. This place is a fire trap."

"It's my place. I keep it how I want. It's no business of yours."

"It *is* my business. It's my responsibility to ensure your safety."

Huck's eyes narrowed. The legs of his chair creaked as he leaned harder into them.

"Get out of my place, you piss ass."

"Mr. Fryman, I can come back with the police if you don't cooperate."

Huck reached for the shotgun he kept under the desk. He leveled it at the intruder and closed his bad eye to sight down the barrel.

"Get the hell out of my place before I blow a hole in your ass."

The fire chief backpedaled down the narrow aisle.

"Jesus! They told me you were odd. But this is way past eccentric."

"Don't come back. Next time I'll shoot you on sight."

Huck watched through the hole in the window as the fire chief's pickup went bouncing up the lane. He ground his cigar butt into the dirt floor with the heel of his good leg and lit a new one.

Jack Willis? He turned the name over in his mind groping for a connection. Had to be Buck Willis' boy, he decided. Was old Buck still around? Most likely not, with his bum heart. No one that he grew up with was still above ground.

"Buck'll be rolling over in his grave with you pointing that old relic at his son."

"I'll be rolling over in *my* grave if you don't stop sneaking up on me. Lord, woman, make some noise already—especially when I'm holding a shotgun."

"Is the confounded thing even loaded?"

"Damn right it's loaded. And I'll point it anyone I damn well please."

"And when they come for you with a posse?"

"Let'em come. Piss asses every one of them. Not a full set of balls between 'em."

"You promised me, Huckleberry. A year ago to this very day, you promised me you'd stay out of trouble."

"I don't go looking for it. But if it finds me that's no fault of mine."

"Trouble finds people who want to be found. You promised me, Huckleberry."

"Alright, alright. Enough said. Let me be for a bit. I still have work to do."

Huck picked up the motor sitting on the desk and began to disassemble it. His gnarled fingers fumbled over the small parts, searching for a dexterity which time had stolen from them. Contentment softened his perpetual scowl.

An hour and a half passed in this fashion. From time to time he rummaged for spare parts on the desk or in wooden crates on a shelf behind him. An uncharacteristic patience guided his movements as if the ramshackle shed was a sanctuary where time held no sway.

Another vehicle sounded in the lane kicking up a dust cloud behind it. Huck frowned at the interruption. He stood to peer out the window. A jolt of pain ricocheted up his leg which gave way under him. He toppled into the chair with a mumbled curse.

"It's Kevin, Huckleberry. Now you be nice. He's the only one of our three that still comes to visit."

"In that damn Japanese car. Why he can't buy what's made here, I don't know."

"Kevin says they're built right here in Canada now."

"Still foreign to me."

"Be nice. Send him in to see me before he goes."

The door to the shed creaked open. Huck crossed his arms and hunkered down in his chair.

"I swear, every time I come here this damn aisle gets narrower. Do you ever sell any of these, Dad?"

"You looking to buy?"

Another wave of pain shot up Huck's leg all the way from the ankle to the hip this time. He closed his eyes to fight it off.

"That leg gets worse every time I see you. I don't suppose you'd let me take you to the doctor?"

"I've made it through 80 years without seeing a doctor. I'm not about to start now."

"You're 85, Dad. You don't even know how old you are."

"You come all the way out here to tell me my memory is bad? I could have saved you the trouble."

"Jack Willis called me. He said you pointed a shotgun at him. You can't do stuff like that, Dad."

"Why the hell not? It's my place."

"You just can't. There are laws and they apply to you just like everyone else." Kevin's eyes swept the shed again. "This has to end, Dad. Enough is enough."

"My place. My rules."

"No, I'm not taking that crap anymore. I have your power of attorney, Dad. Don't make me use it."

"Power what?"

"Power of attorney. It means I can make your decisions for you."

"The hell you can."

"What do I have to do to get through to you? You can't be on your own anymore."

Huck took another long puff on his cigar and fixed his stare on the wall behind Kevin.

"For Christ's sake, Dad, put that cigar out. One spark and this whole place will go up."

"Ain't happened yet. I expect no one will much care if it does."

"You're not leaving me any choice. I'll do what I have to do. I'm the only one of your sons who still cares enough to do it."

Huck shifted his gaze to the ceiling. Kevin shook his head and started for the door.

"Go in and see your mother before you go. She'll blame me if you don't."

Kevin stopped in his tracks. Sadness ebbed from his eyes as he turned to face Huck again.

"Mom's gone, Dad. She died a year ago. You know that. You didn't say a word for a month after the funeral. She's gone, Dad."

Consternation leaked from Huck's eyes and spread across his grizzled face. Snatches of memory flashed like heat lightening. A hospital room in sickly white. A rattling breath, another, and then silence. A church half full of grim-faced mourners.

Huck willed his memory's eye to close. He picked up the motor on the desk in front of him and hurled it in Kevin's general direction.

"Goddamn it, Dad!" Kevin ducked away from the missile. "You're incorrigible. There's no talking to you anymore. Say goodbye to this place. The next time I come it'll be to take you to a nursing home where you belong."

Kevin stalked through the shed door leaving Huck in a vacuum of silence. Huck waited for Vera's voice to fill it. The silence grew thunderous as he waited and waited for the only thing he had left in this world.

"Huckleberry, my sweet, incorrigible Huckleberry. Come be with me."

A weight fell from Huck's shoulders as his heart rose to the long awaited invitation. He pulled the whiskey bottle down from the shelf behind him, took a long swig, then another and several more until the bottle was dry.

He waited patiently for the fog to descend to blur his senses and dull the pain. When his eyes were heavy and he could not hold them open any longer, he picked up the cigar butt from the table and flipped it onto the newspaper pile beside him.

A thin wisp of smoke rose from the newspapers and spiraled gracefully toward heaven. Huck's eyes closed as the peace of love everlasting lulled him to sleep.

Hurricane Ike

Eddies of leaves swirled around the state trooper where he stood in the doorway. The windows hummed menacingly, the trees in the yard moaned and the rain came in sideways driving sheets as the wind gathered velocity. Gibra Lucie Muller thought of the first night she had spent in this house seven years ago, under such strange circumstances, and wondered if tonight would be the last.

"Listen to me," the trooper insisted. "Hurricane Ike *is* going to make landfall on the Texas coast. Everything from Bolivar Flats north is going to be hammered. There's an evacuation order in effect. You have to leave now."

"We're staying," Ike Thomas declared. His seven foot, 340 pound frame dwarfed the trooper in the doorway. "We'll ride it out here. I'm not going to run from a hurricane named after me."

The trooper shook his head, leaned sideways to look around Ike and frowned at Gibra.

"God help you. You're going to need it."

Gibra's faith in their decision faltered as the trooper disappeared through the wall of rain.

"Maybe we should leave, Ike. I heard on the news that this hurricane killed seventy people in Haiti." She knew, even as she voiced her doubt, she could not leave. High Island was her last stand. There was nowhere to run from here.

"Trust me, Gibra. I'll protect you." Ike pulled her into his massive arms. "High Island may be just another Texas town with an odd name to the rest of the world. But it's our home. We're staying put."

In the shelter of his arms, she felt safe from anything man or nature could summon. When the telephone rang, she knew it was Kate and Jeff, her children by her first husband, making one last attempt to convince them to leave.

"Hello, Kate. Hello, Jeff."

"Mom, for God's sake! Why are you still there?" Jeff demanded. "You're right in the hurricane's path."

"We've made up our minds," she answered, with a calm that surprised herself. "We're going to ride it out here."

"Is this because we wouldn't come and live with you and Ike all those years ago?" Kate asked. "Please mom, don't punish us this way."

"No, Kate. It has nothing whatsoever to do with all that. You were right not to come. I—"

The line went dead before Gibra could finish. It was just the two of them now, she realized, against the hurricane that was bearing down on them with murderous intent. It was ironic that her heaven-sent protector and the hellish storm shared the same name. The legacy of her name, dubious as it was, might offer them aid, she thought.

Her mind slipped into reverse taking her back 1,300 miles to Toronto Island as a ten year old.

"This is it, Gibraltar. This is who you are."

"You mean ... my daddy lives *here*?"

"No, Gibraltar. You have no father. *This* is who you are."

She leaned backwards to take in the odd shaped structure in front of her. It made no sense, like so many of the things her mother said.

"This is Gibraltar Point Lighthouse. I named you after this place. J.P. Radan Muller, your great, great, great grandfather, was a Keeper here two centuries ago. He was murdered and now his ghost lives here. I brought you here so you would know who you are."

"My teacher says there's no such thing as ghosts," she protested. But her mother was not listening. Her mind had disengaged and gone to that far off place.

"We're special, you and I, Gibraltar. We've lived many lives before, but always together. This place is where all our lives converge."

"I don't believe you. You're making it up. I want to go home."

Her mother took Gibraltar's face in her hands.

"Listen, Gibraltar. He's speaking to you."

"Who, mom? Who is speaking?"

"Your grandfather. J.P. Radan Muller."

She tried as hard as she could to listen, wanting more than anything else to enter that special world her mother inhabited. But it was not to be.

***

"Gibra! Gibra!" Gibra awoke to Ike's urgent voice amidst the roar of wind and rain. "She's coming and she's a bitch. We've got to get onto the roof."

She heard a high pitched whine in tune with the wind.

"It's a siren, Ike. Help is coming."

"No, Gibra. That's the wind. It's blowing through the gates of hell out there. The roof is our only chance."

"Ike, the window."

As she pointed at it, the glass appeared to bend as if it was made of wax paper. A crack raced horizontally from one side to the other.

"Gibra—"

Before Ike could finish, the window shattered inward showering them with glass. Wind rushed in with a ferocious groan driving a sheet of rain that drenched them. Tex, their Jack Russell Terrier, yelped and jumped into Ike's arms.

"Go! Go! Go! There's no time to waste!"

Ike dragged Gibra through the house with Tex tucked under his arm. As he reached for the front door, it blew off its hinges careening over their heads. The wind slammed into them and water rushed in

194

over their feet. Ike wrapped his free arm around Gibra and herded her to the side of the house where he had the extension ladder tied up.

"Up, Gibra, as fast as you can! We have to get onto the roof before it hits."

At the top of the ladder, as an immense flash of lightening illuminated the night, Gibra looked to the south and froze in terror. A raging, twelve foot wall of water was surging toward them. Ike pulled her down onto a wooden object she could not make out as the water swept them away. She tried to scream. But Ike's arm wrapped tightly around her trapped her breath. She heard Tex barking and caught a glimpse of him clinging with all his might to Ike.

The surge tide drove them forward as an ungodly wind threatened to wrest their makeshift life raft from beneath them. Gibra realized it was the picnic table they were riding on as it spun in tight, dizzying circles. Thunder crackled and lightening burst through the darkness. Blue black clouds were spinning maniacally above them. The deafening roar and electric whine of the wind lodged in her brain like an evil presence.

"Smith Oak Woods!" Ike bellowed in her ear.

She saw the branches of the great Live Oaks above the water. Yes, she thought, Smith Oak Woods. But of what consequence was that now?

"I'll come back for you! I promise! Go!"

Ike's mighty shove propelled her toward an approaching Oak. Gibra grabbed hold of a large branch, wrapped her arms around it and held on for dear life.

"Ike! Ike!" Gibra screamed. But in an instant he was gone. She clawed her way upward to a fork in the branches and wedged herself firmly there. Lightening flared, giving her one last glance of Ike in the distance, before darkness closed in again.

Hang on and survive until Ike can return, she told herself. No other earthly soul would have a chance. But Ike, who came into her life when hope was nearly gone, would surely find his way back to her.

***

Ike lost sight of Gibra the moment he let go of her. The picnic table crashed against a tree trunk, spun crazily and nearly threw him off.

"Gibra's in your hands now, Lord," he whispered. "Keep her safe until I get back."

Onward through the night, driven by the surge tide, Ike battled with his namesake. The bellowing wind tortured his ears as the rising pressure threatened to pierce his ear drums. He was consumed and held hostage by the maelstrom of wind and torrential rain. But throughout the battle, Gibra never left his thoughts. She had come into his life, in the most unexpected of places, answering a prayer he had all but given up on.

"I'll never give up!" he swore to the devil of the night. "You can't take Gibra from me!"

On the heels of that oath, his battered raft went airborne. He held on like grim death as the table did two full end-over-end flips, before crashing down again on something hard. He peered over the edge and was astonished to see that for a moment his raft was balanced on the back of a bottlenose dolphin driven inland by the tide.

In a matter of seconds, the wind mysteriously relented. A mystical stillness replaced the howling storm. The spinning clouds vanished giving way to the moon. A warm rush of air descended like a spring morning. It was as if God had waved his arm in an impetuous flourish and wrought serenity from madness.

"What is this?" Ike puzzled at the transformation. "Am I hallucinating?"

In this vacuum of peace, Ike thoughts turned of their own accord to his father, long dead now, and of a father-son talk that foretold his future.

"Ike, we need to talk. I've been putting this off for too long."

"This isn't the sex talk again, is it, Dad? I think I got that covered."

"This is serious. You're only thirteen but you're already six feet tall and 240 pounds. You're going to be a giant of a man."

"You mean I'm freakishly huge. Tell me something I don't know."

"Ordinary is not all it's cracked up to be, Ike. Don't ever be ashamed of who you are. God made you this way for a reason. It may be a long time before you find out why."

"Whatever, Dad. Can I go now?"

The sky erupted in fury again as unexpectedly as the calm had descended. It was not a hallucination, Ike realized. He had only passed through the eye of the hurricane. The short reprieve, and the reminiscence it spawned, renewed his determination to get back to Gibra.

"You can't kill me, you bitch!" he bellowed his defiance. "I'm the man they call Tank! God made me a giant and now I know why. You can't take Gibra from me!"

***

Gibra's faith waned as the remnants of the hurricane moved further inland. The moon peered apprehensively through the clouds, mimicking her fears. What if Ike had drowned and been pulled back by the tide into a watery grave in the Gulf of Mexico?

"Is this how it's going to end for me, God? Was my fate sealed when my crazy mother jumped off the island ferry and left me orphaned at sixteen? I've tried to live up to my name. But what was I supposed to do when Tom died—after he moved us all the way to Galveston for his new job—and left me with two children to feed and a mountain of debts? I had to give up my children to my in-laws. I had to beg favours to survive. It was Ike who rescued me. If he's gone, what was it all for?"

The moon broke free from the clouds. Gibra watched in awe as it glimmered over the expanse of water creating a pathway of luminescence. Was this the pathway Ike would follow back to her? It eased her fear to believe that Ike was at the other end of it. Her mind slipped a gear and retraced time back to the day Ike came into her life.

She had moved to the town of Winnie to take a job as a maid at a local motel. It was the first weekend of October. One-hundred thousand people had assembled for the Texas Rice Festival—the annual celebration for Texans who made their living flooding fields to grow rice. She had volunteered to serve at the barbecue cook-off.

Gibra remembered the scene vividly. The two men, both falling down drunk, grabbed at her every time she passed them. No one seemed to notice or to care if they did.

"That'll be enough, Jimmy. You too, Ricky. Leave the lady alone."

When she turned and saw Ike standing there, she was taken aback by the sight of him.

"The mighty Tank speaks! What are you gonna do, Tank? Huff and puff and blow us down?"

"Don't make this difficult, boys."

"We're not your *boys* and we damn sure aren't afraid of you."

Jimmy grabbed a chair and swung it head high. Ike brushed it aside, lifted his leg and mule-kicked Jimmy in the chest. The force of the kick sent him sprawling in a backwards somersault. Ricky took a running start and tried to tackle Ike. Ike grabbed him by the shoulders, hoisted him in the air and tossed him away. He crashed back to earth demolishing a small table in the process.

Gibra did not know what to make of this giant who had come to her aid.

"Sorry about that. Those boys needed to be taught a lesson. The name's Ike, though most folks call me Tank."

"I'm Gibra. Thank you. I hope they didn't hurt you."

"No worries. I'm too strong for my own good sometimes ... Gibra. Never heard that name before."

"It's short for Gibraltar, although I don't go by that anymore. I was named after a lighthouse."

The startled look on his face made him appear vulnerable in spite of his size.

"Did I say something wrong?"

"No, it's just such a coincidence. Lighthouses are a hobby of mine. There are about fifty of them left along the Gulf Coast. I've been to see all of them: Aransas Pass, Halfmoon Reef, Brazos River, Heald Bank, Sabine Pass. I always figured I would have made a good Keeper. The solitary life would suit me."

"My great, great, great grandfather was a Keeper. I'm named after his lighthouse."

"Well, this is quite the twist of fate. There's a lighthouse not far from here at Bolivar Point. They say it's haunted by the ghost of a young man who killed his parents. It's privately owned now, but I know the owners. Would you like to see it?"

"Yes, I would. I would like that very much."

Gibra came back to High Island with Ike that night never to leave, believing that fate had cast their lots together. He became her provider and protector. She became the light in the night that gave him purpose.

Ike would find his way back to her, she reassured herself, if only she kept the faith.

***

Ike surveyed what remained of his life raft as the wind throttled down.

"Well, Tex, it's smashed all to hell. Half the top is about all that's left. I suppose we're lucky. We would have sunk like a stone when the wind let up if it were all still in one piece."

The water had dropped two feet from the peak of the surge tide as the current gradually reversed direction towards the Gulf. Ike spied something in the distance amongst the flotsam drifting on the flood water. He scooped a board from the water and used it as a paddle to steer toward the object.

"Well I'll be damned, Tex. It's a rowboat."

He reached out with the board, levered the boat right side up and recoiled in horror. A body was hidden under the boat with one mangled hand tangled up in the oarlock.

"God forgive me. This boat can't help the poor soul now. But it's the answer to my prayers."

Ike used the board to dislodge the body. He set Tex down on the seat before carefully manoeuvring his 340 pounds into the boat.

"Hang on, Gibra. We're coming. Keep a lookout, Tex."

He began to row with long, powerful strokes. Tex stood straining forward in the bow keeping watch.

***

The sun climbed higher in the eastern sky breathing life into Gibra's slim grasp on hope. Her perch in the fork of the Oak was now several feet above the retreating water. The towering Live Oaks emerged around her, stripped of their smaller branches but still largely intact.

High above Gibra a pelican appeared soaring on thermals left behind by the hurricane. It swooped down with an odd grace on its nine foot wingspan and landed on a branch a few feet from her. The pelican surveyed her for a few moments and took off again. As Gibra watched it fly away, she spotted an object far off to the north. It gradually grew larger and took the form of a small boat. It had to be

Ike, she decided. Who else would be rowing through the flood water toward Smith Oak Woods? The size of its inhabitant, as the boat drew nearer, left no doubt. Tex began barking excitedly at the sight of her.

"You're a sight for sore eyes, Gibra," Ike shouted as he turned toward her. "I said I'd be back and here I am."

Gibra freed herself from the fork in the tree and edged down the trunk to another fork at the water level. As her feet touched the water, she heard Ike bellow "GATOR!!" and gasped at the sight of the alligator gliding through the water towards her.

The rowboat rocked wildly as Ike launched from it. A few powerful strokes brought him face to face with the beast. He wrapped his arms around its snout and squeezed with every ounce of strength in him. The gator instinctively went into a death roll. Gibra watched in horror as Ike disappeared beneath the water.

"Ike! Ike!"

Ike emerged with the gator still in his grasp. Under he went again, back up and under a third time. When the gator rolled right side up again, Ike was nowhere to be seen. Gibra's heart clutched in her chest. After all they had been through, was this how it was to end?

"Let me die too," she prayed. "Let this be the end. Where Ike dies, I'll die."

Ike broke the surface once more, eye to eye now with his adversary. He lunged forward and struck a mighty blow between the eyes of the beast. The stunned gator thrashed about for a moment before sinking below the surface.

Ike, too exhausted to speak, struggled the few feet to Gibra. He caught hold of her leg to rest and catch his breath. Gibra laid her hand gently on his head.

"Hurricane Ike. That's what they'll call you now. And you're mine, all mine."

Five For Luck

Is this extravagance I'm willing into existence something to be proud of or just the foolish indulgence of an old man desperate for a legacy?"

Jake Wolfe posed the question to himself, knowing he was past the point where the answer mattered. He wished he could appeal to Anneliese for reassurance. But three years had gone by since she passed away.

He picked up a flat stone the size of a soup spoon, weighed it in his hand a moment as he fixed his mind's eye, and gave it a sidearm flick. He watched intently as it skipped across the sleek plane of the water before piercing the surface and disappearing.

"Another six weeks and we'll be skipping stones for real, Tessie. Won't that be grand?"

Jake ruffled the hair on the back of the Golden Lab's neck. Tessie let out an enthusiastic *woof* and thumped her tail on the ground.

"There's a hurdle we have to clear first. Shaun and Danielle will be here soon, if their flights were on time."

Both of his children, but Shaun in particular, had urged him to sell everything when the offer came from the developer. At 72, they argued, he was too old to be living by himself on the farm. But he had held his ground, literally and figuratively, keeping five acres as well as the barn and the house. He had no use for the barn now. But it was too much a part of him, too chock full of memories, to consider parting with.

Someone had obviously tipped off Shaun and Danielle about the large payments from his bank account. Why else would they both come for a visit out of the blue?

Jake shifted his eyes to the pile of boulders and envisioned the bulldozer moving them into place. Each one was a marker that declared his allegiance to this land. His farming days were behind him. But that did not mean he had to stop living. What good was the windfall from the sale of the land if he did not use it to make a future for himself?

Tessie's head swiveled toward the house. A cloud of dust signaled the arrival of a car up the lane. She looked up at Jake and whimpered pleadingly.

"Go girl. Go say hello."

Tessie bounded across the yard. By the time Jake rounded the corner of the house, Danielle was out of her car and roughhousing with the dog.

"So good to see you, Danny." He gave her a long hug. "I hardly ever see you kids anymore."

"It's tough to get away, Dad, with work and the kids. It's a long trip from Calgary. Even longer for Shaun from Vancouver."

"I know. You have your own lives to live and that's as it should be."

"Why is your pickup truck parked halfway up the lane? Did it break down?"

"No, I just leave it where it's most convenient for me, that's all." A necessary deception for the moment. "I thought you and Shaun would be coming together from the airport."

"I suggested it," she replied. "But you know Shaun. Always has to do things his own way. Some things never change."

Nor should they, he was tempted to answer. But he shuffled aside the urge. "Let's go inside. Tessie, settle down. Let Danny get by."

He ushered Danielle into the living room. Her profile, as always, recalled Anneliese which caused his heart to lurch. Three years and these bittersweet flashes of her still persisted. He feared the day when they would stop happening.

"There's coffee on in the kitchen. Let me get it for you."

"Sit, Dad. I can get it." She settled him into his recliner, giving his hand an affectionate squeeze for things unsaid, and went into the kitchen.

And so it begins, Jake whispered, counting down the seconds.

"What in God's name is that?" Danielle stepped out into the hall with her finger pointing through the kitchen.

"That would be my kitchen."

"Don't play dumb with me, Dad. I'm talking about that huge crater out behind the barn."

"Oh, that. It was the damnedest thing. A meteor crashed there a couple of weeks ago. Caused quite the fuss."

"*Dad.* Get serious. *What* is that huge hole?"

Jake drew a deep breath. He had hoped to go through this only once with both of them.

"That's my lake. Or the start of it, at least."

"Your lake?"

"Yes, I'm building a lake. Although I guess *building* isn't the right word. It's actually more of an excavation."

"A lake? A lake." She was stuck on the word.

"You have to picture it full of water, Danny. Otherwise, it's just a hole in the ground."

The ring tone on Danielle's cell phone sounded as she stared at him.

"Are you going to answer that?"

She shook her head to refocus herself, and slid the phone out of its waist clip.

"Hello ... Hi, Shaun. Yeah, I just got here." She stepped back into the kitchen as she spoke. Jake cocked his hand to his ear to make out her muffled words. "Well, yes. Apparently he's building a lake ... Yeah, you heard me right. A lake ... I don't know. Like I said, I just got here ... No, right now it's just a ginormous hole in the ground out behind the barn. You really need to see it for yourself ... Alright ... Yeah, alright ... Goodbye."

Danielle stepped back into the living room and fixed Jake with her gaze. "You do know that Shaun is going to go off the deep end over this, right?"

"Not yet, I hope. It would be better if he waited until there is water in it."

Danielle rolled her eyes affectionately. "You should have stuck with the meteor story, Dad. It would have been an easier sell."

Jake shrugged and smiled back at her. "You may be right about that."

***

Shaun wheeled into the lane in a dark green SUV. He skidded to a stop behind Danielle's rental car, jumped out and crossed the distance to the porch in half a dozen strides.

"What's this about a lake? What kind of crazy scheme is this?"

"Don't I at least get a *hello?*" Jake countered. "I haven't seen you in almost a year."

"Yeah, okay. It's good to see you, Dad. Sorry it's been a while." Shaun cast a questioning glance at Danielle as he greeted his father. She mouthed the words *go easy* in response.

"So I guess you want to see it up close," Jake offered. "Come around back. It's not much to see yet, but I'm pretty damn proud of it."

Jake glanced surreptitiously at his watch as he led them around the house and past the barn.

"There she is," he gestured with his hand. "She covers about two and a half acres. The excavation is done. They're working on the grading now."

Shaun and Danielle took a moment to take it in. It looked much larger now that he viewed it from their perspective.

"Okay, Dad. Who talked you into this?"

"Nobody talked me into it, Shaun. I just decided I wanted it."

"You don't just *decide* you want something like this. It's not normal."

"Who says everything I do has to be normal? I'm 75. I've lived long enough to be a bit eccentric if I chose."

"Obviously somebody found out about the money and conned you into this scheme. Why didn't you—"

"Shaun," Danielle intervened. "I think we should let Dad explain before we start jumping to conclusions."

Shaun sucked in an impatient breath. "Alright Dad, explain away."

Jake cast a glance over the excavation as he gathered his thoughts. He would only have this one chance to make his case.

"You know how I love fishing. It's one of the few joys I have left in life. I used to go to Lake Scugog all the time with Denny Andrews and Sam Logan. But they're both gone now. That's what happens when you get old. The people you love die off. One day you wake up and find yourself all alone."

"Correct me if I'm wrong, Dad," Shaun cut in, "Lake Scugog is still there, isn't it?"

Danielle tilted her head toward Shaun and narrowed her eyes.

"Yes. But my eyesight is going to hell. I know, when I go for my license renewal next month, they're not going to give it to me. So even if I wanted to go by myself, I won't be able to anymore."

Danielle took Jake's arm in hers. "Dad, you know you can come and live with Doug and me. All you have to do is ask."

"That's good of you, Danny. But I'm too old and set in my ways to pick up and move halfway across the country. When I leave here, it'll be in a pine box."

"Okay, Dad," Shaun countered. "We get it. You're lonely and you can't get around like you used to. But this—", he pointed to the excavation, "— is not the answer. Somebody conned you into thinking it was."

A car horn sounded from the laneway.

"Ah, that will be the reporter from the Sun-Tribune. They got wind of what I'm doing. They want to do a story on me ... Back here! Behind the barn! Come on back!"

"That's just great, Dad. Tell the whole world about your crazy idea."

"Shaun, don't talk to Dad that way."

Shaun lifted his hands in a gesture of exasperation as the reporter came around the barn and jogged up to where they were standing.

"Jason Highland from the Sun-Tribune." He held out his hand. "You're Jake Wolfe?"

"That's me. These are my kids. My daughter Danielle from Calgary and my son Shaun from Vancouver. Shaun's a lawyer, by the way."

"You both came all this way to support what your dad is doing? That is so great."

"We didn't—" Shaun started to object, but Danielle's elbow dug into his ribs.

"So, Mr. Wolfe. Can I call you Jake?" Jake nodded. "You're building your own lake. That's quite an undertaking. How did all this come about?"

"It's simple, really. Three years ago, the developer of the subdivision made me an offer for my land. Eight thousand dollars an acre. Can you believe that? I had shut down our farm a few years before. So I sold off 45 acres. Suddenly I had more cash than I had ever dreamed of having."

"That is quite a windfall. But what made you decide to build a lake?"

Jake repeated what he had told Shaun, then added: "I was sitting in the house feeling sorry for myself when it hit me. I have all this money in the bank doing nobody any good. So I thought: What if I built a lake on the land I kept, and stocked it? I could walk out my back door and go fishing anytime I wanted."

Jake snuck at glance at his children. Shaun still looked skeptical. But there was a flicker of admiration in Danielle's eyes that encouraged him.

"You make it sound simple, Jake," the reporter replied. "But obviously it isn't."

"Not as complicated as you might think. I spent most of last winter researching it. These days there is someone who does just about anything you can imagine. You just have to have the resources to hire them."

"So, walk me through it. How *do* you go about making a lake?"

"Technically it will be a large pond. But since I'm bankrolling it, I'm calling it a lake. And I'll be stocking bass, not trout."

"Really? That's surprising. Doesn't that make it more difficult?"

"Not at all." Jake was warming to the subject now. "Bass can tolerate warm water and low oxygen levels, so they do well in ponds. They cost a bit more than trout to stock. But they'll reproduce. Trout won't spawn in a pond so you have to keep stocking them. And besides, I've always been a bass fanatic."

Jake saw Shaun's eyes narrow as he listened.

"Anyway, it's not as simple as digging a giant hole and filling it with water. First of all, fish like structure. That's what the grading is about. She'll be about eight feet deep down the middle and on the right side. See that ridge on the left side." Jake waited as three sets of eyes picked out the ridge. "It'll change to three feet there. The north end will be about six feet and the south end will taper from six feet to three feet.

Different depths mean different water temperatures. The bass will move around depending on the season."

The reporter turned to Shaun and Danielle. "Your Dad has certainly done his homework."

"Seems that way," Danielle conceded.

"You have to think of the whole thing as an *ecosystem*. You have to control aeration and nutrients and block the sunlight. It gets pretty technical, but basically it's all about keeping things in balance.

"And you've got to have a food chain. I'll be stocking small bluegills for the bass to feed on. Plus supplemental forage—that means species with different food habits. I'm going with fathead minnows."

Jason tapped Jake on the shoulder. "I have to say, I'm impressed. You've become quite the expert. One question: The logs and boulders over there. What are they for?"

"More structure," Jake replied. "The boulders will go in the south end and the logs in the north end. Any good fisherman knows to look for rocks and deadwood."

"They must have cost you a small fortune by themselves." Shaun chipped in. Jake repressed a smile. He was hoping for that objection to be voiced.

"Actually, they didn't cost me a cent. I made a deal with the developer. He had to clear the land for the houses. Instead of hauling away all the rocks and the trees that were cut down, he just dropped them here. He saves money. I save money."

A smile of admiration spread across Danielle's face.

"What about water, Dad?" Shaun could not contain his displeasure any longer. "Rain alone isn't going to fill that crater, unless you're counting on another biblical flood."

"Part of the land the developer has to clear is swamp ponds. So I made another side deal. Once my lake is ready, they'll run pipes from the ponds to my lake and pump the water in."

Shaun's limited store of patience was emptying out.

"Let's assume for the moment that there is enough water in those ponds to fill up your lake. What happens in a hot summer? Rain isn't going to keep up with evaporation. Your little ecosystem will dry up. All the money you spent will be gone."

"What have I always told you, Shaun? You don't remember? Where there's a will, there's a way. Big housing developments have to deal with rain water drainage." Jake pointed toward the subdivision. "See that large ditch they're making. It's going to connect to my lake which will be the storm water pond for the whole subdivision."

"I think that's Dad two, Shaun zero," Danielle offered, with a sly grin.

"Spare me the commentary, Danny. You're putting too much faith in the developer, Dad. If he gets a better offer, he'll screw you over in a heartbeat."

"Well Jake, I think I have everything I need." The reporter looked anxious to get away. But Jake needed him to stay a bit longer.

"I expect my son is wondering how I'm going to pay for the upkeep of my lake. Just so you know, I have a plan for that too. I made a deal with the Big Brothers organization. Every weekend from July to the end of September they'll have use of my lake. Strictly catch and release, of course, and no live bait. In return, they'll make an annual donation that covers my operating costs."

"That's so great, Dad." Danielle was totally on board.

"Well, I'll be on my way now. I'll let you know when the story is going to run. Nice to have met both of you." He shook Danielle and Shaun's hands as he prepared to make his exit.

"I'll see you to your car," Shaun said, and tagged along with him.

"What's he up to now?" Danielle wondered aloud.

"I don't know. But I'm pretty sure it's not good."

Shaun and the reporter stopped at the corner of the house. An animated conversation ensued. After a few minutes, the reporter waved his hands, cast a glance in Jake's direction and left. Shaun strode purposefully back to Danielle and Jake.

"What did you say to him?" Danielle asked.

"Let's just say I made sure he won't be writing any story. Okay, Dad. It's time to cut your losses and get out of this mess. Give me the name of your contractor. I can't get back what you've already spent. But I'll get you off the hook for anything else."

"This may seem foolish to you, Shaun. But it means the world to me. If it's a bad idea, it's my mistake to make and to live with."

"And we're just supposed to stand by and watch while you squander your money?"

Danielle's expression darkened. She turned on Shaun.

"I don't recall giving you permission to speak for me."

"You can't possibly think this is reasonable, Danny. It's a monumental waste of good money."

"That's your opinion, Shaun. And it's not your money."

"You want me to be the bad guy, so you can save face. Is that it? Fine, play that game."

"Shaun, slow down. Try to see this from Dad's perspective. He has obviously put a lot of thought into this project." She put her hand on Shaun's arm to calm him. But the gesture seemed to unnerve him.

"If you're not going to help, Danny, just stay out of my way."

He pulled his arm away and brushed her aside. A look flashed in Danielle's eyes that made Jake flinch. Her next move was both impulsive and decisive. She took a step forward and threw a right cross that caught Shaun square on the jaw. He staggered and went down hard.

"What the hell? What was that for?" He glared up at Danielle, trying to regain his dignity.

"For doing what you always do. Being a bully. You've been a bully your whole life. That's why you became a lawyer, isn't it? So you could push people around in a courtroom. You get off on it. I'm pretty damn sure that's why your wife left you." She stopped short when she realized what she had divulged. "I didn't mean to say that. But Dad deserves to know."

"And now he does. *Thank you* for that." Shaun got his feet, dusted himself off and turned to Jake with a wounded look. "You wanna blow all your money building *a lake*. Fine, have at it. I won't say another word about it. I've got my own shit to deal with."

***

The last of the sun was sinking below the half-finished frames of houses in the distance. Jake sat on the pile of logs next to the excavation watching it dissolve into darkness. Night approached differently, hesitantly like fog rolling in, now that the subdivision had put its mark on the landscape. The vision of his lake, the oasis of his old age, would not come to him now. The excavation in front of him looked like a scar on the land.

Tessie stirred beside him and barked once. He knew by her bark that it was Danielle approaching. If it was Shaun, Tessie's bark would be sharper and her ears would be raised. Danielle climbed on to the log pile beside him and put her arm around his shoulders.

"Shaun?" he asked.

"He took off. Don't worry. He'll be back when he cools off."

"Is he okay? I mean, about his wife."

"He will be, once he gets past the denial stage. That's a big leap for him."

A single cricket began to chirp in the woodpile beneath them. On its own it sounded plaintive and lost. Gradually others joined from near and far. Each tuned its voice to the solo appeal of the first to sound the call. Within minutes they were a perfect chorus rising with the darkness, tremulous and rhythmic.

"I can't believe you cold-cocked him."

"You have no idea how long I've wanted to do that. But I suppose I could have picked a better time and place."

The faint howl of a coyote drifted in on the breeze. Tessie's ears raised a moment. Jake reached down instinctively to reassure her. She settled again at his touch.

"I'd forgotten how nice it is to sit here and listen to the night come to life, Dad. Nights are so different in the city."

"How so?"

"Restless. Impatient. All those lights that never go out. There's this strange gray glow that hangs over everything. I'd forgotten how soothing country darkness can be."

"Country darkness. There's an expression I haven't heard for a good while."

" ... Mom." There was an echo of unresolved grief in Danny's reply.

"She had a thing about summer nights. We would sit out on the back porch until midnight sometimes. Now and then we'd hear a whip-poor-will calling. She loved the sound. Haven't heard one in a very long time ... Do you miss her?"

"Of course. Shaun does too, more than he would ever admit. Is she the reason?"

"For me doing this crazy thing? In a way, I suppose. Something to fill the empty space. I was planning to call it Lake Anneliese."

Jake climbed down off the logs and stood looking wistfully over his lake in the making. It took several minutes, but he was finally able to summon the image of what it would be in a few weeks. He bent down, sorted through a few stones until he found one to his liking, and flicked it out into the darkness.

"What are you doing, Dad?"

"Skipping stones. I keep trying for five skips."

"There's nothing to skip them off."

"Sure there is. You just have to let yourself see it."

Danielle slid down off the logs and stood beside him. Jake bent down, selected a stone and offered it to her.

"Wanna give it a try?"

Danielle took the stone and jostled it in her hands for a moment to get the feel for it. Jake wondered if she would remember what Annaliese always said before she skipped a stone.

"For Lake Anneliese," she whispered and let it fly. "Five for luck."

Hunting Muskie

F"olle Avoine."

Norman made the observation from his Muskoka chair on the floating dock. It had the air of a non sequitur. But Tom understood it as a ritual his father held to as time eroded those things he held dear.

"Lake of Wild Oats."

Norman nodded in approval and expanded his observation.

"That's what they used to call her before she became Rice Lake. The wild rice was so thick the natives had to paddle back out by the same channel they made coming in. Can you imagine? *Men-o-min.* That's what the natives called the wild rice."

A rattling call came stuttering across the bay.

"Kingfisher," Norman offered.

Tom nodded in turn as he squinted in the late afternoon sun. He tracked the sound and located the kingfisher patrolling the shoreline. The call came again, stitching together joys and sorrows that coexisted in this place. How was it, he deliberated, that a particular sound could become so firmly lodged in one's mind? The roadblocks you consciously placed in its path had no effect.

His memory conjured a precocious night with moonlight wavering on the black expanse of water. Bats were careening past their heads as he and Ben had piloted the boat across the bay only to ground it off the point of the island. They had slept on the island under the stars that night. Life was simple in those days. You took what it offered and made do.

"White Island feels like an old friend to me." Norman cupped his chin in his hand as he spoke.

"It's a sowback formation. Or whaleback."

"Either or," Norman agreed. "But I always preferred *sowback*."

Norman was a geologist by profession and possessed of an enduring love of natural history.

"I've been thinking about selling this place."

"Oh. Really?"

It made sense now why his father had been so insistent about getting together for the week.

"I think it's a good decision, Dad. You'll be 78 this year. I've been worried about you coming up here alone. But I know you'll miss the place."

Norman fixed him with his trademark piercing glare.

"You always had a flare for understatement, Thomas. You got that from your mother. God knows it didn't come from me."

For reasons he could never fathom, Norman had always used their full given names when the family was here.

"We've had some great vacations here over the years. I'll miss the place too. Wish I'd made more time to be here."

"I said I'm thinking about it. I didn't say I'd decided. Anyway, let's not get all sentimental. I'm an old man. I have to start letting go of things. Let's go fishing."

Norman winced as he stood up.

"Are you okay? Did you hurt your back?"

"At my age, there's always something that hurts."

He flinched again as he turned back toward the cottage.

"You sure you're okay?"

Norman did not answer. He dropped his pole and tackle box into the boat and lowered himself in.

"Are you getting in or am I going fishing by myself?"

He reached forward, fired up the motor and started untying the ropes. Tom deposited his gear in the boat and stepped aboard.

"Well, let's get out there. There are fish to be caught." He backed the boat away from the dock and turned it about. "We'll head over to Margaret Island. They tell me the bass and walleye are lively over there."

Norman steered the boat around the narrow handle of spoon-shaped White Island. He looked back at Tom, shaking his head as they passed the infamous grounding spot, as if he still had not forgiven that indiscretion. He was silent for a few minutes as they headed east.

"She's a eutrophic lake. Glacial waters from the last ice age made her."

"The ... Wisconsin Glacier?"

Norman nodded. "Twelve thousand years ago. The islands too. A lot of them are half-submerged drumlins from the Peterborough drumlin field. Drumlin is a Celtic word. Most people don't know that. It means *little hill*."

It appeared to Tom that his father was closing the loop on their years here. He was making peace, in his own way, which was strangely out of character for him. Norman slowed the boat as they passed Hickory Island.

"Your mother always loved hickory trees. I don't remember why. Probably the flowers. Yellow was her favourite colour ... God, I miss her."

"Me too. She went much too soon."

"She did at that."

Norman pushed hard on the throttle and sped on past Grasshopper Island toward the east end of the lake. He resumed his commentary as they approached Margaret Island.

"Sad story. A native girl from Alderville drowned here, way back when."

"She fell through the ice on her way to Keene."

Norman nodded.

"The body washed up on the northwest shore. Gave the island its name." He cocked his head as if searching for a thought. "George and Wellington Ferguson farmed the island back in the late 1800's. Some of their kin are still around here. Always meant to look them up, but I never did. You always think there's time."

Tom pondered this wave of nostalgia in his father. Was Norman's commentary meant for him? Or was he cataloguing his knowledge to lock the beloved images and stories of the lake in his memory? Was he trying to find his place in that history?

"Here we go," Norman said, with a distinct change in his tone, as he killed the motor on the north side of the island. "Time to fish."

Tom watched the quick flick Norman used to send his line gliding gracefully over the water. He could not match the simple elegance of that wrist flick no matter how much he practiced. Ben, on the other hand, had mastered it, which was all the more reason he should still be here.

"Got one!" Norman announced, before Tom had even made a cast. "A walleye. Decent. Couple of pounds, I'd say."

"Fish on the first cast," Tom said. "Ben would have said that's a good omen."

Norman landed the walleye and released it before he responded.

"I call his wife every now and then," Norman said. "Seems like she'd rather that I didn't."

"Everyone deals with loss differently, Dad. I'm sure it's nothing personal."

"Sure as hell feels like it is. Was it my fault his skidoo went through the ice? I told him it was too late in the season to be out there."

"It was nobody's fault—just a terrible accident."

The truth was that Ben had inherited his father's stubbornness as well as his skill with a fishing pole. Once he got an idea in his head, nothing could shake it loose.

Norman made another cast while Tom coaxed his line off a snag.

"If it's any consolation, Dad, she isn't particularly receptive to me either."

"It isn't."

"I think—Oh, got one! Damn, I lost it."

"You didn't set the hook. Thought I taught you better."

"Guess I'm out of practice."

"Hmmm."

The cryptic response puzzled Tom. His father was normally not one to let go that easily. There were certain things that he viewed as sacrosanct. The art of fishing was one of them.

They fell silent now as the rhythmic cycle of cast and retrieve wove a pious spell around them. Watching the line arching gracefully through air, the soft slap of the lure hitting the water and those few anxious moments waiting for it to settle. The long, measured retrieve with the hope and anticipation of a strike. It brought them into a communion that occurred nowhere else. An emerald green dragonfly landed teed up on the tip of Tom's pole. For no discernable reason, it made him think of Arianna back home in Edmonton and what she might be doing at this particular moment.

Tom saw Norman wince again as he cast. It worried him but he let it pass. Norman narrowed his eyes and surveyed Tom.

"You don't seem yourself, Thomas."

"How so?"

"You just don't. Are the boys okay?"

"They're fine."

"And Arianna?"

"Arianna is ... Arianna."

"Strange thing to say about your wife, Thomas."

"Nothing much to say. Same old, same old."

"Same old what?"

"Can we talk about something else?"

"No. I think we'd better stay on this subject."

Tom let his line go slack.

"Marriages go stale, Dad. It happens."

"Bread goes stale. Marriages—they go south. Are you two breaking up?"

"No, just ... adjusting our expectations."

Norman dropped his pole in the boat and turned abruptly to Tom.

"You listen to me. Life is too short. If it's gone bad between the two of you, end it. You're only 47. You've got a lot of years ahead of you. Don't goddamn waste them!"

Norman started the motor without waiting for a response. Tom got his line out of the water just in time as Norman steered the boat in a sharp curve to the west.

As they sped past Hickory Island again, Tom pictured Arianna on the day he left for this trip. There was an expression on her face he could not decipher at the time. She had tried to conceal it. But he knew every nuance of her after eighteen years of marriage. In the clarity of distance, he solved the puzzle. It had been relief, he realized, that she would not be seeing him for a week.

Norman slowed down as they passed between Sugar Island and Rack Island. Tom assumed he was going to swing right and head for the mouth of the Indian River where largemouth bass gathered. But Norman held straight as he looked sideways at Sugar Island.

"They found an Indian settlement on the north-east end of Sugar. Burial mounds too. Over 6,000 years old. Must have been quite something to discover that."

"Yeah, must have been."

Tom knew it was a poor response. But he had no other knowledge of the island and could not hold up his end of the exchange.

"Take a lesson from that. Life is short. Infinitesimal, in the scheme of things. You blink and it's over. All you have left are your regrets."

Norman opened the throttle again and steered for the middle of the lake. They sped past three small, unnamed islands strung together like an ellipsis.

"Where we headed?"

"Black Island."

"Ah, the great white."

Norman nodded but kept his eyes fixed on the water ahead. Tom occupied himself switching poles and rigging up for muskie. They were silent until they came to Tic Island and the sunken railroad.

"Largest railway bridge in the world back then," Norman observed. "All the way across from Harwood to Picnic Point. But the winter ice did it in. Now it's just a ghost. Nothing lasts forever. The older I get the more truth I see in that."

"Arianna and I just need to find a new equilibrium. We'll figure it out."

"Hmmm."

***

"Go big or go home," Norman declared, as he rigged his eight inch Lil Ernie Deep Diver.

"You think it's still out there?"

"We'll see."

Norman had hooked into a huge muskie in exactly this spot a few summers earlier. He had battled it for ten minutes before it spat the lure and escaped.

Tom watched as Norman cast his Lil Ernie far out along the rock ridge that ran below the surface. He cast his own line on the other side of the boat as the look in Arianna's eyes flashed in his mind again.

"I've got cancer."

Norman made the announcement as he cast his line a second time.

"What?!"

"Kidney cancer. Renal Cell Carcinoma, if you want to know the official name for it."

"My God, Dad." Tom let his line go limp in the water. "When did you find out?"

"Does that really matter?"

"Well ... they can operate, right? You can live with one kidney. Lots of people do."

"It's already metastasized. It's in both kidneys."

"Damn. When do you start treatments? You're going to need help. I could take a leave of absence."

"Chemotherapy? I'll tell you the same thing I told the Oncologist. I'll be damned if I'm going to spend what time I have left feeling like hell warmed over."

"But you can't just give up. You've gotta fight it."

Norman cast again.

"The sixth island from the head of the lake. An oval island, remarkable for its evergreens."

"Yeah, I know. Catherine Par Traill describing Black Island in one of her stories. I remember everything you taught us. Are we going to talk about this or not?"

"Not."

"Then why even tell me?"

"Muskie take their prey head first. One gulp and that's all she wrote."

"So we're talking about muskie behaviour now?"

"At my age, Thomas, cancer is like a muskie. Once it has got its teeth into you, you're not getting away. Why would I even want to? Your mother is gone. Benjamin is gone. You live 2,000 thousand miles away. And I'm too old to keep coming up here. I may be stubborn. But I know when it's time to bow out gracefully."

A wave of guilt assaulted Tom. He had become too absorbed in his own life, and its fraying edges, to see that his father's life was unraveling to the end of its spool.

"I'm sorry, Dad. I didn't know it was so hard for you."

"I'm not complaining. If one of us had to go early, I'm glad it was your mother who went on ahead. I would not have wanted her to be the one left behind. But Benjamin ... A father should not outlive his son. It just isn't right."

"Even still, I think you should reconsider. There are–"

"Whoa!"

Norman reefed back hard on his pole. It bent like a bow as line went screaming off the reel.

"Muskie?"

"Bet my life on it. Nothing else runs that fast. There's the head shake. Get your line in. We're in for a battle."

"Do you think?" Tom asked, reeling in as fast as he could.

"We'll know soon enough."

Norman cranked hard on his reel to make up ground. The muskie started another run, dead straight for thirty feet. It broke the surface, erasing all doubt, in a majestic, gravity-defying leap.

"My God, it's huge! A four footer, maybe."

"Oh, you beautiful thing! I'll have you in this boat if it's the last thing I do in this life."

Norman glanced at Tom with a grin on his face even as he winced at the effort.

"I'm glad you're here to see this, Thomas. This is how I want you to remember me. Not lying in a bed waiting to die. Out here hunting muskie."

Tom saw his father's life, and his own, in a new light. Muskie were the stuff of legend—the fish of ten thousand casts. You could go your whole life without hooking one. But when you did, and the hook was set deep, a muskie would always claim the dignity of fighting to the end.

"Give her hell, Dad. She won the first battle but this one is all yours."

Folle Avoine. Steeped in history, witness to the fall of one culture and the rise of another, too wild to be bridged, too maternal to give up her dead. As good a place as any to bow out gracefully, Tom decided, and, for that matter, to start anew.

Flights of Deliverance

"Sorry to be late, Emma, although I suppose where you are, time is not really a concern."

Malcolm Leatherby set up his folding chair beside the grave and lowered himself into it—grimacing as his hip locked up momentarily.

"Miranda kept me on the phone for forty-five minutes. I haven't told her about my vigil. You understand. I will tell her eventually. But not until my penance is finished."

Each day since Emma's internment, Malcolm arrived at her grave at noon and remained there in quiet reverence until three o'clock. It worried him that Day Eight felt no different than any of the preceding days. Such was the nature of serving atonement, he reasoned, trying to bolster his faith. But if deliverance did not come, what then?

The sweet, slurring notes of a chipping sparrow, accelerating like a bouncing ping pong ball, stirred a memory from over 50 years ago.

"Do you remember that day, Emma? We were newlyweds. Sitting on the plane at Heathrow minutes from leaving England forever for a fresh start in Canada."

Malcolm recalled how a sense of unease had stolen over him as the plane began to taxi. Was it possible that the state of affairs he now found himself in was preordained—the wheels already in motion that day? Nonsense, he told himself. Events of this magnitude could not be so easily explained away.

Malcolm became aware of a man approaching. He was disconcertingly tall, on the plus side of six and a half feet, with a wiry, athletic build and a farmer's tan. His purposeful approach implied that he had a story he needed to tell. Malcolm hunched down in his folding chair and avoided eye contact in the hope that the man might keep on walking. But his efforts were to no avail.

"Your wife?" the man asked.

Malcolm nodded.

"My name's Anson. I'm sorry for your loss ... Such a ridiculous thing to say, isn't it? As if you'd misplaced your wallet or your watch." Again, Malcolm only nodded. "Was it sudden?"

"It's always sudden, isn't it? She went peacefully."

It was the Anson's turn to nod knowingly. "People say it's better that way. But what do they know? Until you've been there, you can't judge." His eyes narrowed against the sun. "My wife passed away a month ago from a heart attack. I wasn't there when it happened."

Malcolm studied his shoes.

"I was in Tokyo," Anson continued, "on the fifth hole at Shishido Hills, when I got the message. I'm a golf pro, although not a particularly good one. I've been all over the world on just about every tour there is—the Canadian Tour, the Challenge Tour in Europe, Web dot com Tour, Asian Tour, EPD Tour. I've been at it for over twenty years."

"Seems like a nice way to make a living." Malcolm made eye contact with Anson for the first time.

"You'd think so. But I never have made a living at it. Most of the time I barely make enough money to pay my way to the next tournament. Angie juggled two jobs, on top of looking after our boys, to keep us afloat. But she never once complained ... I didn't have enough room on my credit cards for the flight home. I had to borrow the money from one of the guys on tour."

"But you made in back in time?"

Anson shook his head. "My plane was landing at Pearson just as she died. I don't think my sons will ever forgive me. As far as they're concerned, I drove her to an early grave by making her carry such a load."

Malcolm pondered what could be spurring this grieving man to pour out his confession to a total stranger. "I was going to quit. Didn't have it in me to go back. But I thought of all the times I was tempted to pack it in and Angie would talk me out of it. So I'm going back on tour. I don't mind telling you that I'm scared. But I'm going to keep grinding away until I win a tournament. I owe her that."

He paused now and studied Malcolm. Was there something in his own eyes, Malcolm wondered, that betrayed his secret? It startled him when Anson touched his shoulder and smiled encouragingly.

"Don't let anybody talk you out of coming here. You have your reasons. Whatever they are, trust in them."

As he turned and walked away, a butterfly coasted by, looped once around Anson and again around Malcolm.

"Look, Emma. A monarch. I wish you were here to see it."

***

"Where are all the monarchs, Malcolm? It's August already. They should have arrived weeks ago."

Malcolm was used to these repeated questions which Emma posed as if for the first time. The progression of Alzheimer's was painfully evident. He had learned to be patient with her mental lapses.

"I don't know if many of them are going to get here this year. We read about them in the newspaper. How the drought last summer hurt them—and their winter colonies in Mexico being so much smaller. Anyway, it's only late June."

"Late June? It's not August?"

"No, Emma."

A look of consternation washed across her face. It pained him to see it appearing more and more.

"You know how much I love them, Malcolm. It won't be summer without monarchs."

"I'm sure at least a few will make it here. We just have to be patient."

"Maybe if we go to the cottage, we'll see them."

"The cottage was sold last year, Emma. It was too far for us to drive at our age."

Emma's head swiveled towards him. There was indignation in her eyes.

"You sold the cottage without telling me?"

"No, Emma. We talked about it and agreed it was the right thing. It's okay if you don't remember."

Her eyes clouded over and her hand reached for something that was not there. Malcolm took her hand and cradled it in his own.

"We sold the cottage. We sold the cottage." She repeated the words as if searching for the truth in them. "Yes, I remember now. It was a nice young couple with twin boys who bought it. I'm glad about that. The boys will so love fishing off the dock."

Malcolm did not have the heart to contradict her. What did it matter if she did not remember correctly? If she reinvented the memory in a way that was more comforting, there was no reason to take that away from her.

"Yes, I'm sure they will."

He reached over to brush away a bee that was circling Emma's head. She did notice the gesture.

"I wonder what ever happened to Colin. Do you suppose he's dead?"

Emma's question left Malcolm dumbfounded for a moment.

"Do you mean *that* Colin?"

"Yes, the one who tried to kill me."

They had not talked of the incident since their arrival in Canada, honouring an unspoken agreement to bury it in the past. It had happened several months before they met. Colin was an ex-boyfriend of hers, violent and possessive by nature, who had broken into her flat one night and stabbed her. It was a terrible part of her past that was undeniably linked to their life together. For Malcolm, it had been love at first sight. He had proposed after only three months. Her response was imprinted in his memory.

I'm fond of you, Malcolm, but I don't love you. But if you take me to Canada, where Colin can't find me, I'll marry you.

"I think he probably is dead. He lived a violent life. It would make sense that he would die young."

Malcolm felt the inadequacy of his response, but tried not to let it show. Emma weighed his reassurance. She turned to him with more clarity in her eyes than normal.

"I may be falling-apart but I know that I love you, Malcolm. You've given me a good life."

Tears welled in Malcolm's eyes. He clasped her hand in both of his and leaned over to kiss her on the cheek.

"You're all I've ever needed, Emma."

Weeks later, in the clarity of hindsight, he would remember this moment as the de facto end of the Emma he knew. He was coming up the stairs from the basement a week later when the first episode occurred.

"Malcolm! Malcolm! Oh my God, it's him! Malcolm! Help me!"

He stumbled on the stairs, bruising his knee as he tried to take the steps two at a time. Emma screamed again as he reached the hall and lumbered toward the bedroom. She was hysterical when he reached her and pulled her into his arms.

"It's him, Malcolm! Outside the window. It's him!"

"Who Emma? Who is it?"

"Colin! He's found me. He looked in the window. He has a knife and he's going to kill me!"

Malcolm looked toward the window. "There's no one there, Emma."

"Don't you tell me that he's not there! I saw him. He's going to kill me!"

Malcolm did a full circuit of the outside of the house, for his own peace of mind, and returned to Emma.

"It's been raining all day, Emma. The garden outside the window is muddy. There are no footprints. There was no one there."

"I saw him, Malcolm. Don't you think I would recognize the man who tried to kill me even after all these years?"

Three days later the scene was repeated. Soon it became a daily occurrence. Their family doctor confirmed Malcolm's worst fears. Emma was moving into the final stage of the disease—slipping away from him in larger increments now. The most Dr. Holland could do was prescribe a sedative.

Emma slept most of the day but always awakened with the same delusion. Miranda, their daughter, came as often as she could to help. But when she suggested putting Emma in a nursing home, Malcolm steadfastly refused.

"What kind of husband would I be if I abandoned her now? I brought her across an ocean to keep her safe."

"It's too much for you, Dad," Miranda pleaded with him. "You can't take care of her now. You're 76 yourself."

"She's my wife and, by God, when it's her time, she'll die in my arms. We've spent 45 years together in this house. Delusions or no delusions, this is where she will stay."

***

"Excuse me. Ae you okay?"

Malcolm had dozed off in the afternoon heat and awoke with a start. His heart fluttered as he looked up into Miranda's eyes. But the illusion passed. It was not Miranda—just a stranger whose voice happened to sound like hers.

"Your wife?" she asked.

"Yes."

"What was her name?"

"Emma."

"Oh, I thought for a moment you said *Emily*. My name is Emily. I've seen you here before. My brother is buried over there. I lost him six months ago. Tragically."

"Death is always tragic, and sudden," Malcolm replied.

"I suppose so. But Daniel ... well ... he took his own life."

Malcolm wiped beads of perspiration from his brow as he puzzled over this latest uninvited intimacy. Was this part of his penance—to be made to listen to the grief stories of total strangers?

"He had schizophrenia. It was terrible at times—the delusions, the voices. They put him on medications that stopped all of it. But Daniel said they took away his soul. He couldn't feel anything at all. No emotions, good, bad or otherwise. He called himself the walking dead."

"I'm sorry," Malcolm replied, recognizing a grief that mirrored his own. "How old was he?"

"Twenty-one when he was diagnosed. He took the meds for two years before he stopped. Our parents begged him to go back on them. They threatened to have him committed." She made a gesture of brushing a strand of hair away from her face. Malcolm saw that she was really wiping away tears. "They can't forgive me for taking his side. They blame me now for his suicide."

"Blame is a selfish emotion." Emily looked puzzled. "When you get to my age, Emily, when you've seen as much of life as I have, you'll understand."

"How long were you and Emma together?"

"Fifty-four years. I wanted more. But I couldn't be that selfish."

Emily leaned down and touched his hand. In that instant, something passed between them like an electrical charge.

"I think it's wonderful that you're here with Emma. People will say it's strange or eccentric. Don't you believe them. If this is what brings you peace, stay as long as you need to."

"Thank you, Emily. I'm so sorry about your brother. I understand more than you know."

"I don't think I got your name."

"Malcolm. A good old British name."

Emily nodded and smiled. "Maybe I'll see you another day."

As she turned, the monarch fluttered by, looped once around her and continued on. Malcolm thought to raise his hand and tempt it to land. But it moved on before he could.

***

Malcolm awoke one morning, near the end of July, to find Emma awake and staring intently at him. He braced himself for an episode.

"Malcolm, what have I done to you? You've aged ten years in the last few months."

"You haven't done anything to me. It's just what happens. One day you look in the mirror and think: *How did I get old so fast?*"

"Malcolm, I want you to do something for me."

"Anything, Emma. You know I'll do anything you ask."

"I want you to kill me."

"My God, Emma! What are you're saying?"

Malcolm sat up in bed and reached for his eyeglasses.

"Colin has been looking for me all these years. Now that he has found me, he won't leave until he kills me. I don't want to die that way. Don't you see? If you do it, it will be an act of mercy."

"You're confused. It's the medications. You don't mean it."

"What good am I to you? I'm just a broken-down old woman you have to take care of like a child. You deserve better, Malcolm."

"Taking care of you is not a burden, Emma."

Malcolm held her in his arms, praying for deliverance from her suffering, as she drifted back to sleep. Throughout the morning he roamed the house haunted by her words and questioning his motives. Was it selfish of him to want to keep her with him? A nursing home might be the best place for her now. The delusions might fade away if she was out of the house. Was keeping her here really for her needs or for his?

As the grandfather clock chimed noon, he tried to reconcile himself to the idea that she needed more care than he could provide. And yet, how could he balance that against the responsibility he had taken on when he agreed to take her away? Was that not a *till death do you part* commitment? There were no extenuating circumstances that could possibly override it.

"Oh, God! Malcolm, help me! He's here! He's trying to kill me!"

Emma's scream tore Malcolm from the seesaw battle of his thoughts. He rushed to the bedroom and took Emma in his arms. But she fought him and pushed away.

"Emma, it's me. It's Malcolm. It's alright, I'm here."

"Help! He's hurting me. Malcolm, where are you!"

Emma struck him in the face in her frantic state. Malcolm fell backwards on to the bed as they struggled. He tried to take hold of her arms but she flailed wildly. In that moment, he realized that she was no longer Emma. What little grasp of reality she had been clinging to was gone.

"Get away from me! Malcolm! Malcolm! Where are you? I need you!"

He tried again to subdue her. But she fought him with a strength he did not know she still had left in her. There was terror in her eyes as she gasped for breath between screams. He had waited too long. Emma's screams came in waves. Her right arm struck the headboard as she flailed. Malcolm heard the distinct crack of a bone breaking. From somewhere within him came the realization that she would not survive this episode. He had a choice: Watch her die slowly and painfully, or mercifully end her suffering. He could not fail her now.

Malcolm reached for the pillow, levered himself back onto his feet and sidestepped Emma's flailing arms. But his will faltered as he raised the pillow over her head. It was impossible. He could not take her life. Malcolm was about to pull the pillow away when Emma saw it. Calm descended over her as she looked up. The veil of delusion lifted and she stopped resisting. He could not deny what he saw in her eyes now— gratitude and a deep, abiding trust in him to do what was needed.

He expected her to struggle as he pressed the pillow gently over her face. But she remained perfectly still. How long did it take to suffocate someone? It would be terrible to pull away too soon. He held the pillow in place for several minutes until there could be no doubt.

Malcolm stumbled into the living room, his heart pounding in his chest, and collapsed in a chair. *What have I done? Dear God, what have I done?* Grief and horror rose in an accusing tide within him. As he fought to keep from being swept away by it, the reality of what had happened lost its clarity. Surely he had not done such a thing. It was no more than a trick of the mind. Emma must still be alive.

Malcolm crept back into the bedroom and listened for her breathing. But the room was veiled in silence. He staggered back into the living room, fell into the chair and passed out.

***

"Mr. Leatherby? Mr. Leatherby? It's Susie, the home care girl. I'm so sorry, Mr. Leatherby. I'm so very sorry."

It took a moment for Malcolm to gather himself. He had no sense of how much time had passed.

"You didn't answer the door. I got the spare key from the neighbours and let myself in. You know, don't you? You know Emma is gone?"

"Yes."

"Doctor Holland is here. I called him. He came right away."

Malcolm turned his head and saw Dr. Holland. It must have been some time since he had passed out. Time enough for what he had done to be discovered.

Doctor Holland knelt in front of him. Malcolm saw a question forming in his eyes. Did he know? Were there signs a doctor could detect? He decided in that moment he would not deny it if asked. There would come a time for penance. For now he would be grateful that Emma was no longer suffering.

"It was sudden?" Dr. Holland asked. "No time to call for help?" Malcolm saw the barely perceptible nod of his head. He understood how he was being led to answer.

"Yes. Very sudden. There was no time."

Dr. Holland nodded. "It happens that way sometimes. I'm so very sorry for your loss. Emma is at peace now. You did your best."

Malcolm let his eyes fall closed. Emma's suffering was over.

***

"Who is it?"

Malcolm had nodded off again. He opened his eyes to a young boy standing in front of him pointing at the grave.

"Who is it?" the boy asked again.

"My wife. Her name was Emma. And who are you?"

"I'm Jake. Was she sick? Like, for a long time?"

"Well, yes. And no."

"Well, was she or wasn't she?" The earnestness in Jake's eyes softened the harshness of the question. "Did she have B-R-C-A-1? It's this thing that, if you have it, you get cancer. My Mom had it, and now she's gone. She's buried over there. That's my Dad."

Malcolm's eyes followed Jake's finger. The boy's father was kneeling before the grave as if in prayer.

"Why are you sitting here in a chair? That's weird. Are you a crazy old man?"

"I might be. I did something that some people would say you'd have to be crazy to do."

Jake puzzled over that answer. His brow furrowed and his lips curled.

"I think you're just real sad because your Emma died. I'm sad too."

"At least you still have your Dad."

"Yeah ... Do you have anybody?" Jake posed the question with a seriousness that belied his years.

"I have a daughter. Her name is Miranda."

"I'm sorry that your Emma died. My Mom said that you go to this other place when you die. Maybe your Emma and my Mom are friends there now."

"I'd like to think that they are."

"I have to go now." Jake started to walk away, but stopped to watch as the monarch sashayed past. He looked back at Malcolm and pointed at the butterfly.

"Maybe that's your Emma. It could be."

"Jake, what are trying to say?"

"It's called ... " Jake screwed his face into a knot as he tried to remember. "Recarnation?"

"You mean re-*in*-carnation?"

"Yeah, that's it. My Mom told me about it before she died. She said she'd become a bird so she could sit by my bedroom window and sing to me. And she does. So that butterfly, it could maybe be your Emma."

Malcolm held out his hand. The monarch coasted in and perched in his upturned palm as the trill of the chipping sparrow sounded again. Jake stretched on his toes to see with eyes wide in wonder.

"See. It's your Emma!" He clapped his hands and ran off to tell his father.

Malcolm drew in a long and purging breath. Deliverance was more about surrendering to what was beyond your own judgment than it was about being set free. Decisions made in the urgency of the moment, and in the name of love, answered to a higher authority that dealt in deeper things than guilt or innocence.

He gently raised his hand to launch the monarch into flight. It looped once around him, weaving an invisible thread that released him from his vigil, before fluttering off toward the field and places unseen.

Acknowledgements

Authors are influenced and shaped by countless people in the course of inventing themselves as an artist and in weaving the stories they are irresistibly driven to write.

I am indebted to my editor Shane Joseph for showing faith in me and for patiently editing my stories, diplomatically pointing out my sometimes overly indulgent writing habits and coaxing me to excise the *little darlings* that I so loved but which did not advance the plot. His insights made each story measurably better and the collection as a whole more cohesive.

Special thanks to Jake Hogeterp who edited the first iterations of most of these stories and saw the many flaws I overlooked.

I owe much to my lifelong friend and fellow artist Edgar Thatcher. He steers me through the technology challenges that modern authors must navigate. More importantly, he has continually inspired me with his passion for life, his courage through life's trial, his artistic integrity and his unwavering loyalty.

I would be remiss if I did not thank my family who put up with having an artist, an eccentric and a nonconformist in the family.

And finally, I acknowledge the many people, nameless here but essential nonetheless, from whom I borrowed life experiences (taking great liberties in the process) in fashioning the stories that make up this collection.

Author Bio

Michael Robert Dyet is The Metaphor Guy. Novelist, short story writer, closet philosopher, chronicler of life's mysteries—all through the lens of metaphor. He holds an Honours B.A., Summa Cum Laude, in Creative Writing from York University and was awarded an Arts Acclaim Award from the Brampton Arts Council in 2010.

He is also the author of *Until The Deep Water Stills: An Internet-Enhanced Novel*—a traditional print novel with a unique and ground-breaking online companion featuring text, imagery and audio recordings, which was a double winner in the *Reader Views Literary Awards 2009*.

Michael's online co-ordinates:

Author Website
www.mdyetmetaphor.com
Novel Online Companion
www.mdyetmetaphor.com/blog
Metaphors of Life Journal Blog
www.mdyetmetaphor.com/blog2

CPSIA information can be obtained
at www.ICGtesting.com
Printed in the USA
LVHW02s1746040118
561822LV00014B/1287/P